MARRY, KISS, KILL

Advance Praise

"Raymond Chandler meets Chelsea Handler — a hard-boiled, sexy, funny book."

— **David Hyde Pierce,**
acclaimed Broadway actor and star of *Frasier*

"Anne Flett-Giordano is a writer who constantly surprises and delights me. The real mystery here is: why hasn't she written a mystery before now? *Marry, Kiss, Kill* is dead-on!"

— **Tom Fontana,**
creator of *Oz, Copper,* and *Borgia*
and award-winning writer of *St. Elsewhere,*
Strip Search, The Philanthropist, and many more

"For those who like their mysteries more breezy than brooding, Flett-Giordano delivers the goods. *Marry, Kiss, Kill* is a fun, twisty romp that keeps the tone airborne even when detailing a murder that suggests how Titus Andronicus might have behaved if left in charge of a day spa. I enjoyed its cast of soldiers, schemers, and seducers but most of all Nola MacIntire, a shrewd, self-deprecating sleuth who knows that, for Santa Barbara blondes, the real killers are sun, carbs, and time."

— **Joe Keenan,**
author of *My Lucky Star* and other novels
and award-winning writer of *Frasier, Desperate*
Housewives, and other TV shows and films

MARRY, KISS, KILL

Anne Flett-Giordano

PROSPECT
·PARK·
BOOKS

Published by Prospect Park Books
2359 Lincoln Avenue
Altadena, California 91001
www.prospectparkbooks.com

Distributed by Consortium Books Sales & Distribution
www.cbsd.com

Library of Congress Cataloging-in-Publication Data
Flett-Giordano, Anne.
Marry, kiss, kill / by Anne Flett-Giordano. -- First edition.
    pages ; cm
ISBN 978-1-938849-49-7 (softcover : acid-free paper)
I. Title.
PS3606.L488M37 2015
813'.6--dc23
                        2014041277

Simultaneously printed in hardcover and softcover editions
Hardcover ISBN 978-1-938849-53-4

Cover design by John Roshell
Page layout by Amy Inouye, Future Studio
First edition, first printing
Manufactured in the United States of America

With thanks to my indulgent friends and family who allowed me to assign their names to sometimes-vile characters, with whom they share no actual traits whatsoever. If your name is in this book, it's because I love you. This includes the city of Santa Barbara, which is truly heaven on earth. I can't imagine a lovelier, safer place to live. That, however, would have made for a very dull book.

One

"I see a sloe-eyed lady…
'Bout five-foot-three I'd say…
The way she works that long black hair…
She takes my breath away…
Oh, Doctor…"

The pretty woman smiled bashfully as Charley flashed his infectious grin but made no move toward her purse as she passed his open guitar case.

"But baby, she ain't stoppin'…
Got no time for me today…
Got a ticket for the movie…
And that film's about to play.
That's why I got the blues…
That's right…
The Santa Barbara International Film Festival blues, blues, blues…
Yeah, we got JLaw, Pitt, and Gosling…
And don't forget Penelope Cruz, Cruz, Cruz."

As often happened, the woman stopped, darted back, made a hurried, almost embarrassed donation, then flitted away again.

"Thank you, Miss."

Thank you and then some. It had been a dog's life since the sixteenth president had graced Charley's guitar case. The bad economy had trickled down from bankers and brokers to teachers and shopkeepers and hit street musicians smash-mouth in their drinking money. Even the farmers' market crowd had started slipping their change back into the pockets of their skinny jeans. Not that you'd know it tonight. The film festival was in full swing. The crowd outside the Arlington Theater was drowning out the mariachis at Carlito's across the street, and a Batman beacon lit up the sky. Somehow they'd managed to churn out another one, with Ben Affleck as the dark-knight superhero donning his cape to rid the world of Comicon villainy.

A Batman with a utility belt full of Lipitor seemed AARPathetic to Charley, but *No Crime Stopping for Old Men*, or whatever it was called, was catnip to the excited crowd. Cheers went up as glittering movie stars stepped out of their limos. They waved and smiled, then disappeared under a swarm of paparazzi like so much sequined roadkill under the weight of a million flies.

Charley had always liked the Arlington. Its vaulted forecourt provided a shady retreat where a homeless man could come in outta the sun. On hot afternoons he'd stake a spot on the cool Spanish tile by the fountain and smoke a bone or lift a brew. Tonight his spot was covered with a sea of red carpet and mingling VIPs sipping champagne, but Charley didn't mind. He was happy just being part of the general hustle and flow.

Pocketing the five, so the crowd wouldn't think he was so flush they could afford to miss him with their quarters, Charley strummed his old guitar and struck up another rhyme.

This time he singled out two hipsters in stingy-brim fedoras and expensive kicks, each trying to outshout the other on their iPhones. There was no shortage of junior nobodies, up from L.A., this time of year. Too ironically T-shirted to be agents, too freshly showered to be writers, they were all Bluetooth and no bite.

Normally Charley chose some flattering aspect of a person's appearance to sing about, not only because they were more likely to pony up for a compliment than a slam, but also because he enjoyed making people feel good. The kind of good they might pay forward as they went about their day. But these two iHeads offered precious little to inspire any random act of musical kindness, and tonight Charley couldn't resist having a little fun.

"Now here we got two big wheels...
Their iPhones say it all...
But they ain't making big deals...
It's their mamas made them call...
Yeah, they got the blues...
The Santa Barbara International Film Festival
blues, blues, blues...
From their ponytails and Prada...
To their iron-on tattoo...oo...oos..."

The crowd laughed. One of the hipsters, annoyed at being singled out, tossed him a dime in disdain, but before Charley could thank him kindly, the ushers threw open the doors to the theater, and the rush was on to get in and score a good seat.

Later, after the people lucky enough to have wrangled tickets were inside watching the movie and the rest had started to straggle home, Charley scooped up his night's earnings and returned his guitar to its case. A little quick addition put him close to twenty-eight bucks up, twice his usual take off the college kids on dates outside the Fiesta Five.

As he made his way toward Dargan's Pub, he marveled at how good it felt to have coin in his pocket. Adding to his pleasure was the fact that it was another warm California night. Crazy warm for February and already smelling of jasmine, a combination that always made him feel nostalgic. For what, he didn't know. Surely not his childhood, growing up in Chicago. If he was there now, he'd be fighting snow and cold just to keep alive. Nah, Santa Barbara was the town for him. The pink-tinged adobe and the courtyards full of bougainvillea made him feel like he was in Mexico. Not the Mexico with drug-gang killings and Montezuma's stomach grinder, but the one you saw on travel posters. Warm and lazy and anxious to serve up a cold cerveza. Maybe tonight he'd spring for a Dos Equis when he got to Dargan's instead of his usual Bud. *Why not?* he thought. Tonight he could afford it. Yeah, life was good. And then it wasn't.

Lying on the wet grass, one eye open, blood running from his mouth and two gaping holes in his chest, Charley stared at the Batman signal in the sky. Even if help was out there, he knew it would arrive too late.

The police report was short and to the point. African-American male, late forties, found dead. Two bullet wounds to the chest. Sunken Lawn Courthouse.

TWO

Nola MacIntire let go of the tiny handfuls of skin she'd been pinching back behind each ear and watched her smile lines bungee-jump back into place in the bathroom mirror. Geez, where had they all come from? She must have spent the last twenty years giggling like an idiot. But there was no time to indulge her nasal-labial fixation today. Thankfully, she had a murder to solve.

Tall, tan, and born-again blond, having accepted L'Oréal into her heart when she started going mousy brown in high school, Nola was also Deputy Chief of Detectives for the Santa Barbara Police Department. Back in college she'd wanted to join the FBI, but her friendly beach-babe demeanor, and the fact that she was a card-carrying liberal, had prompted the recruiter to conclude her first and only interview with a remark about how much money a pretty girl could make just doing the weather on TV.

Fortunately, the local P.D. had come to prize what the Feds had overlooked. Nola was a tenacious puzzle solver, and the puzzle she liked solving best, the one that sent a sharp little tingle up her spine every time, was who murdered whom — and why.

The five a.m. homicide call had landed in her lap like Christmas in July. Three weeks with hardly more to show than a little drug-related stabbing in the rundown college playground of Isla Vista had left her with far too much time to think, and what she thought about was growing old.

She'd pushed it to the back of her mind at twenty-eight, rationalized it at thirty, and tried to broker peace with it at thirty-two, but on the eve of her thirty-seventh birthday, her eyes welled up when she passed the pretzel place that had once been her favorite Betsey Johnson store. Nola had long ago transitioned from Betsey's colorful hooker couture into Tommy Hilfiger's All-American Girl, which she could already feel morphing into Donna Karan, the last stop on the road to Chico's and death. Even the luckiest Cinderella only got one shot at her twenties.

"Knock, knock."

"Who's there?"

"Your thirtieth birthday. I'm afraid I'm going have to take away all your silly party clothes."

"Oh, my God! Even the accessories?"

"Yep. The skintight skin, the boundless energy after midnight, it's all gotta go."

"But why didn't you warn me?!"

"I tried, ma'am, but you were too busy dancing."

"'Ma'am'!?!"

Benjamin Button had it right. Aging in reverse was the way to go. Getting younger and stronger every day. Sure, you still ended up in diapers, but you were little and cute, with people lining up to bounce you on their knees. It was a win-win.

Slapping on some ridiculously expensive moisturizer, hoping "Miracle Lift" wasn't just corporate-code for how much cash it lifted out of a gullible blonde's wallet, Nola ran a hairbrush through her loose, shoulder-length hair, grabbed a lipstick and mascara, and called it a morning. If God didn't want women to apply makeup at stoplights, he wouldn't have invented rearview mirrors. Checking out her amber-eyed reflection in the mirror one last time, she smiled and thought, *Oh, what the hell. If Betty White can be fabulous at any age, so can I.*

Back in the bedroom, she slipped into a Rag & Bone Valentina sweater and black pants, then tossed her closet looking for any two sandals that might pass as a matching pair. She kicked both shoes off at the same time every night, so how was it possible that they never managed to land in the same place? Finding a match, she slipped them on, grabbed her phone from the charger, pursed her gun to avoid the bulky shoulder holster, and headed out the door. In the hallway waiting for the elevator, she did a few calf stretches. Inside the elevator she did a couple of toe raises. Morning workout, done and done.

The air outside the condo complex was nipple-freezing cold. The warm winter night had been swallowed up by a thick layer of fog blowing in off the ocean. Across Cabrillo Boulevard, the volleyball poles on East Beach rose ghostly in the mist. It was pretty as a postcard but hell on her hair. She'd have to keep the top up on the T-bird till the sun came out and burned away the gloom.

Climbing into the little black Ford, she pressed the ignition, blasted the heat, and wondered how much longer she could go on having "Fun Fun Fun" before she'd start craving the comforts of a more grownup car. Time, she realized, not Daddy, would take the T-bird away. Cranking up her favorite vintage Beyoncé, she gunned the little convertible's big engine and shot up Cabrillo toward the scene of the crime. "*Who runs the world, girls…*"

Santa Barbara's elegant courthouse was smack in the center of town and a major tourist attraction. People stood in line to climb the clock tower, and concerts were held on the vast sunken lawn. Now the lawn was cordoned off with yellow police tape, and generator-powered work lights were infusing the early morning quiet with a sinister hum.

Nola pulled up and parked in front of the Coffee Cat. The kids inside, just firing up the espresso machines, were agog at the activity across the street. Wishing caffeine came in handy inhalers, like asthma meds, she resisted the urge to go in and order a double nonfat cap and sneak a meaningful glance at the muffins. The familiar blue Audi parked up ahead of her meant she was already late to the party. Stepping out of the car into the dusky overcast, she crossed the street and headed toward the lights.

Three

Detective Lieutenant Anthony Angellotti stood waiting by the body. Halfway across the damp lawn, Nola stopped to remove the orange and red Kate Spade slingbacks she'd eventually located behind a gym bag in her closet. All those seminars at the academy about emotional and physical burnout, but not a word about how hard homicide was on your shoes.

"Too pretty not to buy, even though they're killing your feet?" Tony called out.

"Too expensive to be ruined by wet grass," she called back.

"Sorry, forgot to spread my cloak," he said, doffing an imaginary Musketeers hat as she crossed the wide lawn to join him, shoes in hand.

"If chivalry were any deader, we'd run out of crime-scene tape." She laughed, marveling at her partner's radiant good humor, in spite of having been dragged out of bed at the crack of dawn to view a freshly decomposing former human being.

In addition to his perennially sunny disposition, Tony had the kind of boyish, Paul McCartney good looks that never seemed to get old. He and Nola had slept together a couple of times in the early days, but the relationship thing had never kicked in for either of them. A blessing in disguise, since it had allowed them to remain friends for more than fifteen years. Fifteen years? Where had they gone?

"Betty White," Nola's inner voice chastised her age-obsessed brain as she grabbed some nitrile exam gloves from Tony's scene case. Just lighten up and focus on the corpse. But when she looked down at the face of the victim, her heart sank.

"Oh no."

Tony shot her a puzzled look. "You know him?"

"I don't know him, know him. It's that sweet street singer who makes up songs outside Café Roma. Why would anybody want to shoot him?"

"Ours is not to reason why, ours is but to catch and fry," he replied, holding up an evidence bag with two .38-caliber shell casings. "Found these underneath the archway."

Nola followed Tony's gaze to the massive stone archway at the far side of the lawn. It was roughly the distance of a city block. The killer was definitely someone who knew how to shoot.

"Anything else?" she asked, running her eyes over the body.

"Nothing overtly visible to the naked eye." Tony recognized a familiar look on her face. "Okay, what are you already seeing that I don't?"

"It's what I'm *not* seeing. Where's his guitar?"

Tony shrugged. "This is just how the patrol officer found him. The man was traveling light."

"Doesn't make sense," she said, snapping on the exam gloves. "That guitar was his livelihood. I never once saw him without it. It had a strap with a green feather on it. You can still see the chafing marks it left around his neck." She knelt and gingerly pulled down the T-shirt, revealing the strap marks still visible on the rigored flesh.

"Maybe he left it home last night," Tony said, squatting

down at her side for a better look.

"Good theory if he'd had a home. And I'm guessing he was far too savvy to leave it at the shelter."

Tony signaled to a police photographer to come get a clean shot of the chafing marks, then turned back to Nola. "So, you think some sleazebag offed the poor guy for an old guitar and some spare change?"

"I hope not, but we better send an e-alert to the pawnshops just in case. Jeez, I've smiled at him a million times, but I never had a clue what his name was. Any ID in his pockets?"

Tony handed her a dog-eared card. "All we found were a couple of old roaches, more lint than pot, and this library card."

Nola read the name on the card. "Charles Beaufort." It sounded Southern, apropos of the smooth, warm baritone and the Mississippi-wide smile that had been Charles Beaufort's best feature back when he was still breathing.

"What's Alex's call on the preliminary time of death?" The question was asked more out of habit than need to know. Nola had been around enough victims, algor mortis, to recognize the stages of body cooling and muscle stiffening, even without the medical examiner's assessment.

"He's guesstimating between seven and nine last night. Cause of death is most likely those two sizable bullet holes to the chest." Tony nodded toward the ME's ambulance parked under a wide-leafed fig tree. "Alex is having his morning blood clots in syrup, waiting for us to give him the okay to remove the body."

"It's beet juice with ginseng," Nola laughed.

"Whatever it is, it creeps me out," he said with a shiver.

"The guy makes his living Ginsuing dead bodies. Being creepy is pretty much part of the job description."

Tony stood and helped Nola to her feet as he continued to fill her in on the prelim investigation of the scene. "Evidence team ran a detector over the lawn, but so many tourists tromping through every day, it's a forensic stew. Going to be hell sorting it all out. Juan and his guys are doing a door-to-door for witnesses, but I don't expect much help there either."

Detective Juan Garza always got the canvassing detail. Thin and dark with a wry smile, Juan had a natural knack for putting people at ease. A cop at the door usually remained at the door; Juan was regularly invited in for coffee. But Tony was right. If there had been a witness, he or she would most likely have come forward already. Nearly ten hours after the fact, the best they could reasonably hope for was that someone had heard the shots and mistaken them for fireworks from the festival. At least that would help them pinpoint the TOD.

By the time Nola and Tony finished assessing the crime scene, the sun was already glinting off the courthouse's red-tile roof. The bell tower clock chimed seven-fifteen. Charles Beaufort had been lying out in the wet grass all night, and his killer wasn't likely to have hung around waiting to see what happened next.

Nola shielded her eyes and smiled at her handsome partner.

"Nothing more to do here. Shall we head over to the shelter and see if we can verify that Charles Beaufort was his real name, and hopefully discover that somebody had a better motive for killing him than stealing a beat-up old guitar?"

Tony took a last look at Charles Beaufort's lifeless body being bagged and tagged. "What's the difference at this point?"

"The difference," Nola said, grabbing her sandals off the

stretcher to make way for sadder cargo, "is that if the world's really that messed up, I'm not sure I want to Zumba in it anymore."

"Zumba? Is that one of those words only women know, like Pinterest?"

"It's a Latin dance exercise thing. You get too old to go to clubs, you got to get your salsa on somehow."

"Oh, we're in midlife-crisis mode again. So how 'bout, before we hit the shelter, we swing by Max's for some cheer-up pancakes and bacon?"

"Italian, please. A woman over forty has to get an hour of sustained aerobic exercise every day just to *not* gain weight. You'd be cheering me right into my fat pants."

"Since when are you over forty?"

"I've decided to start rounding up so it won't be such a killer shock when it happens."

"Okay, then, how 'bout you get some tasteless eggwhite-y thing, and I get double pancakes, extra bacon, and you can have fun telling me about how many empty calories I'm consuming?"

"I love the way you get me."

Four

The gray-ponytailed woman on duty at the shelter dabbed tears from behind her wire-rimmed glasses. She wished she could give Tony more information. Women always did. Nola had long ago learned to just hang back and let her partner work his charm. She studied the small group of transients loitering nearby, anxious to hear what had befallen one of their own, while the woman told Tony what she could about the late Charles Beaufort.

"Charley was originally from Chicago."

Not the South, Nola thought. *Well, that's the first thing I got wrong.*

"He had a happy way about him. The first night he came in for a bed, I asked if he liked to be called Charles or Charley, and he said, 'Ma'am, you can call me anything but late for supper.'" She fished under her sleeve for another of her seemingly endless stash of sweater tissues, but came up empty.

"Any idea where Charley might have been going last night, or who he might have been seeing?" Tony asked, as he passed her more Kleenex.

The woman blew her nose and said she couldn't be certain. He'd been at the Arlington most nights that week, playing for the folks in town to see the movies, but beyond that she had no idea. The gathered transients under her care had little more to offer. None of them knew if Charley had been meeting up with anybody or why anybody might want to kill him. Always in a good mood, Charley had steered clear of the petty arguments that occasionally flared up among the dispossessed, often making up songs that soothed the commotion and made everybody laugh.

Nola studied their tired faces, weathered by drugs and disappointment, and tried to imagine them laughing. She reminded herself for the thousandth time to be grateful for what she had, to quit whining about what she missed, and to always wear sunscreen.

"...*watching the detectives...*"

Elvis Costello's funky drawl drew everyone's attention to Nola's knock-off Chanel tote. She'd realized her ringtone was too cute by half the first time it went off, but she kept forgetting to change it. They watched as she pawed through pens and makeup and a million loose receipts and finally came up with her cell.

It was Kesha at the station. The e-alert had paid off. A twitching junkie was trying to pawn an old guitar at a shop on Haley Street. Nola flashed on Charley's big, warmhearted grin, snuffed out for the price of a little bit of high.

"Excuse me. Tony, we've got a possible hit on the guitar."

Outside, the street was filling up with news vans. The local press was being outflanked by reporters up from Los Angeles to cover the film festival. "Murder at the Movies!" It was just the kind of tie-in that would send the mayor and the city council sledding down freak-out mountain shrieking, "Noooo!"

On her way to the shelter, Nola had popped the top on the T-bird, a decision she was currently regretting. As she started to pull away from the curb, Rachel Palmer, a petite Action News reporter with alabaster skin, raced over, grabbed hold of her steering wheel, and stuck a microphone in her face.

"Detective MacIntire! Who were you here to interview? Do you know who the shooter is?"

"Well, I can't say for certain, Rachel, but it's usually the guy with the gun." Nola revved the T-bird's engine. "You want to let go of my steering wheel now?"

Rachel's skin was even more flawless in person than it was on TV. Invisible pores and no lipstick-catching lip lines — it was every woman's dream. Under different circumstances, Nola would have been tempted to ask what C serum she used, but Rachel was more than just a pretty face. Her tiny hand remained doggedly attached to Nola's steering wheel as she fired off another question.

"According to my sources, Mr. Beaufort was last seen outside the Arlington Theater before the *Batman* premiere. Do you believe his murder is somehow related to the film festival?"

Nola didn't dare be glib this time. "We have absolutely no reason to believe that Mr. Beaufort's murder is in any way connected to the festival. He was a street performer, so naturally he gravitated to large crowds. Last night the largest crowd just happened to be in front of the Arlington."

"Have you spoken to the festival organizers?" Rachel pressed.

"The police department has no further comment at this time," Nola replied as she eased the T-bird out of Rachel's grasp and into the street. Looking back in her rearview mirror, she saw Rachel and her colleagues descending on the shelter like a pack of sound-bite-hungry wolves. She hoped the occupants, long accustomed to being shunned and neglected, would enjoy their fifteen minutes of fame, but the full-court press meant the push would be on to solve this one fast.

"...*watching the detectives*..."

It was Tony calling from his Audi up ahead.

"Excited you're going to be on TV?" he asked, knowing full well she'd rather gargle with pushpins.

"I almost pulled Rachel's arm out of her socket trying to get away. She's trying to establish a link between Charley's murder and the film festival."

"Well, we had to know that was coming. Think we'll get lucky and this junkie at the pawnshop will turn out to be our guy?"

"As Cassady probably once said to Kerouac, 'Beats me, Jack.' But I'm sure starting to hope so."

Five

It was a short drive to the pawnshop. The owner, a sharp little sparrow of a man, had kept the suspect haggling while his plump, bedazzled peacock of a wife called the cops. Walking through the dust-caked door, Nola felt like she was passing through a portal to an older, dingier era. Cases full of cheap jewelry, stacks of used DVDs, and a jumble of battered luggage filled every inch of the cramped space.

The junkie was cowering against a counter in the back. He was high as a kite and about as sharp as a marble, but he was clearly no killer. The stringy little guy was shaking like the San Andreas Fault inside him was shifting plates, but there was no mistaking the blood on his tattered sweatshirt and Charley's guitar with the feather on the strap.

Nola and Tony flashed their badges and took turns asking questions.

"I'm Detective MacIntire. I need you to tell me where you got that guitar."

The junkie started scratching a scabby patch of skin on the side of his neck. "Wasn't no point leaving it with a dead man."

Tony picked up the guitar and played a chord. "You know how he *got* dead?"

"Dude just shot him, click, click, click." The scratching grew more intense.

Nola's eyes lit up. "You saw the shooter?"

"Under the circle by the pink flowers. Shot him and just ran away," came the disjointed reply.

The stone archway where they'd found the shell casings was bordered by pink hibiscus. So far the junkie's story was fitting perfectly with their reconstruction of the crime. An eyewitness, even one with tweaker vocabulary issues, was still worth his weight in circumstantial evidence. If he could give a halfway decent description of the shooter, they could get a police sketch out on the street by noon.

"What did this dude look like?" Tony strummed another chord.

The junkie stared at the old guitar like it was his next fix. "Wasn't no point leaving it with a dead man." He was scratching so hard now, tiny fissures in the scabby patch were opening up and starting to bleed.

Nola took his dirty hand from his neck and gently held it. "Relax, okay? You're doing great," she said, channeling her inner nurse. "This dude, was he tall, short, white, black?"

"Dude just shot him, click, click, click."

No matter how they framed the questions, the methalated answers always came back the same. Thirty minutes later they were no closer to a description than they were when they'd started. Obviously the little crank vulture had seen something and heard plenty before he picked Charley's bones clean, but it was impossible to glean anything from his ramblings beyond, "Dude just shot him, click, click, click."

Nola and Tony passed him off to a patrol car to be taken in and booked for theft. Hopefully he'd babble something more coherent once the drugs playing badminton with his brain cells started to wear off.

Tony struck a final chord on the guitar and grinned. "And so the handsome detective and his intrepid female partner were back to square one."

Six

Nothing new broke that afternoon. As expected, Juan's canvass of the area around the courthouse hadn't produced any new witnesses. Nola and Tony interviewed the street people who congregated near the Trader Joe's parking lot, but nobody knew of anyone who had beef with Charley. For the price of a dollar in an old Starbucks cup, one entrepreneurial soul sent them in the direction of Dargan's Pub, where Charley liked to drink, but the bartender there told the same sad story. Charley had been a model patron, no fights, no attitude. He just drank a few beers and made up songs.

"Why would anybody want to kill a nice guy like that?"

Nola assured him they'd do their best to find out, but with nothing to go on but the musings of a strung-out junkie, the prospect was looking bleak.

She was back in the squad room, wrapping up an email about Charley to Chicago P.D., when she was summoned to Chief Johnson's office. Tony had already gone home, and she'd been two minutes from doing the same. Passing Kesha at her desk, she smiled and sighed.

"So close."

Sam Johnson had been Nola's boss for a little over five years. Most times their mutual respect and fondness for each other made working together a breeze. This wasn't one of those times. Sam started off calm, but five minutes into their "discussion" he was ready to wring her pretty neck. The shit, in the form of the six o'clock news, had hit the fan. True, it could all be managed with just a little cooperation, but blind cooperation wasn't exactly her strong suit. She watched Sam's corn-fed, country-boy complexion turn from healthy pink to over-ripe plum as she refused for the umpteenth time to charge the junkie thief with Charley's murder.

"This isn't just me asking," Sam huffed. "The city's elected pains-in-the-asses are on my phone every five minutes! We've got a town packed with celebrities and a murder right outside the damn courthouse!"

"I understand that," Nola said calmly, wondering what color would come after plum. Puce, maybe?

Sam crossed and stood over her chair like an angry gym teacher. "Well, try to understand this. If you charge the junkie, we can make it clear to the press that this was just an isolated case of homeless-on-homeless crime. The filmies will go back to La La Land and tell their friends that Santa Barbara's still a safe place to go to the movies, and maybe you and I can keep our jobs!"

Nola knew better than to try to out-shout Sam in his own office, but he was coming off like some clichéd captain in a TV drama berating the detective beneath him for not playing ball, and it was starting to piss her off. To avoid sending him into full cardiac arrest, she tried to adopt a tone somewhere between Sincere English Teacher and Ruler-Wielding Nun.

"I'm sorry, Sam, but I'm not going to arrest a man for a crime he didn't commit."

"How do you know he didn't do it? He had the victim's blood on his clothes! He was pawning his guitar! He's a meth addict, for God sakes!"

"So's Charlie Sheen. He's hanging by the pool over at the Bacara — should I arrest him too?"

"You think you're funny?"

"In a winsome kind of way."

"Well, maybe for a change you could try being pragmatic?"

"You mean like stop carrying a purse and start wearing a fanny pack? Sure, it would make chasing bad guys easier, but it's never gonna happen."

"*I mean* like charging the little tweaker with murder so the film freaks won't go home blabbing to anyone who'll listen that Santa Barbara's got a crazed killer on the loose!"

"That's not pragmatic, it's lying, and I don't lie."

"Really? Shall we check your real weight against what I'm guessing it says on your driver's license?"

"That's different. Highway Patrol just assumes women lie, so they automatically add ten pounds. We know they do it, so we have no choice but to play the under. It's a vicious circle."

Sam plopped down in his ergonomic chair and stretched his arms across his desk. "Look, just charge the junkie now so everybody'll calm down. I'm not asking you to end the investigation. Later, if we find out he's innocent, which I highly doubt, we'll drop the charges. It happens all the time."

"Not on purpose," Nola countered, her patience wearing thin. "Crackheads are rarely crack shots, and this one's got junkie-Parkinson's so bad he can't hold a thought straight, let alone a .38. And where's the gun?"

"Who knows? Maybe he ditched it?"

"He ditches a five-hundred-dollar gun and tries to pawn a forty-dollar guitar? Now, if you wanted me to charge him with being the dumbest junkie ever... Sam, I'm telling you, he's not the guy."

"Well thanks for your opinion, but I happen to disagree."

"Then you charge him! I don't want any part of this!"

Frustrated, she stood up to go; then remembered she needed his permission to leave.

Sam gave it one last shot. "Come on, Nols, you caught him. If I charge him, it's just going to look weird. Can't you for one moment think of the greater good?"

"There's nothing good about charging the wrong guy."

"Fine, if you're so sure he didn't do it...go on. Get out. You're dismissed."

"Quite frequently," she replied on her way to the door, "and by many people, usually as just another airhead blonde, but I won't lie about murder." She'd wanted to sound tough, but even at rounded-up forty, she couldn't quite get the little-girl whininess out of her voice when she got mad.

Outside Sam's office, Nola was met by the surprised faces of her fellow officers. Clearly the walls were thinner than she thought. Kesha was holding out Nola's mock-Chanel tote. "I thought you might want to make a quick getaway."

"Thanks, Kesh," Nola said, grateful for intuitive girlfriends. On her way out of the squad room, she chided her colleagues. "Okay, folks, move along. Nothing to see here."

Rehashing the argument on her ride home, Nola imagined herself saying the millions of things she wished she'd said, in that sexy Kathleen Turner growl that reduced tough guys to marshmallows. *This ain't over, bub.* But the image burst when she pulled into her parking space and dropped her purse getting out of the car, then spent what seemed like an eternity down on her knees, fumbling under the wheelbase for her MAC berry lip gloss, a carton of Tic Tacs, and her badge.

When she finally opened the door to her condo, she kicked off her shoes, not giving a rat's ass where they landed, and collapsed on the sofa with a belly full of mad.

Her spirits lightened a little when her phone whistled,

signaling a new text. But it wasn't Chicago P.D. getting back to her about Charley. It was a message from a guy she hadn't seen in years saying if she wasn't married yet, he'd like to fly her to his place in Telluride for the weekend.

When women got lonely, they repainted their bedrooms and had lunch with their friends. When men got lonely, they panic-texted old girlfriends.

Nola was grateful that men still found her worth the price of a lobster bisque and a crisp Pinot Grigio at Brophy's, let alone a ski trip to Colorado, but she couldn't help missing the boys they used to be. The carefree guys who'd laughed too loud and played too hard and replaced each other so effortlessly in her heart that it was hard to tell where one relationship had ended and the next one had begun. All except for Josh. But then every girl needed a good eight-year cry in her life. How else would she understand pop music?

It was a sad ending to a frustrating day. She knew she was getting old, but old-boyfriends-start-texting-you old? She might as well take up scrapbooking. When she texted back, she was surprised to find it was actually fun catching up again, but she made it clear that a ski-trip booty call wasn't in the cards. "No, no, u r not the 1 4 me."

Seven

Nola was stretched out on her living room rug listening to the outré fabulous Chrissie Hynde and rereading her case notes on Charley when she heard a knock at the door. It was after nine. Tony was at dinner with his latest thing, her girlfriends would call before dropping by, nothing was due from Amazon, and she hadn't buzzed a serial killer up in weeks. Maybe, if she just lay quiet, whatever Mystery Achievement was out there would give up and go away. The second knock was louder. On the off chance that it might mean Thin Mints in her future, she planked off the rug and went to peep out the peephole.

Outside in the hallway, a petite, pixie-cut brunette in Bluefly overalls and a pink crop top was staring sheepishly down at the carpet. One of the cluster of twentysomethings who had just moved in down the hall, she probably wanted to borrow a scissors or a sofa or something. They hadn't looked all that put together when they moved in. Putting on her best meet-the-new-neighbor smile, Nola opened the door and said, "Hi."

"Hi. I'm Nancy. I was wondering if you had a hammer and screwdriver I could borrow?"

Nancy was as cute as a button, if the button had big brown eyes that had recently been crying. Tactfully pretending not to notice, Nola swung open the door. "Yeah, sure, come on in."

Nancy followed Nola into the kitchen to the everything drawer, where useful items like obsolete phone chargers, loose batteries, and stale Chinese fortune cookies lay dormant for months.

"I'm Nola MacIntire, by the way," Nola said, remembering her manners as she rooted through the drawer for the tools. A hammer and a screwdriver, no wonder the poor girl had been crying. Do-it-yourself construction projects were about as much fun as outside-your-comfort-zone sex. Sure, they both started out exciting, but eventually you found yourself twisted into some ridiculous position, trying to fit the right part into the wrong hole, hoping it would all be over soon because you forgot to record *Scandal*.

"Phillips head or regular?" Nola asked, holding up both.

"I don't know," Nancy replied in a voice that was holding back tears.

"Hey, it's okay. We'll figure it out. What are you putting together?"

"It's a bookcase thing from Ikea." A tear broke free and made a run for her cheek.

"Looks like it's putting up quite a fight." More tears came chasing after the first. Nola tore a paper towel from a roll on the sink and handed it to the tiny stranger who had unexpectedly become the focal point of her evening. "Sweetie, are you okay?"

"My boyfriend broke up with me today."

"Oh, I'm sorry. Can I get you a glass of water or something?"

"In a tweet."

"O-kay, margaritas it is."

Two boxes of Kleenex and one bottle of Skinnygirl margaritas later, Nola was totally up to speed on the ill-fated romance of Nancy and Ken. They'd met at an art show. Nancy had been working as a cater-waiter, and Ken was covering the event for the *Santa Barbara Reader*. Nola loved the *Reader*. A free weekly that survived on advertising, it was a perfect blend of hard news, horoscopes, community awareness, and movie listings.

Unfortunately, its owner and managing editor had a daughter. Nancy had sensed something was going on between Ken and his boss's offspring, but like most people who cheat, Ken had lied and told her she was crazy. She'd believed him because she loved him. She still loved him. In spite of his 140-characters-or-less breakup tweet, in her eyes he was still Ernest Hemingway, the God Apollo, and a Jewish Johnny Depp all rolled into one. Nola thought of how Josh had once seemed like all that and more to her own twentysomething eyes. Moles, near blind from birth, were VEGA 3 electron microscopes compared to young women in love.

As sure as Nancy was that she'd never get over Ken, Nola was equally sure she would, but strangers crying their hearts out in your living room tend to be a tad resistant to even the most well-reasoned arguments. The best she could do was maneuver Nancy away from her beige linen sofa to a more snot-resistant rattan chair and parcel out platitudes between drinks and drinks between sobs.

"You've got to be Taylor Swift. You know, just 'shake it off.'" It was late, and she was clearly running low on cogent advice.

"I don't know what I should do," Nancy sobbed. "Maybe I should text him, or go over to his apartment. Do you have a baseball bat?"

"Sorry, I never let my guests drink and drive high fly balls."

"Too bad, 'cause that's just where I'd be aiming. Oh God,

I love him so much. I really need some pot."

"Ah, you know, this might be a good time to mention that I'm a detective with the Santa Barbara police department."

"Seriously?"

"Yeah, I get that reaction a lot. Look, you don't need this guy. He sounds like a thoughtless egomaniac who probably got *way* too much love as a child. "

"His mother framed his bar mitzvah suit. It's hanging in her bedroom."

"Really? Wow. Well, there you are. I'd rather arm wrestle ISIS than deal with that brand of crazy. There are a million great guys out there, Jewish, Japanese…Argentinean, so sexy, am I right? Trust me, one day you'll be bodysurfing or at a party, and suddenly you'll realize you haven't thought about Ken for a few days, and that's when it'll all start to turn around. How long were you two together?"

"Eight months."

"Then the general rule of thumb is to suck it up and focus on your work, and in half that time, maybe less if you get a promotion, meet a new guy, or get a really spectacular haircut, you'll be over him."

"I don't want to be over him."

"I know, but the good news is, you will be. In the meantime, no pot. Not 'cause I'm a cop, pot will just make you hungry. Ken's already done a number on your heart. Don't let him mess up your thighs. Best breakup food: kale salad with salsa. You can binge for days and still look good in your breakup bikini. Did I mention you need to buy a breakup bikini?"

"You should write a book or something. *Breaking Up for Dummies.*"

"You're not a dummy. This happens to everybody."

Nancy made a halfhearted attempt at a smile, but the tears were still falling. Nola patted her shoulder and carried their margarita glasses into the kitchen. It was time to transition from Mexican beta-blocker to Colombian caffeine.

The clock on the coffeemaker read 12:45. Less than twenty-eight hours ago, Sam hadn't been furious, Nancy hadn't been heartbroken, and Charley Beaufort had been looking forward to a long, full life. Back in the living room, Pink came up on the iPod shuffle. *"Darlin', who knew?"*

Eight

Augustus Gillette the Third was a big man, both physically and in the moneyed circles he traveled in. As chairman of the Santa Barbara Coastal Commission, multimillion-dollar deals rose and fell with the bang of his gavel — his "second dick," as it was jokingly referred to by the dot-com commodores he slapped backs and downed single malts with down at the yacht club.

Married thirty-seven years to his Yale sweetheart, Gus felt he'd earned his divorce and the gorgeous new arm charm he laughingly called his "Viagra wife." Her name was Haven, and she was everything that name suggested. Twenty-two years of Santa Barbara sun had produced the kind of warmly tanned tits and ass that a man pushing sixty could happily retreat and retire to. But tonight Gus was far from the lee shore.

His father had often cautioned him to be outwardly genial but inwardly leery of the "hail fellow well met" members of his own class, the theory being that only people you innately trusted were in a position to cheat you. But Gus had trusted: in the old boys' club, the rich boys' club, the Yale boys' club. And the result had been an economic collapse of catastrophic proportions.

Upon hearing they were broke, Haven had taken to sleeping in a guest room on the pretext that Gus's snoring kept her awake. An excuse not worthy of her guile, since the impending loss of his expertly tailored Savile Row shirt had robbed Gus of any semblance of sleep for the past six weeks.

Alone in his darkened bedroom, Gus lay pondering his folly. He was a big man made small by the vastness of his king-size bed. Not a standard king, but one custom designed to be just a few inches bigger than the next guy's. Even in sleep, he'd strived to get an edge. But now he was sleeping alone. He pictured Haven lying awake on the other side of the thick Venetian plaster, calculating how much she might still get her manicured claws on in a divorce.

The cause of Gus's ruin was awaiting trial in federal prison. Nicholas Ridener-Howe Esq., aka Nicky Boy, aka First Class Son of a Bitch, had turned out to be a Ponzi schemer of Madoffian proportions. Gus chuckled to himself imagining Nick, who'd once refused to give him a lift to the Super Bowl because sharing a G6 made him claustrophobic, trapped in an eight-by-ten-foot cell with whatever tattooed homie the cat dragged in.

When the world first caved in, Gus had cursed his fair-weather wife and the phony financier, but now he could afford to laugh, because now he had a secret, one that rendered both his bankruptcy and his impending divorce moot.

He was shaken from his thoughts by the sound of the bedroom door. There she stood in all her gauzy, backlit, baby-doll glory. *So,* Gus thought, *she couldn't even wait until dawn to break the news.* He wondered how long she'd been rehearsing her speech. "It's not you, you did your best. It's just I…I…"

Of course, there'd have to be a suitable pause for tears before she segued to the topic of her financial settlement. The see-through negligee was a sinister touch, but he couldn't really hate her for that. The fact that Haven often went to absurd lengths to look devastatingly sexy in any situation was one of the prime reasons he'd married her. It had flattered him to think, "Here I am, almost sixty, and I can still get that."

Haven lingered in the doorway, letting the hall light that was shining through her nightie give maximum play to her curves, before whispering, "Baby, are you awake?"

Gus decided to keep the tone light. "I'm not snoring, so I guess I must be."

She crossed to the enormous bed, looking chastened and ashamed. "Oh, daddy, I'm sorry I've been such a bitch."

Gus's hope started to stiffen. Was it possible he'd misjudged the depth of her lack of feeling for him? She slipped under the covers, all kitten warm and female softness.

"It was just the shock of learning you'd invested so much without even discussing it with me. And then you tried to hide it from me...I know I'm not a brainiac like Angry Susan, but I'm just as much a wife to you as she was. I was hurt that you didn't trust me."

Gus's mind raced. "Of course I trust you, sweetheart." He hoped the lie would buy him time to divine what she was up to.

"I wanted to apologize last night, before the movie," she said, running a finger along his jaw. "But then someone took you aside somewhere, and with all the excitement of meeting Ryan Gosling…"

And there it was, a motive as transparent as her nightgown. Words exchanged out of sight of prying eyes. She must have sensed a little bribery was afoot. After all, how many yes votes in front of the commission had been followed by long vacations in Tahiti and shopping sprees in Paris? Of course, things were different now, but Haven didn't know that. She didn't know the secret.

Gus smiled down at her impossibly pretty face as he tallied

up the cost of their short life together. Marriage to Gold Digger Barbie...half his assets to his ex-wife, Susan...her young flesh yielding to his aging carcass...the dream mansion in Hope Ranch and the huge diamond on the hand now gently stroking his chest...the pleasure of telling her she was going to have to kiss the mansion, the diamond, and all the rest of it goodbye — ahhh, something far too delectable to rush. The higher she hung her own rope, the more pleasurable it would be to pull the chair out from under her.

"I do trust you, sweetheart. I was just ashamed," Gus lied.

"Shhh," she cooed. "Don't say that. Nicky fooled a lot of smart people." The hand with the diamond slid lower.

"Thank you, but smart people don't lay themselves open to be conned. It was a hard lesson, but it stuck. The 'someone' you saw me with tonight offered to solve all our financial problems if I'd endorse a certain development project that's before the commission. Even offered to cut me in on the deal."

"Really? What did you say?"

Her voice was cool, not a trace of mendacity, but Gus could hear the hum of the cash register in her head. He savored the words on his tongue like fine cognac before finally whispering, "I turned it down flat. I've even written a speech against the project to ensure the other board members will have no choice but to vote no along with me."

The look of stunned fury he'd imagined failed to materialize. No frown lines marred her perfect features, no storm raged in her ice-blue eyes. Confused, he pressed on. "I've been greedy and unprincipled my whole life, and look where it's gotten me. I've decided it's time to make a change."

"Good for you, baby." Haven stretched her arms over her head to better showcase her breasts, a clear sign she was still expecting sex.

"Good? I turned down cash that would have saved our

ass, and you're okay with that?"

"Better than okay, I'm proud of you. Never mind about the money. We'll find some way to get by."

The hot slap of shame Gus felt for having misjudged her took the stiffness out of his sails. Haven held him, small and flaccid, both literally and figuratively, in the palm of her hand.

"But we're going to have to do better than this if we're going to celebrate." She took a playful nip at his earlobe, then rolled across the bed to a drawer in the nightstand. "I bought a new toy."

She must have hidden it earlier, but when? A question Gus instantly pushed aside to make room for one far more tantalizing. Six weeks of celibacy were about to end with whatever she was reaching for in that drawer. They'd already graduated from handcuffs and spankings to leashes and dog collars. Even in Susan's best days, she'd only wanted run-of-the-mill sex, but Haven's taste in kink was all-embracing: a cuddly stuffed animal disguising a dildo, a cat-o'-nine-tails, Woody Allen's vibrating egg. Whatever it was, she'd bundled it under the covers and was slinking back toward him with it. His salacious imagination was working like a little blue pill.

"Are you going to tell me what it is?"

"It's more fun if you guess."

"Not even a hint?"

"Close your eyes, give me your hand, and I'll slide it in," she whispered, and like any good lap dog doing tricks for a treat, he obeyed.

By the time Gus felt his finger against the cold steel of the trigger, it was too late for guesses. She squeezed her hand hard on top of his, and the gun went off.

Haven recoiled, less horrified by the Picasso she'd created with bits of blood and brain on her favorite Frette sheets than by the noise a gun makes when you actually blow somebody's head apart with it.

Although, technically, Gus had shot himself, and there'd be powder burns on his hand to prove it. Of course, she had powder burns, too. She'd shielded her face with the pillow, but her hand and arm were exposed, and there was blood spatter on her nightie. But it could all be explained away if she just kept her nerve. Ears still ringing, she suppressed her gag reflex and steeled herself for what had to come next.

Well, I've had to do worse things in bed with the big dope, she thought as she lay herself down on top of Gus's bloody body and rocked back and forth. It was only natural that, hearing a shot and finding her husband dead, a young widow, overcome with grief, would throw herself on his body, sobbing till the police arrived. As for motive, an old man distraught over losing his money: He obviously just couldn't live with the disgrace.

Peeling herself off the sticky corpse, Haven looked down once more with regret at the exquisite sheets, the only memento from her trip to Milan. Then, with genuine tears in her eyes for the lost linens, she reached for the phone and called the police.

Nine

The inside of Nola's T-bird was like a meat freezer. The dashboard clock read three a.m., meaning it was really two a.m., since she never bothered changing it for daylight saving time. She'd barely said goodnight to Nancy and climbed into bed when the call came in. Another cold morning, another cold-blooded murder or possible suicide. The truth was still TBD. Sam would naturally be hoping for suicide, since there probably wasn't a convenient little junkie to pin it on this time.

Tony's blue Audi was idling in front of the electric gates, waiting to be buzzed in, when Nola pulled up behind him. If she'd known the length of Augustus Gillette the Third's driveway, she would have suggested they carpool to save gas.

The imposing pile of bricks that Gus and Haven called home was surrounded by six acres of avocado trees, and the front lawn was just a few feet shy of the ninth hole at Augusta. As they climbed out of their cars, Tony let out a low whistle. "Maybe the guy killed himself over the water bill."

"I'd laugh, but my brain's on energy save."

"Drinking alone last night?"

"No."

"Come on, you can't hide those Visine eyes."

"I was drinking, just not alone."

"New guy?"

"New neighbor. Her boyfriend broke up with her in a tweet."

"Really, is that cool now?"

"NO! Same goes for email, Facebook, Tumblr, and smoke signals. Why do guys think 'easiest way' is synonymous with 'best way'?"

"You'd understand if you'd ever peed standing up."

There was an empty patrol car and an ambulance already parked outside the house. Tony knocked on the window of the meat wagon. The paramedics inside were packed up and ready to roll. They'd been in and out, and there was nothing they could do. When Alex arrived to officially examine the body, he'd take it back to the morgue in his own ride, so they figured they might as well be heading home. Their unanimous opinion was "very messy suicide" by gun. The patrol cops who'd arrived on the scene first had come to the same conclusion.

"Are they inside now?" Tony asked the ginger-haired ambulance driver.

"No, they're checking the grounds for signs of an intruder, just doing due diligence, I guess. She's in there by herself."

"You mean the victim's wife?"

"I mean ... oh, hell, I don't know what I mean," the guy said, laughing. "But I'm probably going to hell for what I'm thinking."

Tony wanted clarification, but Nola was shivering and central heating was just a few hundred feet away. She thanked the paramedic and spun Tony toward the house. "Whatever he meant, we'll find out inside."

The carved mahogany front door was high and wide enough to accommodate a small parade float. Nola rang the bell as Tony covetously eyed the layout.

"Jealous much?" she asked, rubbing her hands against

her arms to get warm.

Tony didn't have time to answer. The sight of Haven, looking like she'd just come in first in a bloody-wet-nightie contest, hit him like a stroke. Nola felt a momentary pang of envy and was instantly ashamed. *Envious of a beautiful young woman covered in her dead husband's blood? Am I really that screwed up?*

Nola made perfunctory introductions and "sorry for your loss" remarks as Haven ushered them into a foyer that was roughly the size of Versailles. Tony regained his senses enough to express his own condolences and politely ask to be shown to the body.

"It's horrible," Haven murmured, before tossing back a million-dollar mane of highlighted hair and leading them up the five or so miles of stairs to Gus's bedroom.

As they climbed the staircase, Tony threw Haven a few softball questions about the night's events, and Nola took notes. The results were as follows.

PRELIMINARY WITNESS ACCOUNT: HAVEN GILLETTE.

Asleep in adjoining room.

Awoken by gunshot shortly after one a.m.

Immediately went to victim's room.

Recalls no signs of intruders.

Believes gun in victim's hand to be victim's gun from library desk.

Collapsed on body, distraught.

Has Detective Angellotti eating out of her pretty little hand.

When they reached Gus's bedroom, Tony asked Haven to please remain outside and not wash any evidence off her body till the crime unit arrived. The "perfect" before "body" was implied.

Nola's first grim look at what was left of Gus Gillette

seemed to back up most of Haven's statements. Victim in bed, no signs of a struggle, gun in hand, shot distance consistent with distribution of bone and gray matter all over the, *wow*, really gorgeous sheets. From the other side of the enormous bed, Tony was coming to the same conclusion.

"Looks like she's probably telling the truth," he said as he counted up fragments of skull.

"Maybe," Nola replied, wondering if things were really as straightforward as the evidence suggested. For a woman who had thrown herself on her husband's body in grief, Haven had remarkably un-smudged makeup. Either she had magic mascara or there was more to her story than met the eye.

"Ba ba bump."

"What?" Tony asked.

"Rim shot. I made a bad pun in my head."

"You're a very odd woman."

"So I'm told."

The forensic unit arrived. Alex began his investigation of the body and various pieces of its head. The crime scene was coming to life. Nola nudged Tony when she caught sight of a boner on the fat cop swabbing Haven for gunpowder residue.

"There's something you don't see on *NCIS*."

"Hey, every guy in this room is waging that war. He just happens to be losing."

When Haven was done being mopped and swabbed, Nola escorted her to her bathroom so she could shower off the blood that was beginning to dry and crust on her dazzling Dior nightie. On her way back, Nola was waylaid by Sebastian Jones, SBPD's straight-outta-Caltech crime geek. Nola had always wanted a puppy, but her condo had a strict no-pets rule. Shaggy, sweet, and anxious to please, Sebastian was proving to be the next best thing. He was so naturally lovable that whenever his forensic cyber-spying helped solve a case, she was secretly tempted to tousle his hair, coo "Who's a good boy?" and toss him a Snausage.

Haven had given them permission to search Gus's laptop in the den for a suicide note, but claimed she didn't know Gus's password to get in. Judging by the mile-wide grin on his face, Sebastian had worked out the magic words, or at least bypassed them.

"Hey, good news!" Sebastian shouted, stopping just short of bowling Nola over in his excitement to reach her.

"You cracked the laptop?"

The words flew out of Sebastian's mouth like bullets from a machine gun. "Yeah. First, I found a shitload…I mean…a bunch of emails from Gillette to that Ponzi-guy, Ridener-Howe. They start out tough, threatening to go all Tony Soprano if Howe doesn't give him his money back, but the last couple are just weak."

"Weak?"

"Yeah, guy's begging like a little bitch." A flush of red started at Sebastian's neckline and raced toward his forehead. "Not 'bitch' like a woman, 'bitch' like —"

"Yeah, I get it. Keep talking."

"Right, sorry. Well, everyone knows to diversify, right? But your dead guy —"

"The deceased."

"The deceased went all in with Howe and lost everything. His bank statements were bleak. Dude's surviving on fumes, or at least he was till he whacked himself."

"*If* he whacked himself."

"Right, if."

"How'd you crack his password so fast?"

"Old people keep it easy, so they won't forget. He had a picture of his boat next to his laptop. The back of the boat said *I Got Mine*, and that got me in."

"He named his boat *I Got Mine?*"

"Yeah, the guy, I mean the deceased, was pretty much an A-hole."

"Okay, first rule of policing is 'never dis the victim,' and yeah, sounds like he pretty much was. Anyway, great work."

"Thanks, but like I said, it was easy. Old people always leave obvious clues."

"So weak," Nola said, making a mental note to move the engraved photo of her adored childhood cat, Gracie, from its obvious spot by her Mac.

"Find anything else interesting?" she asked.

"There was the usual porn stash, nothing you haven't seen a million times before." Sebastian blushed again. "I don't mean you *personally* have seen a million times, I mean *you* as in someone who's seen a lot of porn. Which, of course, wouldn't be you."

"Really? Why not me?" She couldn't help teasing. It was too adorable watching him struggle to get his paw out of his mouth.

Sebastian hemmed and sputtered and finally gave up. "I have no idea what to say right now."

Nola laughed. "You're doing great, dude. Anything else?"

Relieved to be out of his porn spiral, Sebastian came quickly back online.

"A draft of a speech to the Coastal Commission recommending they okay the sale of some beachfront property to the Wyatt Development Corporation, and some pretty ugly IMing with his ex-wife, Angry Susan."

"Angry Susan?"

"That's what he calls her. They fought a hella lot about money."

"Alimony?"

"Can't get blood from a stone, bitch." Sebastian's smile froze. "...is what he wrote to her, I wasn't saying that to you, obviously."

"What'd she write back?"

" 'Piss off, Fuck Face' — Uh, again, that's her to him, not me to you. Oh, and there's one more thing. I think he had pancreatic cancer."

Nola took a mental step back. "Wow, didn't see that coming. What do you mean, 'you think'?"

"Well, he had a follow-up appointment with an oncologist yesterday, and his browsing history is riddled with panc-cancer info. It's kinda blatant, really."

"Sebastian, I need you to print out the doctor's address and number, ditto on the angry ex-wife. In fact, print out everything on the guy's hard drive for me, except the porn — well, maybe just the really nasty bits."

Nola threw the stick and Sebastian chased after it. "Um, is there anything special you're into, or should I just kinda do a random sampling?" Realizing he had a mouthful of stick, Sebastian blushed for the third time. "Oh, right. You're kidding. I'll get the stuff printed out right away."

Nola watched Sebastian bound down the endless staircase two steps at a time. All that energy at three-thirty in the morning — maybe he was half puppy. Leaning against the balustrade watching Sebastian disappear, she started formulating workable scenarios to account for Gus's death.

The first was that Gus had simply chosen to off himself in the comfort of his own opulent bed rather than spend his remaining days wasting away, broke and humiliated, in some county hospital for the indigent. A group he'd undoubtedly voted against helping in every election while simultaneously attending every boozy fundraiser thrown in their honor. But if that was the case, why no suicide note? And why bother drafting a speech to the Coastal Commission that he never intended to deliver?

The second scenario was that Gus's ex-wife, Angry Susan, had hated him enough to have killed him for the sheer joy of it. She most likely knew from their past life together where he kept his gun and what night he gave the servants off. Checking Angry Susan's alibi jumped a notch ahead of a quick stop at Sephora to pick up S.O.S. Morning Eye cream on Nola's perpetually re-prioritizing to-do list.

Then there was gorgeous possibility number three. Haven could easily have taken Gus's gun and popped a cap in the old guy's head, hoping to salvage whatever was left of his dwindling fortune for herself. A sleek bronze hyena scavenging scraps from the safety deposit box after the banks had secured the lion's share. The flaw in this theory was that Haven stood to gain more if Gus had a life insurance policy and she let him die of cancer. Of course, maybe he hadn't told her about the cancer. Or maybe she knew the insurance policy had lapsed in the financial meltdown. There were a lot more questions Mrs. Gillette would need to answer.

Tony came out of the "suicide" room and joined Nola in the hall. "Wicked-sexy widow's still in the shower?"

"Yeah, she'll meet us in the 'Great Room' when she's dressed. How we're supposed to tell one great room from another in this joint I don't know — guess we'll have to guess. In other news, Baz cracked our victim's laptop." Nola eyed the bottomless staircase. "I'll fill you in while we hike down to base camp."

"You think we should risk it without a Sherpa and some bottled water?"

"If we get lost and die waiting for help to arrive, at least I'll have gotten my cardio in."

"I'll try to find a coffin that doesn't make you look fat."

"Actually, I want to be cremated. It's my last chance to hit my goal weight."

Ten

When the Forensics had been bagged and tagged and Gus's body was on its way to autopsy, the cadre of cops went home, and a mausoleum-like quiet descended over the big, lonely house. Nola and Tony had found the 'Great Room,' which turned out to be an understatement, and were waiting for Haven, who was still upstairs showering off Gus's blood. Or was it her guilt? Nola still wasn't sure, but if Haven *was* guilty, it was going to take a Lady Macbeth–size loofah to exfoliate that hot mess.

Nola yawned. It had been a long, virtually sleepless night, and dawn was already beginning to break. A brilliant wall of windows was gradually revealing a giant swath of the Pacific Ocean. Pink and purple light glinted off the Channel Islands. The distant offshore oil rigs glowed like a flotilla of shiny little boats. Staring out at them one drunken night from an Isla Vista beach, Jim Morrison had been hit with the inspiration for "Crystal Ship."

"*The Crystal Ship is being built, a thousand girls, a thousand thrills…*"

The old song drifted through Nola's mind as she stared out at the beginning of a brand-new day. "Beautiful, isn't it?" She sighed.

"Almost as good as the real thing," Tony replied, his eyes fixed on a dazzling oil painting of Haven over the fireplace.

"I was talking about the view."

"So was I. Stimulating. Don't ya think?"

"I imagine it keeps the crows away."

"Is it me, or can you almost see through that dress?"

"It's you, and every other guy who isn't gay," Nola replied. "Strikes me, there's something a little predatory behind the evening gown and pearls."

"Really? 'Cause I'm thinking this may be one of those cases where the smokin' hot widow ends up falling for the sexy, boyish detective."

"I suppose it could happen...if you start opening car doors, leaving the toilet seat down, and suddenly inherit a billion dollars. This one's not your usual catch and release."

"Maybe I'll keep her."

"Please, you'd have to sell a kidney to afford that painting of her. And I can't see you honeymooning in a conjugal trailer."

"You think she did it?"

"It's a definite possibility. Why? You buying the suicide?"

"I am."

"Lightning round fact-off?" Nola proposed.

"You're on," he said, rubbing his hands together with cartoon relish. Tony lived for competition, and outside of softball, poker, and fishing tournaments, Prove Your Case was his favorite game.

"Even though I'm a lady, I'll let you go first."

"Thanks. Since you're really more of a broad, I will. FACT: Sick old guy loses his net worth in a very public swindle. CONCLUSION: Guy figures volcanically hot babe of a wife won't be jonesing for his wrinkled rocks in the poor house, so he offs himself. Makes perfect sense."

"Why no suicide note?" Nola challenged.

"His problems were so obvious he thought a note would

be redundant."

"Oh, but drafting a speech he never planned to give made sense?"

"The suicide may have been spur of the moment."

"On the servants' night out?"

"He wanted the volcanically hot wife to find him."

"The volcanically hot wife who was *sleeping* in a separate bedroom?"

"Now you're making my case *for* suicide," Tony said. "Round one goes to me."

"You wish," Nola scoffed. "You proved nothing. I still think she did it."

"Hey, midlife-crisis girl, yesterday you insisted a junkie with the victim's guitar and blood on his sweatshirt was innocent, today you're ready to convict young Miss Good-thighs without a shred of proof. Hmm, now what could we deduce from that?"

"Okay, I admit, one glance at that girl and I spontaneously developed early-onset menopause."

"And now you're planning to bring her down with your Super Dryness Force?"

"That's funny. I bet her husband would laugh his head off, if he still had one. The fact that I wish I had her youth ... and her beauty ..." Nola glanced up at the portrait again. "And that dress has nothing to do with the fact that I think we should at least entertain the idea that this might be murder, and she might be a suspect."

"Fine, she's a suspect," Tony said. "How 'bout I tail her for a year or two?"

"You couldn't keep up with her."

"That's what you think. I could follow that girl with my eyes closed."

"Ah! See? You're the one who can't be objective because

of her looks. You're mentally sexting her right now."

"I do like soft things," he said, smiling.

"Bet you could strike a match on what's underneath," Nola replied, doing her best Lauren Bacall.

"Actually, Grandma, people use lighters these days. You gotta try and keep up with the cool kids."

"LMFAO," Nola smirked. "Okay, round two, my turn."

"Okay." Tony mimed limbering up. "Aside from the fact that she's incredibly young and so smeltingly hot that you're insanely jealous, tell me why you think she's guilty."

"FACT: I just spent three hours with a girl whose boyfriend dumped her. Real grief is messy, ugly, swollen, and red-nosed. Your Miss Goodthighs is crying like she couldn't get the spray-tan appointment she wanted. Which, by the way, she doesn't need because she has a spray-tan setup of her own in that airplane hangar she calls a bathroom."

"No kidding."

"She probably has one of the maids hose her down every morning before she leaves the house. CONCLUSION: It's pretty damn obvious she didn't really love the dearly departed."

"Proves nothing." He waved his hand dismissively. "If *not* loving something made you guilty, you'd get arrested every time I dragged you to a Dodgers game."

"I go for the hot dogs."

"Hopefully she does, too."

"Uck, and might I add, uck. And stop getting off point. FACT: She doesn't love him enough to sleep in the same bed with him, yet she claims to have cradled his bloody body till the EMTs got here? CONCLUSION: She's lying. Why would she hug a man's corpse when she wouldn't hug his living, breathing body?"

"Shock reaction? Latent vampire tendencies. Tripped

and fell into the viscera? There's a million plausible explanations."

"Yeah, like mucking up the evidence to fool forensics. That's the one I'm going with."

"Objection," he said playfully. "The witness is arguing facts that haven't been introduced into evidence."

"What? Are you her lawyer now?"

"I didn't realize I needed one." Haven's voice was cool and matter of fact.

She was standing in the arched entrance way wearing a white terry robe that was so short Nola half expected her to announce she was ready for her waxing. Too pussy-punched to think on his feet, Tony stood in silent admiration, leaving Nola to make their apologies.

"I'm sorry, Mrs. Gillette. It's nothing personal. At this point in an investigation, we have to regard everyone as a suspect."

"Do you usually look for suspects when a desperately sad man commits suicide?" Haven asked caustically.

"Things aren't always what they seem," Nola said, with an apologetic smile. "Take a suicide home after last call, and sometimes you wake up with a murder."

Haven wasn't amused. She fixed Nola with a superior look that said, *Really? That gun with those shoes?* then turned the full force of her babeliciousness on Tony. "And what do you think, Detective?"

Too smart to take sides in any girl-on-girl subtextual power plays, Tony deflected. "I think maybe we're getting off on the wrong foot here."

Nola hiked back up to the high road. "I know this is a terrible night for you, but I'm afraid there are still a few more questions we have to ask."

Haven's eyes remained zeroed in on Tony. It was the

classic hot-girl-in-high-school move, signifying they were the only two people in the room who mattered. When she answered, it was directly to him. "You mean, questions, like, why did I kill my husband? That's simple, I didn't. Why would I? Certainly not for money. The banks are taking everything, this house, the yacht. I don't even know where I'm going to be living next month."

Tony was instantly taken in. His concern for her welfare, where she could go, who she might call, was totally undermining the interview. Another minute of steady eye contact and he'd be handing her a get-out-of-jail-free card. Suppressing the urge to Cher-slap him and shout, "Snap out of it!" Nola soldiered on with the questioning: "You and your husband were sleeping in separate bedrooms. Were you having marital problems?"

Haven released Tony from her ice-blue trajectory beams and flashed a withering glance at Nola.

"Just his snoring. You think I killed him over that?"

"You wouldn't be the first," Nola quipped.

Anger sparked somewhere deep and dark. "My husband just blew his brains out, Detective. Pardon me if I don't think this is the best time for jokes."

The rebuke stung, mostly because Nola knew she deserved it. Tony shot her a look that said the comedy club was closed. Retreat with what little credibility you have left, and don't forget to tip your waitress.

"I'm sure my partner didn't mean to be disrespectful," he said, in a vain attempt to smooth the waters. "Sometimes we get a little hardened in this line of work."

Haven produced a pristine tissue from the pocket of her terry robe. There weren't any real tears to wipe away, just a new little throb in her voice when she answered him. "It's just this whole thing is like a bad dream, and then to hear myself being accused…if I'm guilty of anything, it's not being the kind of support Gus needed in his time of crisis. If I'd known what to do or say, maybe he wouldn't have done this horrible thing."

Nola saw a chance to play the C card while still sounding sympathetic. "I'm sorry for being glib, Mrs. Gillette, it was entirely inappropriate. And try not to be too hard on yourself. It's difficult for anyone to know what to say when someone they love is dying of cancer."

"Cancer?" Clouds of confusion blurred the Cover Girl countenance. *Ah*, thought Nola, *so you didn't know.*

"I'm sorry," Nola said, feigning regret. "I assumed you were aware that your husband was ill."

"No, Detective, I didn't know."

Haven crossed to the wall of windows and stared mournfully out at the ocean to buy time to think. So, the big blowhard had cancer — no wonder he didn't take the bribe. All that crap about wanting to be a better man. A better man wouldn't have let his life insurance lapse, leaving her with nothing. Obviously, she should have gone through his computer more thoroughly. But she'd only been looking for his speech to the Coastal Commission. The one she'd cleverly rewritten to support the Wyatt Development deal. The one the cute boy-cop had undoubtedly discovered. Pretending not to know Gus's password and placing the photo of the *I Got Mine* by his laptop before the police arrived had been a last-minute stroke of genius. Believing she had no prior access to the speech, they'd have no reason to be suspicious when she presented it to the commission in Gus's place. But how best to respond to this new bit of cancer news? She dabbed another fake tear as she thought it over.

Not buying Haven's "sad thoughts at the window" bit, Nola shot Tony the "can you believe this crap?" look they always shared when it was obvious a suspect was faking. When he didn't give her the usual nod back, she knew he was lost.

"We're sorry you had to find out this way, Mrs. Gillette," he said in a voice so sweet it should be dodging humming-birds.

When Haven turned back from the window, she was the living image of the brave, philosophical wife. "Terminally ill, with no money and no health insurance. I guess I can't blame the poor man for taking his own life," she said, chin held high.

Nicely done, Nola thought. She had to give her props, the girl had game.

Tony ended the interview with what had to be the un-derstatement of the century: "I think we have all we need for now, but I'm sure we'll be in touch."

As they walked back to their cars, Nola was close to bursting. "Well, that was a perfectly vomitous display. Since when are you such an all-day sucker for a pretty face?"

"If you'll keep your voice a notch below fishwife, I'll tell you. Much as I hate to admit it, I think there's a chance you may be right. There's something not quite kosher here."

"Then why were you playing good cop, smitten cop?"

"Because you were playing bad cop, bat-shit-jealous cop. One of us had to seem normal."

"Sorry. Seeing you falling for that eye-contact trick made me go all Single White Female. Nice acting, by the way. I really thought you wanted to sleep with her."

"I do."

"You just admitted she might be a murderer."

"So? Afterwards I just won't remove the handcuffs."

"I don't know why I always just assume you're joking."

"Yeah, I don't know either."

Haven watched from the windows that flanked the big front door till Nola and Tony were safely in their cars. When she lost sight of their taillights, she went to the kitchen and felt around the Sub-Zero for the disposable cell she'd duct-taped there earlier. Removing the sticky silver tape, she dialed a number and waited for a sleep-addled voice to answer. It was the voice that was going to make her rich again.

Eleven

The remainder of the day was swallowed up in background checks, interviews, and ballistics reports. Nola reminded herself that being a good detective was like being a good mom. With children and victims, it was never cool to play favorites. Still, she'd been more than a little disappointed when Sam had sent Tony to further investigate Charley's case, leaving her to follow up on Gus. Nothing she'd learned about Augustus Gillette the Third had made her very sympathetic to his plight. Charley, on the other hand, had been a fixture in her life without her even being aware of it. His smile and songs and random compliments had been part of the charm of State Street. Since his death became public, people had been leaving flowers, candles, and cards on the sidewalk spots where he used to play. In a few weeks, the cards and flowers would be gone. People would forget. The bell had tolled on Charley's brief life, and Santa Barbara was the lesser.

The fact that Charley had been so popular was making Tony's job close to impossible. No one he interviewed had a clue why anyone would want to kill such a nice, harmless guy. The reports from Chicago P.D. were all good. Charley didn't have a record, just a devastated mother who couldn't afford to fly his body home to be buried. A jar was passed around the squad room and a notice put in the local papers asking for GoFundMe donations, which were already pouring in.

There was no indication that Charley was involved with drugs, save the raggedy old roach in his pocket, and if he'd been at the bad end of a romance gone wrong, he'd kept it so far on the down low that nobody knew a thing about it. Ballistics confirmed he'd been clocked with a .38 auto from a distance that suggested the killer was highly proficient with a gun. Ergo, the possibility that the shooting had been accidental was, fittingly, a long shot.

With nothing new to go on, Sam had gone ahead and filed a murder indictment against the little misery they'd arrested at the pawnshop. Further interrogation had yielded no new information — the guy was sticking to the only part of the story still velcroed to his brain. "Dude just shot him, click, click, click."

Nola periodically texted Tony to keep apprised of his progress, while she conducted her own go-nowhere investigation on Gus.

Alex's autopsy report gave the suicide theory two bloody thumbs-ups with no mitigating facts a gal could hang a hunch on. No ligature marks, scrapes, or skin scrapings under the fingernails to suggest Gus had been bound or attacked in any way. No sedatives or signs of poison in his system. The pancreatic cancer was stage four, but there was no evidence of medication. To make matters worse, the trace-evidence report indicated there was indeed gunpowder residue on Haven's suntanned skin and nightie, but it was consistent with her having cradled the body postmortem. Haven one, Nola zero.

When Nola questioned Gus's oncologist, he confirmed the autopsy findings. Gus's cancer had only recently been detected during a routine physical. Prior to the tests, Gus had chalked up his dwindling energy and appetite to the overwhelming stress of losing his financial empire. In spite of the oncologist's dire warnings, he'd refused to initiate any form of treatment, saying he'd rather go out high on morphine than sick on chemo.

"Do you know if his wife was aware of his illness?" Nola asked. She was positive Haven was clueless, but he *was* a doctor, and it never hurt to get a second opinion.

The oncologist set Gus's chart aside on his desk. "I never met his wife. But when I asked if he'd like me to speak with his family, he laughed. Frankly, I'm not surprised he chose an early out."

"Actually, we're not quite ready to rule his death a suicide."

"Really? From what you've told me, I can't imagine why not."

Annoyed by his imperious tone, no doubt derived from years of being deferred to by patients and staff, Nola still had to admit the man had a point. Aside from Haven's magic mascara and reality-defying story — hugging the headless corpse of the husband she didn't love — there was no evidence to suggest she'd been anything more than a witness after the fact to Gus's death.

The next stop was Gus's yacht club, where his buddies lifted a rare Sherry Oak Macallan single malt in his memory. Nola got the feeling glasses were raised every day about that time anyway. There were dent marks in their elbows from leaning on the bar. Eyes lit up when she mentioned Haven. They didn't have much to say about her, but what they'd clearly like to do to her would probably get you beheaded in most Muslim countries and Kansas. It irked Nola's feminist pride to admit it, but maybe her maudlin fear of middle age *was* making her a little too eager to cast the younger, far prettier girl as a modern-day Clytemnestra.

Gus had lost his money and his health. He had a gorgeous child bride with an American Express Black card where her heart ought to be, and a bunch of friends who didn't give a damn about him. It didn't make for a heartfelt eulogy, but that's the way it was. What ex–fat cat in his position wouldn't consider turning to a little Remington Steele for relief? Just one question continued to be a burr under her saddle. Why no suicide note? Important men, accustomed to being the center of attention, were usually loathe to shuffle off this mortal coil without at least *trying* to get in the last word. Judging by the length of the speech Gus had drafted for the Coastal Commission, he was a man who liked making other people listen, so why at the penultimate moment of his existence — silence? It didn't make sense. Haven just had to be involved.

Nola had one last person to interview before she'd have to quit swimming upstream of popular opinion and give up and go with the flow. But getting an interview with Gus's ex-wife, Angry Susan, was proving to be a huge pain in the ass. Susan was out at Two Bunch Palms, a luxury spa in the high desert, and had only agreed to drive back to Santa Barbara after Nola threatened to have a couple of cops from Palm Springs come and drag her out of her meditative mud bath by force. That had been hours ago. Susan moved on her own timetable; there was nothing for Nola to do but take a walk on the beach and wait for her call.

Twelve

Ironically, Angry Susan lived in peaceful splendor. Her modest, five-million-dollar cottage was perched high in the foothills overlooking Montecito Village, Santa Barbara's slightly sexier suburb to the south. Rather than invite Nola inside, Susan had a maid usher her out to a tranquil Zen garden in the back. Nola followed the maid down the white marble "thinking path" to a secluded spot where single-stemmed plantings and muted green lounge chairs sat quietly in the shade. In a nearby reflecting pool, languid koi swam in dazed circles through the water, never raising a ripple. The serenity was so oppressive even the birds were afraid to chirp. The only sound in the garden came from a small fountain under a lemon tree, where a happy Buddha contemplated the water gently trickling through his bowl. It was the kind of Prozac landscaping an anger-management professional might design for an insane asylum.

The maid produced passion fruit iced tea and assured Nola that "Mrs. Susan" would be joining her momentarily.

Earlier in the afternoon, while Nola was waiting for "Mrs. Susan" to return from the desert, she'd done a little internet research. Unlike Gus, Susan hadn't tried to make up what she'd lost in the divorce by investing in any get-richer-quick schemes. In fact, while not as flush as before the split, she was still sitting pretty. Nola sipped her sweet iced tea, breathed in the even sweeter smell of lemon blossoms, and waited. She was still soaking up the vibe when a snapping-turtle voice abruptly broke the spell.

"So the bastard shot himself. I don't see what right that gives you to ruin my spa trip."

Susan was clearly a woman who liked coming to the point. Smallish, late fifties, she'd let her short hair go gray but still managed to pull off bangs. Her tanned body was slim and tight as a violin string. She was dressed in moss-green silk. A loose blouse draped over flowing pants with matching Prada slippers. *Soft clothes for a hard woman*, Nola thought, as she rose to introduce herself.

"Deputy Chief Nola MacIntire."

"Well, who else would you be?" Susan snapped as she sat down and poured herself a glass of tea. Nola was pretty confident that as long as Susan was holding the glass, the ice would never melt.

"Sorry to spoil your vacation, but the city budget wouldn't cover me driving all the way out to the desert to question you."

"I don't see why you have to question me at all. The stupid jerk lost his money, so he killed himself. Isn't it obvious? Case closed."

"Not quite. You see, we're not totally convinced the scene wasn't arranged by someone to *look* like suicide."

"I see. So I'm a suspect, am I?"

Nola knew a woman like Susan was far more likely to outsource a murder than go the do-it-yourself route, but the standard questions had to be asked.

"Not if you have an alibi for last night between midnight and two a.m."

"Well, that's an idiotic question. I was in bed in my bungalow at the spa. I didn't even know Gus was dead till your call this morning interrupted my *qi*-regeneration exercises."

Nola was glad she hadn't had to send the Palm Springs Police to drag Susan back. They would have been hard-pressed to tell her apart from the rest of the thorny old cacti in the desert. Of course, maybe she hadn't been quite so prickly before Gus dumped her for the second Mrs. Gillette the Third. That would be a tough row for any woman to hoe.

Nola pulled a small notebook and pen from her purse. "Is there anyone who can corroborate that you were in your room at that time?"

"Well, I wasn't sleeping with my tantric breathing instructor, not that it's any of your business. If you'd bothered to check, you'd know there are security cameras in the parking lot, and my car didn't move all night. Frankly, I'd be the last person to kill Gus for the very simple reason that I wanted him alive." She paused to let the weight of her words sink in.

It dawned on Nola that Susan's hazel eyes perfectly matched her moss-green slippers, which perfectly matched the cushions on the lounge chairs.

"I assume you've met Gus's new eight-by-ten-glossy whore of a wife?" Susan spit out the question like sour milk.

Yep, Nola thought, *green was definitely her color.*

"Actually, she's the one who found his body." Nola sipped her iced tea and waited for the next outburst. She didn't have to wait long.

"When Gus divorced me, he wasn't satisfied just marrying her at the club in front of all our friends. He bought a new yacht for their honeymoon."

"Right, the *I Got Mine*. There was a picture of it on his desk."

"Of 'her.' Ships aren't 'its,' they're always referred to in the feminine. Anyway, Gus named her that just to spite me.

He was furious about our settlement, so he was throwing his new life in my face."

"Harsh. But how does that prove you wanted him alive, as opposed to, say, on a spit with an apple in his mouth?"

Susan smiled for the first time. "The banks are auctioning off Gus's assets to pay his creditors. I was planning to buy that yacht even if I had to mortgage this house to do it. Then I was going to have a handyman drill a hole in her hull, throw the biggest party that yacht club's ever seen, and raise a toast while she sank to the bottom of the harbor. The perfect symbolism can't be lost, even on you, Detective."

Nola bristled at the implied slight. Immune to other people's feelings, Susan continued to vent. "Of course, now that Gus's dead, what's the point? I can still buy the knife, but without his big fat back to plunge it into, where's the fun? He died before I could humiliate him, and I *really* wanted to humiliate him. As far as I'm concerned, I'm the real victim here."

"I'm not sure the coroner would see it that way, and I don't appreciate that bitchy remark about how even *I* could appreciate the symbolism, but you're upset that your revenge plot's a wash, so I'll let it slide. But don't sell me too short. Under all this honey blond, I'm a pretty smart Mint Milano. I know about your car, and I also know it would be simple enough to have a taxi pick you up on the road and have a second rental car waiting nearby. I've got people checking on that now. I've also got them checking your bank accounts to see if you've spent a little of your mad money on a hit man." Nola paused, but there were no nervous tells. If Susan *had* killed Gus, she had a poker face that could stand up to any high-stakes game in Vegas.

"On a separate note," Nola continued, "were you aware your ex-husband had cancer?"

The hazel eyes went wide as quarters. "Seriously?"

"Terminally."

The quarters shrunk to narrow dimes. "Now I really wished he'd lived. I would have had two ways to watch him suffer."

"Wow. Did you write your own wedding vows? Because 'till death or I get to really watch him suffer' might have raised a few red flags."

"Someday you may realize how funny that isn't. Don't judge me, Ms. MacIntire. At least until *you've* wasted forty years of your life with a man who dumps you for a cunt with cheekbones. Then see if you aren't bitter."

Nola cringed at Susan's casual deployment of the C word. Apparently those *qi* exercises hadn't quite kicked in yet. She knew the smart thing was to just let it go, but if she always did the smart thing, there wouldn't be a tiger-striped monokini hanging in her closet.

"Well, in forty years I'll be nearly eighty, so I guess I would be a tough sell on eHarmony, but if you don't mind my saying, stockpiling anger and dropping C bombs doesn't seem to be helping you on your quest for inner peace. Didn't your fountain Buddha say something about how, when you grasp a hot coal to throw at your enemy, you only end up burning yourself?"

Susan took another sip of tea. "I trust you can see yourself out, Detective."

Asking Susan to stop being bitter was like asking passion fruit iced tea to stop being sweet. Nola had enough seemingly lost causes to deal with at the moment, so she left Angry Susan with her happy Buddha and returned to the T-bird.

Pulling out of Susan's polished-slate driveway, she thought about all the ways she'd seen love go wrong. A guy who doped his girlfriend's Smart Water…a wife who added a pinch of live blow dryer to her husband's hot tub…a gay man who suffocated his partner with a cloth he'd been embroidering for an AIDS quilt. Forget carbon monoxide — that person calling you sweetheart was the real silent killer. Still, despite its clear and present danger, love was the heroin of the heart, and everyone was always jonesing for a fix. It had only happened to Nola once, and there was no telling if it ever would again. Thankfully, there was a handy substitute right nearby. Back on Coast Village Road, Nola pointed the little T-bird toward her favorite cupcake joint. Frosting: the methadone of desire.

Thirteen

When Nola got home, she found a blue Post-it thank-you note from Nancy, accompanied by a mix CD. The first song on Nancy's playlist was by Swedish House Mafia.

"Don't you worry, don't you worry child..."

Great advice, but how could she help but worry? The day had been an epic fail. No new leads had opened up. The newspapers and television stations were reporting whatever they could and getting most of it wrong, and when she'd stopped at Crushcakes on her way home, they'd already run out of red velvet. She only ate the frosting off the top...but still. There was nothing to do but go out on the balcony and talk it over with a glass of chardonnay. Unlike most people, who had an annoying proclivity for amping things up, wine had a quiet way of putting things into perspective.

It was another warm night. The ocean fog was graciously waiting offshore for midnight to roll in. Out on her tiny balcony, she listened to the music and the waves and let the wine slip a ball gag over the mouth of her constantly yapping inner critic. She wondered if Tony had made any progress on Charley's case since their last text. Anything big and he would have called, but still...

She reached into the pocket of her old gray cardigan. It was drab and shapeless and amazingly comfortable. She only put it on when she was home alone, and even then it was always with the silent prayer that she wouldn't choke on an almond or something and literally be caught dead in it. She pulled out her cell and hit speed dial.

Tony answered on the third ring. "Hey."

"Hey back. Glad you answered, I was afraid I might be interrupting a date."

"You are."

"Is she hotter than me?"

"They all are."

"You might not think so if you could see the sexy little number I'm wearing now."

"You may look great, but she'll have sex with me."

"I guess some girls just don't have any standards."

"Amen to that. So, how'd it go with Angry Susan?"

"Uck. The woman's a kidney stone with a voice box. She was super pissed that I ruined her spa vacay, and even madder that Gus's gruesome death put the kibosh on her evil-ex-wife plans for revenge. Which, in a crazy side note, were pretty effin' elaborate. She had it planned right down to the color of the cocktail napkins."

"You writing her off as a suspect?"

"Yeah, Juan called on my way home. No cabs reported picking up anyone fitting her description at the resort, no second rental car was listed in her name, and no hit-man money was missing from her Chase account, which is pretty much what I expected. If Haven ran to Gus's room as soon as she heard the shot like she claimed, she would have noticed a hired killer sliding down a drainpipe. And speaking of Haven, no new clues pointing her way either. My whole day pretty much added up to less than zero."

"So why are you calling me at this cop-blocking hour?"

"Relax. If Hotter Than Me thinks you're talking to an-other woman, it'll just make her want you more. I called to see if you got any new leads on Charley."

"Only more testimonials about what a decent guy he was. I'm starting to wonder if he may have stepped in front of a couple bullets meant for somebody else. Gangbangers up from Oxnard maybe?"

"Maybe, but we'll have to come up with something more concrete if we don't want Sam to let the little tweakster fry for it."

"You know, there is one other possibility."

"Don't even say it. It's too scary. Go back to your date."

"They're pretty fun, dates. You ought to try one."

"Can't tonight. George Saunders has a new story in *The New Yorker*, and I'm sure by now a million friends have Instagrammed their lunches, so you see, there's just no time. See you mañana, amigo."

After she hung up, Nola pondered that other possibility. The one so scary she hadn't even wanted Tony to say it out loud. If some psycho had started getting his jollies by killing innocent homeless people like Charley, he could be out there on the prowl again tonight. Click, click, click. Nola pulled the ugly gray sweater a little tighter around her shoulders. How was it possible for such a warm night to suddenly feel so cold?

Fourteen

Sixty miles up the 101 Freeway from Santa Barbara, Vandenberg Air Force Base sits aside a stretch of coastline deemed "primo" by surfers, despite the fact that it's also a primo hunting ground for great white sharks. While the big fish silently prowl the shoreline, high over the Pacific another kind of sleek, deadly hunter seeks its prey. Operated by Air Force Space Command's 30th Space Wing, Vandenberg is a major missile-testing site. When the Patriot interceptors hit their dummy targets, a swirling kaleidoscope of gaseous colors explodes over the ocean, creating a dazzling aurora borealis in the sky. But as powerful as these mechanized kill vehicles are, it still takes soldiers to fight a war: men and women who sometimes return home with scars not readily visible to the naked eye. And that's where Max came in.

Maxwell Waxman, MD, PhD, dean of the psychology department at the University of California, Santa Barbara, was a leading expert on post-traumatic stress disorder. Short on shrinks and long on heroic personnel who'd been wounded in two wars most Americans no longer cared to think about, the Air Force had readily agreed when Max volunteered to provide group therapy in the evenings at the base's mental health clinic. The room his group had been assigned was standard military drab, but the stories that were told around the table were vivid.

Tonight, a young staff sergeant was recounting the grim details of an IED attack in Kabul. The rest of the group nodded knowingly, but Max was having a hard time concentrating. He wasn't just sitting among them as a therapist this time, but as a fellow soldier, albeit in a very different army, fighting a very different war.

A diehard environmentalist, Max had discovered a fellow traveler among his group, one who had access to classified information that Max had agreed to pass on and make public. But now he was having second thoughts. What if he got caught? What if the information was traced back to him? But it was too late to back out. The soldier had slipped the flash drive so deftly into Max's pocket that he hadn't even realized it was there until he reached for the cigarette he kept, not to smoke but just to roll around in his fingers. It was a little operant-conditioning trick he used to relieve stress. Although he'd quit smoking forty years ago, the feel of a Marlboro in his hand still had a Xanax-like effect on his aging nerves.

By the time the group broke up, Max's shirt was sticking to his back, and the Marlboro in his pocket was a twisted clump of soggy tobacco. As he walked in the dark to his car, he realized he was trembling. If someone had ferreted out the plot, MPs would be waiting at the gate to detain him. Was he really prepared to go to jail for exposing military secrets, even if the public had a right to know? He climbed in his Prius, but he was afraid to start it. He could hear his blood pulsing in his ears. For nearly five decades, Max had been studying bravery and the effects of extreme pressure on the human mind. Now he was about to find out if he himself had "the right stuff." Inhaling deeply, he pressed the ignition. The die cast, he steered the Prius in the direction of the Rubicon.

The beefy guard at the gate gave a cursory glance at Max's

ID pass and waved him through. By the time he remembered to exhale, he was already heading south on the 101.

An hour later, he was curling through the Cold Springs section of Montecito on his way up to Mountain Drive. Signs of the infamous Tea Fire that had scorched the earth a few years back were illuminated in his headlights. College kids partying at the deserted Tea House had been too stoned, drunk, or lazy to properly put out their campfire, and a mighty sundowner had whipped it into an inferno that incinerated more than two thousand acres and destroyed two hundred homes. The county sheriff's department charged the kids with misdemeanors and kept their names out of the press. Meanwhile, farther up the coast, two Mexican day laborers who accidentally sparked a fire clearing brush were named and vilified and ordered to make financial restitution in an amount they couldn't hope to earn between them in a lifetime.

Max pondered the inequity as he coasted to a designated stop on the deserted road. He'd been told he'd find directions that would lead him to the spot where he was to deposit the flash drive. A fluorescent-yellow arrow on the charred remains of a fallen oak tree pointed to a ravine. Could that possibly be the "directions" his shadowy co-conspirators had meant? He'd never met them in person; they were just a name on the net: ROTC70, in honor of the 1970 student radicals who'd set fire to the Isla Vista branch of the Bank of America to protest the Vietnam War, but clearly they weren't the brightest tree huggers in the forest. Fluorescent-yellow paint was an absurd choice in the clandestine world of eco-espionage. Not only did it mar the natural landscape, but anyone passing within a hundred yards would be hard-pressed not to wonder where the Day-Glo arrow led.

Max switched off his headlights, dug a flashlight from

his glove box, and climbed out of the Prius. He'd told them he'd make the drop at dawn, but on the ride down from Vandenberg he'd realized he was too nervous to hang on to the flash drive overnight. Standing on the side of the road, he was gripped by the uneasy feeling that he wasn't alone. Was it possible they were already out there in the dark somewhere, watching to see if he'd come early, wondering if his reaching out to them was just bait for a trap being set by the police?

Easing the car door shut, he cautiously started off in the direction of the ravine. Somewhere down in the dry brush he heard a crack. He froze and listened. The sound had come and gone and now there was nothing. A bird, maybe, or a rabbit. Another crack. Instinct told him to duck behind a narrow outcropping of rock. Not all instincts are good. The startled deer's hoof hit him squarely in the center of his occipital bone. By the time his brain had absorbed the shock, Maxwell Waxman, MD, PhD, was dead.

In the dim light before sunrise, the ragtag band of eco-warriors who'd dubbed themselves ROTC70 were gathered around Max's lifeless body. Ian, a skinny kid with the kind of scraggly facial hair only a nineteen-year-old stoner or an estrogen-starved dowager could produce was digging through Max's pockets while his comrades looked on. Ian had never seen, let alone touched, a dead body, but when Malcolm told him to search the old dude for the flash dive, he cowboyed up as best he could to avoid looking like a pussy in front of his crew.

Monica watched Ian struggling to hide his revulsion as he rifled the dead shrink's pockets. Something she, as the girl, would never be asked to do. She'd sensed the misogynist vibe when she'd first asked to join the group, but with a butt so hot she coulda borrowed it from a black girl, and the fine-boned face of a Clinique model, she knew she was as good as in. She also knew Ian was wasting his time going through the dead man's pockets. Didn't these guys ever watch cop shows?

Monica pointed to Max's hand. "Hey, I, check out his fingers, they're curled around something."

Ian's stomach recoiled. Did Hot Monica really expect him to pry open the dead dude's icy claw? But Malcolm was already nodding in agreement.

"She's right, man, crack open the hand."

When Ian touched Max's rigored fingers, all his future reoccurring nightmares took shape. "I can't do this, okay? I'm like two seconds from puking up everything I've eaten since first grade. Kyle?"

"Dude, you're already down there, just do it," Kyle replied. Another queasy, neo-grunge voice heard from.

The sudden sound of shattering bone was followed by a collective gasp. Malcolm raised his Timberland boot off Max's crushed hand, bent down, and casually removed the flash drive from Max's broken fingers. "Got it, you ass cracks."

Malcolm's piercing dark eyes and sexy, pop-star swagger had already aroused Monica's female curiosity, but with this singular display of Nietzschean will to power, he'd totally sealed the deal.

As Malcolm led the way out of the ravine, he shut down any talk of an anonymous call to 911 to save Max from the coyotes. Cell phones had GPS. "Hell, when I die, I *want* to be left to the scavengers. Circle of life, bros." Seeing the glint of lust in Monica's eyes, he basked in the force of his own magnetism. The alpha male was *so* getting laid tonight.

Fifteen

Three dead bodies in three days! No time for the merry rites of maintenance this morning. The tooth-whitening strips and Latisse eyelash extender would have to wait. Nola dry-swallowed a vitamin E, grabbed her Bliss jelly lip pen and shoulder holster, and headed out the door.

Alex was already examining Max's body when Nola arrived at the scene. She was kneeling by his side, trying to ignore his signature odor, half formaldehyde, half Axe body spray, when Tony appeared, still wet from a shower and relaxed from a night of casual sex.

"Morning, Nols — sorry I was delayed. Is this our corpse?"

"No, he's just trying out a new yoga position. Down Deadward Dog."

"Somebody got up on the wrong side of the crime scene this morning," he said, bright sex-eyes twinkling.

"Just tired." She smiled. "I had unresolved-case-issues insomnia last night, and now we've got dead guy number three. It's officially a hat trick."

Tony looked down at the big purple and green dent in the back of Max's skull. "Looks like he came up on the losing end of a polo mallet."

Alex sat back on his bony haunches and squinted up at Tony in the early morning sunlight. "Actually, he appears to have been kicked. There's dirt under the hair, and the imprint of a hoof, probably a deer. Most likely happened sometime between eleven last night and two this morning."

Nola glanced around the surreal landscape of fire-scarred rock and dry brush. "I wouldn't be caught dead up here that time of night."

"Obviously, this tweed-jacketed gentleman felt otherwise," Alex chuckled, pleased with his own joke.

Tony crouched down to get a better look at the victim. "Why would a dapper, I'm guessing mid-sixties 'gentleman' be up here deerstalking alone at night?"

Alex ran his magnifying glass over Max's right hand. "I'm not sure he *was* alone. Someone stomped on this man's hand postmortem. If you look close, you can just make out the faint tread of a hiking boot."

Nola looked through the glass. The tread mark was light, but she could definitely see it, and something else was wrong. The fingers weren't sitting right. She bent down to get a closer look. "Alex, his fingers . . . ?"

"Are broken. Yes. The hand was already in rigor when it was trod on, which means whoever did it either stayed with the corpse or stumbled across it hours later."

"Curiouser and curiouser," Tony said, borrowing the magnifying glass to get a closer look.

Nola had already inspected the area where the body lay, in situ. Whoever left the boot mark had to have walked away, but the ground was broken bracken and dry grass, so the chances of finding a print that matched were virtually nil. She sent a crew to inspect any nearby trails just in case.

Even if a deer kick was the cause of death, a boot-smashed hand after the fact was a mystery that demanded their attention. It might have been just a random act of sadism, or the victim might have been clutching something the boot wearer was after. "Alex, can you tell if our victim was holding something when his hand was stomped on?"

Alex could only confirm that the fingers had been clutched in rigor at the time of impact. Whether they'd been clutched around something was purely a matter of conjecture.

Tony stood and did a quick 360 of the area. "So, where's the jogger who found him?"

Nola quickly brought him up to speed. "I interviewed her and sent her home in a black and white. Actually, it was her dog that found him. They were out on the road for a run when puppy got a whiff of dead guy down here in the ravine. I've got Baz checking to see if she had any prior links to the victim, but my instincts say no. And there's no way she's our hand crusher."

"You sure? Because there's one philosophical school that ascribes to the theory that bitches be crazy."

"Yeah, and there's another that says it's men who make them that way. But, tabling the chicken-or-egg discussion for a minute, our jogger was supermodel skinny."

"So?"

"So, I've exfoliated more than she weighs. She could have gone Gangnam Style on the victim's hand without breaking a pinkie. Plus, she was wearing Skechers, not hiking boots, and her dog was a shelter mutt. Woman plus shelter mutt equals nice."

Alex smiled. "Sounds like someone wants a mutt of her own."

"I do, but my condo has a no-pets policy. Fortunately, I already have a loyal partner who scarfs his food and ruins the carpet."

"I spilled one beer, like, ten years ago," Tony protested to Alex. "She's got a memory like a supercomputer."

While Alex continued examining the body, Nola filled

Tony in on what she knew about Dr. Max Waxman. She'd found his wallet in his pants pocket, no indication of robbery, his cash and credit cards were still intact. His vehicle registration matched a Prius parked on the road just outside the ravine, so carjack was also a nonstarter. The biggest news she saved for last. In addition to his driver's license and his University of California faculty card, Max Waxman had a civilian military ID.

Tony let out a low whistle as they headed back to their cars. "So we check out his home, his office on campus, and then what, the Pentagon?"

"Pretty much."

"Why do long days always have to come after exhausting nights of great sex?"

"She was great, huh?"

"She was good, but I was fantastic, so it evened out."

"Is this another Kim?"

Tony was a sort of god to the guys down at the station for having successfully juggled three different women named Kim one summer and having lived to tell about it.

"Nope. This was a lithe, hazel-eyed Chelsea who kept me *up to the sun, up for good fun, and up all night to get lucky.*"

"Look at you, knowing a pop song that's not Nickelback. So, if the sex was really that good, your electrolytes must be pretty depleted. Wanna stop at Pressed Juice for soy green tea with acai smoothies?"

"Have I ever? I swear, if Gwyneth Paltrow said she drank motor oil in the morning, you'd have STP dripping down your chin."

"Oh, Gwyneth's gone way beyond diet tips. Now she wants us to start steaming our vaginas. Although she didn't specify how to serve them. Maybe over rice?"

Tony winced. "Oh come on, you really thought I needed

that image in my head? Give your keys to one of the patrol guys, so they can drive the T-bird back to the station."

"Why do we always have to take your car?"

"Because I feel like an idiot climbing out of yours."

"Hater."

"Nut job. You can have your smoothie, but we're taking the grownup car, and I'm driving."

Sixteen

Tony drove while Nola scrolled through the recent call list on Max's iPhone. There was no high volume of calls to any one number, so it was unlikely he was married. She found a Tom Waxman and clicked Call. This was the hardest part of the job, the saddest part.

"This is Nola MacIntire from the Santa Barbara Police Department. I'm afraid there's been an accident."

Tom turned out to be Max's brother. Genuinely grief-stricken over the news, he'd agreed to leave work and meet them at Max's home with a spare key. "Sorry for your loss" never seemed like enough, but she didn't know what else to say. When she hung up, she went back to studying Max's phone for clues that might explain his nocturnal wanderings in the woods.

"Finding anything interesting?" Tony asked as they cruised by the bird sanctuary.

"Actually, I'm finding our victim interesting. He has some very eclectic apps. I think I would have liked him. Hey, wouldn't it be great if first dates were just a ritualistic exchange of smartphones over cocktails? You'd know instantly if you were going to click with somebody. 'Well, I see by your browser history that you're into French cinema and kayaking, that's good…uh-oh, lots of vicious texts from ex-girlfriends…looks like somebody has commitment issues…

waiter, check please!' "

Tony shook his head in frustration. "Geez, even your fantasy relationships end badly."

"Yeah, that's not good, is it? How does your fantasy phone exchange go?"

"Perfectly: 'So, your Facebook profile says you're a born-again Rastafarian, an elephant trainer, and you're into Maroon Five and dead flower arranging — shall we go ahead and order dinner?' "

"*That's* what your fantasy girl is into? Dead flowers and whiny bands?"

"In my fantasy she's mad-sexy, so who cares what she's into?"

Nola sighed. "You have no sense of romance. I'm going back to my phone date with Max. He knows how to electronically court a girl."

Max's stored info revealed that he was a psychiatrist with a large circle of friends who read whatever non-zombie-smash-up was currently on *The New York Times* bestseller list, herb-infused his own vodka, and was not into Maroon Five. So far, Nola and Max's imaginary smartphone date was going pretty well.

She clicked over to his calendar. Last night's entry was just two letters highlighted in red: VD. Screech, pause, rewind. She could feel the neurons in her brain starting to pop. It was doubtful Max had contracted a social disease and marked the occasion by boldly noting it in red. Although, he could have been alone in the hills waiting to confront his STD-transmitting lover. But why would they meet outside in the middle of the night? Maybe it was a married lover? Maybe one who wanted a letter back that he was clutching in his hand? Check that, even aging intellectuals didn't send romantic snail mail anymore. Maybe he'd been clutching a ring or a locket? A locket? Seriously? Did she think he was shagging Jane Austen? Okay, train of thought running off the tracks. It was far more likely that VD was someone's initials, but there hadn't been anyone with the initials VD on Max's contact list. Maybe they were the initials of a place?

"Hey," Tony said breaking her concentration. "What's going on in that feverish little bean of yours? Your eyeballs are bouncing around like martini shakers."

"Last night's entry in Dr. Waxman's calendar is two initials: VD."

"Bummer. Good you're wearing evidence gloves."

Nola didn't bother to respond. She was too intrigued by the next entry on Max's calendar.

"Hey, Tone, listen to this! Tomorrow's calendar entry: Coastal Commission meeting, nine a.m."

"So?"

"So, Gus Gillette wrote a speech in favor of the Wyatt deal that he was planning to deliver at the same meeting. We have a link!"

"Cool your jets, Nancy Drew. That property sale is a pretty hot topic. A whole lot of people are going to that meeting. It's probably just a coincidence."

"Freud said, 'There are no coincidences.'"

"Actually, he said, 'There are no accidents.'"

"I know…I was hoping to slide that one by you. But two guys popping up dead who were both going to attend the same meeting…our mysteries have totally converged!"

"Pretending for a moment that I agree, how would 'murder by deer' and a probable suicide link up?"

"I don't know. Let's start with the meeting. We know why Gus was going. Why would Dr. Waxman want to be there?"

"Well, if he's like everyone else who's going to be there,

he's either an investor who's enthusiastically in favor of the project or an environmentalist who's dead-set against it."

Tony turned the Audi into a cul-de-sac and pulled up in front of Max's modest adobe-brick home. It was a model of self-sufficiency: voltaic solar tiles, double-paned windows, drought-tolerant landscaping, and a "Save the Ocean" sticker on the mailbox.

"Yeah, I'm going to go out on a limb and say environmentalist," Nola said, with her smuggest of smiles, positive now that her link theory had legs.

Billowing purple sage lined the sand path that led to Max's front door. His brother Tom had said Max lived alone, but families didn't always know. When no one answered their knock, they made their way around to the back.

Max's backyard abutted a hillside that had been trenched and tiered like an Incan village to accommodate a thriving winter vegetable garden. Nola rubbed some rosemary together in her fingers and inhaled. "I'd love to have a backyard garden."

"You just hate grocery shopping."

"Good a reason as any to go green."

"You? You empty the whole Castaic Reservoir every time you take a shower."

"You're right. I'm drought intolerant. I wonder if there's a self-help group for that."

To keep it fair they flipped a coin to decide who would search the compost heap and who would search the potting shed for anything that might seem suspicious. When they met up again, neither of them had found anything, but Nola smelled faintly of potato peels, coffee grounds, and something distinctly fishy. Her forensic gloves were tough and flexible but apparently not odor resistant.

"If the brother doesn't show up in two minutes to let us

into the house, I'm going to smash an energy-efficient win-dow and climb in," she said, eyeing the thick glass. "I've got to have soap. I smell like a fertilizer factory."

"You do have a certain air about you," Tony said as they walked up to the back porch.

Luckily a B&E proved unnecessary. They spotted the Frontgate hide-a-key rock almost simultaneously. Any savvy burglar worth his salt would have done the same. Frontgate had been aiding and abetting top-notch crookery for years. Still, paging through its spring furniture catalogue was the easiest way for a woman to achieve orgasm without sex, so...good points, bad points.

The inside of Max's house was a patchwork of bamboo flooring, recycled-tile countertops, and reclaimed-wood furniture. The man definitely had the aesthetic courage of his convictions. Nola scrubbed up in the kitchen, and then joined Tony in the study. He was sitting at Max's desk star-ing at his blank computer, wondering how to get in.

"Any guesses what his password might be? 'Green'? 'Sustainable'?"

Nola's eyes lit on a photo of Max posing in front of Old Faithful. Hoping Sebastian's theory might hold, she gave it a shot. "Try Yellowstone."

"What?"

"Just a hunch."

Moments later they were illegally browsing through Max's patients' case files. Nola was engrossed in Max's notes about a man who had gained forty stress pounds in six weeks when Tony clicked over to the next patient.

"Hey, I was reading that!"

"It has no bearing on our case. The guy got fat. Why would that make him smash Waxman's hand open?"

"Maybe Waxman was holding a doughnut?"

"Why do I get the feeling you're not taking this seriously?"

"Because I don't think we need to be checking his patients. Whatever we're looking for has something to do with that development deal."

"You think that, but you don't know it."

"True, but I do know we could get in big trouble going through doctor-patient files without a warrant."

"Do I look scared?" The words were barely out of Tony's mouth when they heard a car pull up outside. "Okay, yeah, I totally am. Back to the living room, we never saw these."

Tom Waxman was a fair-skinned man in his mid-sixties with curly yellow hair cut so short it looked like someone had superglued popcorn to his head. Though still in shock, he was anxious to be of help. Unfortunately, like most relatives of the unexpectedly deceased, he had a lot more questions than answers.

"I don't understand. Why would Max be walking around the Montecito foothills in the middle of the night?"

Nola took a seat beside him on the non-rain-forest-threatening sofa. "There was a notation in his calendar yesterday that said 'VD.' Did he know anyone with those initials?"

Tom thought a moment before answering. "No one that comes to mind."

"Maybe one of his patients?" Tony asked.

"I don't know. He couldn't talk about his patients. He kept files on them, of course, but those are all doctor-patient protected."

"Right," Tony said, nodding innocently. "We're working on a warrant, so we can take a look at those later."

Tom's shoulders started to tremble. The face beneath the popcorn hair was streaked with tears. "Who do I need to call about the body?"

Nola passed him a Kleenex and explained that the

coroner's office would be calling him to come down and make a positive identification later that afternoon. Then, patting his hand, she asked, "Max's calendar indicated he was planning to attend the Coastal Commission meeting tomorrow morning. Do you have any idea why?"

"He was afraid they might okay the sale of some beach property to developers." Tom managed to get the words out before blowing his nose. "But why is that important? On the phone you said Max had been kicked by a deer."

"Just covering our bases," she said. "Even in cases of accidental death, we try to puzzle out what happened. Actually, I'm going to that meeting myself. I'm very much in your brother's camp. Earth Day every day, right?"

Nola could feel Tony rolling his eyes at her pants-on-fire pose as a hard-core ecologist. But she needed Tom to see her as an ally, someone he might confide in if he had any information tying Max and Gus together. Besides, it wasn't like she was *anti*-green. She recycled and used canvas grocery bags, and no one wished they could afford a super-sexy Tesla more than she did.

Whether the ends of her small fib justified the means was a moot point. She could see Tom was barely listening now. It happened all the time with victims' loved ones. The initial jolt of adrenaline that accompanied the shocking news of their loss would start to wear off, and they'd implode into their grief. Tom was collapsing in front of her eyes.

Tony caught the vibe, too. His last question was about Max's military ID. With heartbreaking admiration in his voice, Tom explained about Max's pro bono PTSD counseling up at Vandenberg. The more Nola heard about Max, the more she liked him. And the more she liked him, the more she was determined to solve the mystery of what had happened to him.

Tom was in no shape to drive, so Nola and Tony took him home to his wife, who thanked them politely before gently taking his arm and helping him into the house.

Back in the car, on their way to the university to interview Max's coworkers, Nola put a call in to Vandenberg Air Force Base. VD? Maybe?

The base operator put her through to a public liaison officer, Captain Taylor. Taylor was shocked and saddened by the news of Max's death and readily agreed to arrange an interview with Max's therapy group. Nola assured him it was purely a matter of form. "Just hoping they might have some idea why Dr. Waxman was alone in the woods last night." She didn't mention the crushed fingers. It sounded too accusatory. Captain Taylor said he'd set up an interview and shoot her an email with the time. She clicked off and was filling Tony in on the conversation when an intriguing thought crossed her mind.

"I wonder if anyone at Vandenberg has a vested interest in the Wyatt Development deal."

"Boy, you're like a dog with a bone," Tony replied as they cruised off the freeway and onto Sandspit Road.

"That's why I'm so right for this job. And why I really hope you'll come to that commission meeting with me tomorrow. Come on, Tony — two deaths, two opposing views on a highly volatile subject. It can't just be a coincidence."

"Sure it can," he said as they headed toward the university gate. "I'll go, but I seriously doubt we'll establish a connection."

"I bet Alexander Graham Bell's buddy said the same thing when they tried out the first telephone. Hey, wasn't his name Watson, too?"

"What do you mean, 'too'?"

"Well, clearly I'm Sherlock, and you're Watson."

"Oh, you deduced that, did you?"

"Yep. You're also the Watson to my Crick, in case you were wondering. You know, I never realized before how many partners have been named Watson. But I'm sure you'll say that's just another coincidence."

"Shall we synchronize our watches?"

"Why?"

"So I'll be sure of the exact time that you officially lose your mind."

Seventeen

The University of California, Santa Barbara, is a renowned research center, one of America's few "public ivies," and ideally located right on the beach.

Tony and Nola parked in the visitors' lot and strolled across campus, both secretly hoping they didn't look like cops. A few days before her seventeenth birthday, Nola had arrived on campus as a freshman; a few months after her nineteenth birthday, she'd graduated as a junior. It wasn't that she was any great genius, she just hadn't seen the point of taking summers off when going to school felt like a learning vacation at a high-end resort. It had been a five-minute walk from her dorm room to the beach. Less on days when the sand was so sizzling hot she'd had to take it at a dash and plunge straight into the ocean.

Her mother, a former sorority girl at Berkeley, was appalled when she saw the tiny, drab cubical that was to be her daughter's new home. "I feel like I'm leaving you in women's prison."

But Nola adored her tiny dorm room. She loved her classes and all her new friends, loved the lectures in the morning and the afternoons she spent studying on the beach. She even loved the tar that oozed up from the sand and caked her feet. But she especially loved the lazy Sunday-afternoon parties on the grass, listening to the Chili Peppers and Snoop, even old throwback Bowie. *"Ch-ch-ch-changes..."*

She was totally baffled when her friends claimed that being in their thirties was the best time of their lives. Having children seemed to produce some kind of memory-eating bacteria that made them forget what real fun was like. A little trick of nature to make toting snacks to soccer games, wiping runny noses, and scheduling carpool more palatable. Just thinking about a kid-centric life made Nola want to knock back a quick Drano and tonic. College had been bliss, and here it was still going on, only now it was going on without her.

The university's motto was *Fiat Lux* — Let There Be Light. But Max's fellow faculty members had very little light to shine on the mysterious circumstances surrounding his death. The general consensus was that he was a brilliant therapist, a respected colleague, and not prone to go walking after midnight à la Patsy Cline.

It was late afternoon, and Tony and Nola had one last interview to go. They were meeting Max's teaching assistants in his office near the dining hall. Walking past the familiar cafeteria with its rows of colorful bike racks, Nola was instantly trasnported back to the day she met Josh: her favorite eight-year mistake. Ponytail, glasses, worn jeans, and a flannel shirt...he'd been sitting on a patch of grass that was currently occupied by a couple of shirtless McConaughey wannabes playing hackysack. Nola had seen him around and liked what she saw, but he wasn't in her circle of friends and wasn't likely to be. He was reading a book in Russian. Not a language textbook, just a regular book, *in Russian*. No way a guy like that would ever be interested in her. He was so cool and cerebral. He was coolebral. He probably only hooked up with laconic brunettes named Sloane and Alexa who played Scrabble in Latin and rolled their own sushi. But to Nola's astonishment, when Josh spoke to her, it wasn't to complain that she was blocking his sun.

"You're a friend of John's, right? You were in our dorm room looking at his photographs."

"Oh, yeah, John's great. I love that shot he took of Cobain at the Bowl."

The rest of their conversation was drowned out by her panicky inner voice. She wasn't really John's friend. In fact, she'd only spoken to him once. Walking by his open door, she'd noticed the photo of Kurt and popped in to ask who took it. Josh had come back from class just as she was leaving. Now when Josh saw John he'd say, "I ran into your friend Nola," and John would say, "Who?" and her stupid nervous lie would be exposed. Her pheromone-rattled brain was IMing her mouth to "shut up and say goodbye," when, in a crazy act of self-sabotage, she blurted: "So, are you a language major?"

WTF? She'd engaged when she should have been signing off. And now she had no follow-up. Abort. Abort. Abort. A few tortured minutes later, she babbled something about having a class, turned tail, and ran.

Somehow her attraction-based nervousness must have come off as cute, or maybe it was just Be Nice to a Nutjob Day, because later Josh appeared at her door with the photo of Kurt, claiming John wanted her to have it. Fortunately, once she stopped worrying about seeming smart, the fact that she actually was smart kicked in, and their romance was off and running. The first few months they were like hibernating bears. Snuggled under blankets, talking all night, having mind-blowing sex, and hating to get out of bed. They even played chess under the covers. She'd been mad-embarrassed when John showed up to get his stolen Cobain photo back, but Josh had just laughed it off: "You ran away so fast, I had to have some excuse to see you." And that had made her like him even more, and like turned to love, and love turned to graduating and moving in together and growing up together and then apart.

Their final breakup was so *Zero Dark Thirty* gut-wrenching that she was ready to pull an Anna Karenina every time she heard the 3:15 Surfrider passing by on its way to Los Angeles. Fortunately, her acceptance into the Police Academy, with Tony there to talk her down whenever she started hearing train whistles, had rescued her from the abyss. But now, seeing the exact spot where they'd first said hello...

"Get your mind out of the past."

Tony had very little patience for wallowing.

"Geez, can't a girl watch two cute guys play hackysack without being accused of wallowing?"

"You are the worst liar. He was a great guy, you were a great girl. Things change, people change."

"Things change, people just get old."

"Okay, understand I say this with deepest love. You need to get one of your colon peel — cellulite — potato cleanse — brain exfoliations or whatever it is you do to stay dope these days, because if you don't step off this midlife crisis, I really will be forced to shoot you."

"Actually, the latest thing is anal bleaching."

"And to that let me add — no more watching *Girls*. In fact, no more HBO, *period*."

"I dye mine to match my shoes."

"Clearly, you think I was kidding about shooting you."

"Are you talking to me? Because you seem to be staring at that Middle Eastern girl."

"She looks like she might have some interesting tats."

"Like what? A tramp stamp in Sanskrit?"

"You're right. Let's get these interviews over with before we both have to register as imagination sex offenders."

Nola took a last look at the shirtless hackysack players and sighed. "Eighteen-year-old boys were just so much fun."

The cutest of the two boys kicked the sack into the grass and shouted to his friend, "Screw this. If I don't find some shawty and get laid, my fucking balls are gonna explode!"

Tony grinned. "You were saying?"

"Okay, I admit they have their drawbacks, but you really have to admire that kind of enthusiasm."

Eighteen

Lisa and Jessica: the interview. There have been some groundbreaking advances in medical science throughout the years — penicillin, the polio vaccine, whatever's keeping Ted Williams's frozen head intact — but for all its triumphs, the CDC has yet to come up with a protease inhibitor capable of stopping beautiful young women from lusting themselves silly over handsome Italian men.

Tony may have been working hard to keep from crushing on the coeds, but there was nothing to keep the coeds from crushing on him. Though genuinely heartsick over Max's mysterious passing, his two lovely teaching assistants couldn't resist the urge to flirt just a little as they answered Tony's questions. Once again, Nola was more than happy to let her partner foam the runway before she landed a few key questions of her own.

Lisa and Jessica echoed everything Tony and Nola had been hearing about Max all day: brilliant, intense, color-blind or laundry-challenged based on his often-mismatched wardrobe, and a dedicated ecologist who'd served on the board of Heal the Ocean long before celebrities made it fashionable with Save the Reef regattas and Casino Nights to save the monkey-faced eel.

Nola realized a real date with Max would have ended the moment she ordered her first bottled water. Being anti-fur and riding her bike when time and packages per-mitted wouldn't have cut it. Max had been the real deal. The errant thought gave her an idea. On a hunch, she asked if he'd been a member of any *less visible* environmental groups. The two young women shared a wary look that spoke vol-umes. Tony instantly kicked the charm into high gear. As a woman, Nola found his patter patronizing; as a cop, she was grateful that it pretty much always worked.

"Come on, ladies, you can't exchange a look like that and expect me to just let it slide," he said with a George Clooney grin that could melt a polar ice cap.

Jessica lowered her eyes and stared into her lap. "I'm sorry. It's just, I wouldn't want to say anything that would hurt Dr. Waxman's reputation."

"I wouldn't want that either, honest," Tony replied. "Look, I promise whatever you say will be just between us. In fact, forget this is an interview. Pretend we're just keeping it tight down at the Beachside Café, sipping mojitos, watching the sunset, every guy in the place jealous of me sitting with two gorgeous women, because obviously that's happening."

The two young women mock-rolled their eyes but were secretly flattered. In point of fact, if they had been down at Beachside, Jessica and Lisa would most definitely be turning heads.

"Not that you notice all the masculine attention…" Tony continued rolling out his silly story. "First, because the waiter just brought us a hella-huge order of mixed apps…" He paused, then pressed on with all sincerity. "But mostly because you'd really like to help us find out why Dr. Waxman was in the woods last night, so maybe we can give his family a little closure. His brother's pretty wrecked right now, and the strange circumstances are making it a lot harder for him. So anything you can tell us, we'd really appreciate it."

Tony let the sad words settle. Nola admired his technique, but it wasn't all Police Acting 101; she knew the sentiment came from a real place.

It wasn't hard for her to guess which Phi Beta beauty would crack first. Jessica's brand of smart came with a dash of cool reserve, Lisa's with a hole in her tongue where a diamond stud no doubt appeared on non-school nights. Daring girls were chatty girls, at least as a rule of thumb.

"Okay, there is this one underground group on campus. They're sort of 'occupy everything that pisses them off,' only they don't actually occupy anything. They just launch these useless hit-and-run attacks."

Yep. Lisa it was.

Nola knew Tony was as intrigued by this new bit of information as she was, but appearing too eager could spook a witness, so he held back a beat before asking Lisa the next logical question.

"Does this merry band of maniacs have a name?"

"They call themselves ROTC70."

"ROTC like the military?" The George Clooney grin was back. "And, remember, a correct answer gets you most of the mushroom caps."

"I only eat chanterelles, and it's ROTC70 in honor of the students back in 1970 who burned the bank and peed on the ROTC building. Like that really changed the world. They use free servers to post a lot of social manifestos onto university websites. Lately, Dr. Waxman seemed to be getting into their quasi-violent ethos."

"Lisa, you are making my day."

Feeling left out, Jessica made a gracious but costly error. "If you'd like, I can go print out copies of their posts."

"That'd be fantastic. Thanks, Jess." Tony grinned.

Flattered by Tony's flirty shortening of her name, Jessica

didn't realize till she was halfway out the door that she'd in-advertently given Lisa a one-on-one advantage until she got back.

With Jessica out of the room, Lisa felt freer to flirt. She crossed her legs, sending her sassy swing dress hiking up to DEFCON 5. She wasn't new to the move or the dress, but she made it sound natural when she blushed and explained the Chinese character tattooed on her inner thigh meant "peace."

Girl knows how to work it, Nola thought, hoping the tattoo artist had the right spelling and Lisa's thigh wasn't sending out a very different message of "piece" than she in-tended. Tony kept his eyes well above Lisa's thigh line and tried to think of baseball. When he asked if she knew how Dr. Waxman might have made contact with the group, she didn't have an answer, just a few best guesses.

While Tony and Lisa talked, Nola started an email to Sebastian, asking him to track down ROTC70 online. The minute she sent it, Lisa's phone chirped. For a second, she thought her message had quantum leaped across the room.

Lisa explained that her chirp was an eco-alert. She and Dr. Waxman were on a list of people who were automatically notified by email of any impending threats to the environ-ment. Then she made a sly attempt to scam Tony's deets. "Are you into environmental issues, Detective Angellotti? Because I could put you on the list, too. I'd just need your email."

"Sadly, Lisa, I had a traumatic experience with the en-vironment as a child…I was whipped by a chilly wind. It…still hurts to talk about it. But my partner Nola here is all about eco-activism. How 'bout I give you *her* email?"

He was so obviously pleased with himself that Nola wanted to smack him. Before she could mount a protest, he was spouting out her Gmail address and Lisa was dutifully typing it into her phone.

A millisecond later, both Lisa and Nola got chirped. It was bad news about oil fracking in Virginia. Nola wondered how many other atrocities might be electronically headed her way.

"Ah, Lisa?" she asked with feigned enthusiasm. "About how many of these alerts will I be getting in a day?"

"About fifty to seventy-five."

Tony grinned like a cheshire cat on ecstasy. "Sounds like the planet's in big trouble."

"It's not the only one," Nola replied with her best 'love you now, kill you later' smile.

Jessica returned with the printouts. Nola asked for the women's phone numbers in case she had follow-up questions. The women asked for Tony's card in case they thought of anything that might be helpful later. Everyone said goodbye, and the interview was adjourned.

As soon as Nola and Tony were out the door, she whacked him in the arm.

"What was that for?"

"I just got another eco-alert."

On the way back to the Audi, she got two more. Tony was laughing his ass off. Nola was not amused. "Why didn't you give her *your* email? She was practically begging for it in English *and* Chinese."

"It wouldn't work out. She only eats chanterelles."

"And you only eat shiitake?"

"Oh, come on, don't be France."

"I have a perfectly functioning sense of humor. Look, the only alerts I want on my iPhone are new diet drugs and Victoria's Secret sales, preferably in that order. If I can't get this junk to go straight to spam, you're going to be wearing your dick in my eyelash curler."

"You can't spam it. I didn't have Lisa put you on that list *just* to piss you off — hopefully you'll get e-bombed by ROTC70."

"You think Waxman was meeting up with them before Bambi became a game changer?"

"Oh, hell yeah," Tony said, holding up the printouts. "Who else besides a quasi-clandestine bunch of self-important teenagers would get off on a midnight rendezvous in the woods? It's Robin Hood meets Rage Against the Machine."

"True," Nola agreed. "And what adult would be dumb enough to mark their meeting spot in Day-Glo paint? You caught that on the rock, right?"

"No! Was there fluorescent paint? Wow, you have amazing powers of observation. I mean, seriously, you're like *The Mentalist*."

"*The Mentalist* was just a rip-off of *Psych*, and don't be so touchy. I just thought your head might have been a little foggy this morning after last night's ho-mance."

"Hey, Chelsea's a nice girl."

"She's not the one I'm calling a ho."

As they climbed into the Audi, Nola's email chirped again.

"Oh, goodie, another opportunity to save the snowy newt. Hang on. It's from Captain Taylor at Vandenberg. He'll have Waxman's therapy group assembled for questioning tomorrow at twelve hundred hours."

"He actually wrote twelve hundred hours?"

"No, he wrote noon, but I sounded cool saying it that way, right?"

"Yeah, you're the bomb."

"So we'll hit the Coastal Commission meeting at nine, then shoot straight up the coast to Vandenberg."

Tony gunned the engine. "You know, all this detecting is

making me hungry again."

"There's an old Cheeto on your floor mat."

"Or, how 'bout we hit Ca Dario on the way home?"

"Can't tonight — Pilates with the girlfriends."

"Ah, Pilates, the ancient art of expensive stretching."

"And it strengthens your core."

"Right. The part of the apple everybody throws out. Why don't you just meet for cosmos like other gal pals?"

"Look at you all stuck in *Sex and the City*. Nobody drinks cosmos anymore. And my gal pals all have chores and kids and husbands who hate being left alone with chores and kids so their wives can go drink cosmos. But if they say they're going out to exercise to keep it tight, there's no argument. Of course, afterward we still go out and drink our asses off."

"So basically, you're a gaggle of strong-cored secret alcoholics?"

"Beats another night snuggled up with my body pillow."

"How is Louis?"

"Still fluffy, thanks. In fact, things are going pretty well. I think he's going to ask me home to meet his parents. They've been on his case to get married. Get it? Case? 'Cause he's a pillow?"

"Oh, Lars, we have got to find you a real man."

Nineteen

Nola woke up just a scooch hung over. She'd had a great time at Pilates till her perfect size-two instructor, Suzanne, decided to end the class by having everyone do a self-acceptance exercise in front of the mirror. As Nola was gazing at her body with unconditional love, she noticed the start of a little elbow droop. When had that happened?! After class she exercised her elbow at Sandbar, lifting wine with her girlfriends, whose own unconditional mirror/love experiences had resulted in Stephanie hating her neck, Pam wanting her eyes done, and Kristin wishing perfect Suzanne kindly into the cornfield.

Oh well. Namaste.

Negative body image just came with the territory these days. They'd devoted a whole segment to it on *Good Morning America*, followed by a crash course on how to get your booty bikini-ready for summer, and a commercial advertising Carl's Junior's latest bacon and cheese: elbow droop in a bun.

Television newsotainment was so dumbed down these days that it was undoubtedly responsible for the soaring number of American women on antidepressants — except, of course, for *The Daily Show*.

In the Marry, Kiss, Kill game Nola's friends played over post-Pilates cocktails, Jon Stewart came up "marry" every time. It was a silly game: One woman named three random men, and the others had to rate them in order of marry, kiss, or kill. Stewart's marrying streak held even when it meant Pam had to kill Justin Timberlake and tongue-kiss the Pope. In good Catholic-girl conscience, she couldn't commit papicide, and Stewart would be such a great husband that, sex-alicious as he was, Timberlake had to go. Jon's surprise retirement announcement had plunged every woman Nola knew into the five stages of grief. Still clinging precariously to denial, she was considering starting a support group.

Cuddled in her bed that morning with fluffy, down-filled Louis, Nola decided to prove to her body that she did love it a little by letting it sleep in for another half-hour. She was just closing her eyes again when she heard a knock. It was rare for someone to be dropping by at six in the morning. Endorphins from last night's workout must have been hanging around in her bloodstream waiting for the after-party, because instead of getting irritated, she grabbed her robe and headed out to the living room to see who it was.

Nancy looked even tinier and sadder in her pink hoodie and black spandex running pants than she had the first night they met. "Oh my God, did I wake you? I took a chance 'cause you said you liked running in the morning."

"Actually, I said, 'sometimes I *go* running in the morning.' I like it about as much as a pap smear."

Nancy's face fell about three feet. Nola decided to suck it up in the name of female bonding. "On the other hand, I did have three glasses of wine last night — I'll run with you for 300 calories, then you're on your own."

The foggy beach was deserted except for a few industrious souls swinging metal detectors for rings, coins, and the odd body-piercing trinket lost in the sand. When Nola suggested they run as far as Simply Reds for coffee, Nancy readily agreed. Nola suspected the running was just a ruse anyway. Nancy's roommates were undoubtedly worn out from hearing about Ken and, like all women post-breakup, Nancy undoubtedly had a whole lot more she was dying to say about him. When relationships crash and burn, there's no black box lying in the rubble with clues pointing to what you did wrong. Negative thoughts bounce around in your head like laundry in a clothes dryer, and the only way to let off steam is to vent.

Trying to ignore the cartilage groaning in her knees and wishing she'd invested in a less pretty, better-built sports bra, Nola suddenly realized she was running alone. About a hundred feet back, Nancy stood frozen in front of a newspaper kiosk stacked with the latest issue of the *Santa Barbara Reader.*

The front-page story by Ken Levine had stopped her dead in her tracks. By the time Nola jogged back, Nancy had already dissolved into tears. "He was always talking about how he'd celebrate his first cover story. Now his new girlfriend's probably blowing him in a bathtub full of champagne."

Nola was so consumed by the headline she decided to let that one go. The bold type sent a jolt though her system: "Top-Secret Bio-Weapon Disappears from Vandenberg."

She kicked up their pace to Simply Reds, found a table with good light, and read the story from beginning to end, twice, while Nancy cried into her chai latte.

According to Ken's "reliable" but unnamed source, the military had developed a super-defoliant more potent than Agent Orange. Its abbreviated name was SE40. After the *New York Times* exposed one of the uglier truths about *The* Iraq war — American troops being attacked by mustard and sarin gasses that had been provided to Saddam in the eighties by firms in Baltimore and South Carolina — the government had grown skittish of all bio-chem weapons, and a congressional subcommittee had scrapped the program altogether. All of the existing defoliant was slated to be destroyed, including twelve canisters that had been sent to Vandenberg. But according to a classified weapons inventory, only ten canisters had ever been logged *in* at Vandenberg. If the information was reliable, two canisters of attack-grade poison were MIA.

Nola's mind was humming like the Hadron Super Collider. A leaked log sheet, a missing bio-weapon, a dead environmentalist with his hand smashed open, and they all connected to Vandenberg. The questions she planned to ask the soldiers in Max's therapy group that afternoon were shape-shifting like sci-fi characters when Nancy's teary voice broke her concentration.

"Ken's wanted a cover story forever. He must be crazy happy right now."

"Yeah, well he may feel differently when I get through questioning him," Nola said, signaling for the check.

Nancy's face flushed. "You're going to see him?"

"Oh hell yes. I need the name of his unnamed source and a detailed account of where he's been the past twenty-four hours."

"He was at the film festival the last two nights, and he worked from home yesterday," Nancy volunteered a little too quickly.

"And you know this how?" Nola sighed.

"I wasn't spying on him. I . . . just happened to find out."

"Yeah, and I'm the blond Kardashian. Sweetie, for your own sake, you can't be cyber-stalking him, or following him in your car, or cutting off his dick and carrying it around in your purse like a chihuahua. Restraining orders are a matter of public record. All a guy has to do is Google. If you ever want to date again, you've got to keep your profile clean."

"I don't want to date again. I just want Ken back," she said sadly.

Nola didn't know if Nancy would get her boyfriend back, but if what he claimed in the article was true, there was definitely going to be trouble.

They ran double-time back to the condo. When they got in, Nola copied Ken's contact info from Nancy's phone, promising on pain of death never to reveal where she got it. The threat of a military-grade bio-weapon having possibly fallen into the wrong hands was just a blip on Nancy's radar, but the threat of Ken being angry with her was more than she could bear. Such was the single-mindedness of love.

"After you see him, will you at least tell me everything he says?" she asked with puffy, puppy-dog eyes that no one could say no to.

"Whatever doesn't pertain to the investigation, yes, I promise."

The story was already blowing up on the internet. The snooze-news would only lag an hour or so behind. Nola emailed, texted, and called Ken's cell, all to no avail. She phoned the *Reader* and was told that Ken wasn't in the office yet. She tried pumping his excited colleagues for information, but if any of them knew his source, they weren't about to reveal it. This was their small-town newspaper's moment in the sun, and they were basking in it. The best she could do was to leave another call-back message: "ASAP!" Ten to one Ken would ignore it, but she didn't have time to stake out the newspaper office and grab him walking in. She had the Coastal Commission meeting in an hour, and the interview with Max's therapy group after that. She'd have to wait until she got back from Vandenberg to track him down.

Eighty-sixing her running shoes, Nola showered and dressed at warp speed. Slathering on truffle-infused eye cream, she wondered if she shouldn't go back to her first beauty regimen, playground dirt and cookie crumbs. She'd had flawless skin as a five-year-old — why had she quit what was obviously working? All through her hurried ablutions, she half expected Captain Taylor, the friendly liaison officer at Vandenberg, to email her, canceling the interviews. They had to be going crazy up there, scrambling to do damage control and find the missing canisters, but so far it was still all systems go.

As she headed to the commission meeting, she tried and failed to see how Gus's suicide might tie into the morning's madness. She reminded herself that just because you couldn't prove something didn't mean it was disproven. If it did, no one would believe in God, parallel universes, or commercials that promised that sexy, scantily clad women preferred guys who drank copious amounts of beer. "*There are more things in heaven and earth, Horatio, than are dreamt of in your philosophy.*" True that.

Twenty

Click, pop, fizz...Ah! There was nothing like the sound of your first beer in the morning. Malcolm raised the icy can and emptied it over his Raisin Bran. Across the room, on a whacked-out futon they'd rescued from a pile of discarded furniture on the sidewalk, Ian did the same.

Malcolm and Ian's student apartment building in Isla Vista was as dilapidated as it was notorious. Erected in the sixties, it had soaked up so much pot smoke over the years you could get high just sucking the THC out of the drapes.

The cash Malcolm's and Ian's parents had bestowed on them for beds and computer tables had gone straight to drugs and video games. Having grown up in the money-cushioned lap of Beverly Hills luxury, Malcolm relished his new life of squalor. Sleeping on a secondhand mattress on the floor made him feel spiritually at one with Che.

Back in the day, Malcolm's grandfather had given up his dreams of being a rock star when a producer at Capitol Records had signed his backup band — ironically behind his back — on the condition that they find a new lead singer. In a master stroke of retaliation, Gramps grabbed up all the songs the band had written together in his cheesy Mar Vista apartment and copyrighted them in his own name. The better musicians had been outsmarted by the better businessman.

In exchange for the use of what were now *his* songs,

Gramps had demanded a job at the record company, and since he'd already shown a natural propensity for being an amoral snake, they were more than happy to give him one. The rest was big-hair, metal-music history.

Gramps had passed his music business acumen on to Malcolm's father, who was a sophomore at NYU when a new kind of music was coming straight out of Brooklyn. With his old man's backing, he started his own label, and the bet had paid off big time, yo! The white kid from Beverly Hills became a gangster rap impresario, accumulating money and wives as fast and furious as his father before him.

Malcolm's slimy stepbrother, Rogan, was following in the family tradition, but seeing his family's poorly paid maids stacking blue Tiffany gift boxes under the Christmas tree to be randomly handed out to his father's rich business associates had turned Malcolm into a theoretical anarchist. And hearing his mother, a pampered piece of beef jerky in tennis togs, berate the gardeners in Spanglish for over-trimming the topiary had turned the theorist into a man of action.

Malcolm's first act of violence had been to cut the heads off his mother's favorite topiary lions. For this wanton act of botanical vandalism, he'd been dispatched to Rodeo Drive's top psychiatrist, who had immediately put him on Adderall. It was a lucky turn of events, since it was a prized commodity among the skinny girls at his private high school who were happy to give a handsy in exchange for the pills that would make them even skinnier.

Eventually, talk of sending him to a Malibu home for troubled teens died down, but Malcolm's abhorrence of the one-percenters, the human termites who gorged themselves on the dwindling resources of a ravaged planet, continued to grow exponentially. Once he hit college, his righteous indignation and rock-star good looks made him a catalytic converter for other disillusioned kids looking for a cause, and ROTC70 was born.

The dozen or so *Santa Barbara Readers* scattered around Malcolm and Ian's living room were firsthand proof that they'd officially made their revolutionary bones. For the fifth time that morning, Malcolm threw back his head and howled like a wolf. "Awoooooo! Fight the pow'a, motherfucker!"

Ian echoed the feral cry, then guzzled his beer bran straight from the bowl.

"S'all good, bro. Except for the old man."

"Newsbots said he got kicked by a deer, accidents happen. Not our fault, I."

Ian wasn't convinced. "What if the cops do that forensics shit and find us?"

"So what? There's no law says you have to report a dead body. Ball up, my mad-genius friend. If the cops catch on, we'll just get our fifteen minutes ahead of schedule. CNN, Buzzfeed, Fox Fake News…we'll be folk heroes, bro."

A text interrupted their beer-fueled euphoria. Ian dug around under an old Scooby-Doo blanket he'd liberated from a thrift shop and came up with his phone. It was from Kyle. Ian relayed the message to Malcolm. "Kyle's got the truck. He's on his way to pick up Monica."

"All right, all right, all right, let's suit up," Malcom said, sending his cereal bowl clattering on top of a huge pile of sink dishes.

"So is Mon your new hookup, or was that just a celebration bang last night?" Ian asked idly.

"I don't know. It is what it is till it isn't." Malcolm shrugged.

Ian wished being the scientific brains of the operation got you laid, but it was still the flash guys like Malcolm who had the monopoly on hot pussy. Just another part of the rampant global hypocrisy. The four richest men in the world now held more wealth than half the population at the bottom, but the average moron was too busy wallowing in Big Macs, Cadillacs, and drone attacks to give a damn. Politicians and religious leaders were all part of the same flesh-eating fiscal greed. The new Pope seemed to be a little more enlightened, but no doubt there were already plots in motion at the Vatican to poison his ass. And smart guys like me, he thought, still have to go bottom-feeding for a fuck. The whole system sucked.

Malcolm's voice shook Ian out of his self-absorbed litany of outrage. "Hey, I, stop daydreaming. Gotta go make some noiz!"

Twenty-One

The Coastal Commission met in one of the loveliest rooms in the courthouse. Lush, color-saturated murals of Spanish explorers, Chumash Indians, and Franciscan padres told the story of Santa Barbara's history. The early inhabitants' faces were so nobly depicted they bordered on angelic. Nola imagined her own face in the murals: scrunched up in disgust, fingers pinching her nose to protect her olfactory senses from the onslaught of bad odors that must have been endemic in the age of exploration. She'd always been grateful not to have been born in older, smellier times. With deodorant yet to be invented, the Franciscan padre raising his arms beneficently over the Chumash children seemed like a crueler assault on the native population than the explorers eyeing their land.

In the center of the room, two rows of dark wooden benches, carved in the early ranchero style, were packed with interested parties from both sides of the Wyatt Development argument. Friends of the beach on the left, friends of development on the right, natch. Both sides were murmuring insults as they scoped each other out, anxious for the proceedings to begin.

Nola and Tony had taken seats in the back, hoping to be inconspicuous. When they arrived they'd been surprised to find Haven seated on the dais with the rest of the commissioners. It looked like a tragic error by the prom committee, seating the homecoming queen with the audiovisual club. One young glamour puss amid six middle-aged men in boring business suits and a lone woman who looked so painfully proper she probably showered in her Spanx.

Haven was wearing a body-hugging, business-appropriate skirt and blazer, and her hair was pulled back in a wedding bun. It was a look that had been stirring men's imaginations since women first joined the workforce. The blazer comes off, the hair falls down and ... *Why, Ms. Carstairs, you're beautiful.*

Nola had been unable to convince Tony that a connection between Waxman and Gillette — both planning to attend this meeting, and both turning up dead — was anything more than a coincidence, so she was hoping Haven's unexpected presence might pique his interest in more ways than one.

Leaving him to it, she scanned the gathered crowd and zeroed in on Lawrence Wilson. The Wyatt Development Corporation's majority stockholder was seated, front row, right, signing autographs. Wilson, the former star of a long-running hospital show, had been dubbed Dr. McDorable by the tabloids, and the name still fit. Known as Larry to his friends, he'd remained Hollywood handsome due to good genes, an Ayurvedic diet, and knowing just how much plastic surgery was enough. Unlike his costars, who had squandered their lucrative network paychecks, Larry had realized that what Les Moonves at CBS giveth, he eventually taketh away. Rather than fast cars and even faster race horses, Larry had invested in land, parlaying his TV cash stash into a small real estate empire that included a string of posh housing developments and a successful winery where tourists flocked to buy his wine, his book, and various hospital-themed souvenirs emblazoned with the name of his once-top-ten show.

Nola nudged Tony. "Check out Dr. McD. Early fifties

and still bringing it."

"So, go flirt," Tony replied, nudging her back.

"Right. After the smile he just tossed to Haven of the d'Urbervilles."

"You're as sexy as she is."

"In what universe?"

"Well, you might have to throw in a set of tires . . . and the Lamborghini that goes with them."

"Gee thanks, but even if he did prefer the beauty that comes with cranky old age, I can't be off sleeping with the enemy."

"Who says he's the enemy?"

"My latest eco-alert. The Green community is up in arms about this proposed development, as you can see by how many people in this room are still wearing Earth Shoes. And frankly, I agree with them."

"You don't see the upside of Dr. McDorable turning unspoiled beachfront property into a thriving country-club community with no rustics allowed?" he said.

"No," Nola said defiantly. And if I wasn't here as a city employee required to stay neutral, I'd stand up and say so."

A woman who'd gone overboard on collagen lip injections shot Nola a dirty look.

"Not so loud," Tony whispered. "You're pissing off Apoco-lips now. Although, I think Madame Commissioner up at the dais is on your side. She's looking at Haven the way you look at me when I wear my Hurleys."

"Can't be sure," Nola replied. "She may just have a serious case of Bitchy Resting Face. Some women just always look like they're watching a grown man trying to pull off colorful cargo shorts."

The meeting was called to order by a stout gentleman whose head was two sizes too large for his comb-over. He led off with a short tribute to Gus that seamlessly segued into a treacly introduction to Haven. He practically gushed as he described how she'd selflessly put aside her grief to honor Gus's memory by delivering his final speech to the commission. When he actually said the words, "Wyatt Development," half the crowd cheered and half the crowd booed. It was an earsplitting example of "democrazy" in action.

The female commissioner's BRF got even bitchier as she watched Haven cross to the microphone like Daria Strokous slinking down the catwalk.

"You're right, Tone." Nola said. "Madame Commissioner is definitely voting my side."

Tony didn't answer. He was watching Haven. And he wasn't the only one; every man in the place was pumping testosterone like a Clydesdale. Even the painted faces on the murals seemed to follow her with their eyes. There was no denying the girl had impact. When Haven reached the microphone, she graciously acknowledged that the speech she was about to read would come as a disappointment to some of the people in the room, but she wanted everyone to know that her late husband had given the matter his deepest consideration before composing it.

Haven read Gus's speech in favor of the Wyatt group like she was auditioning to play a part in a movie, the part of somebody who actually cared. Nola's spidey-senses were tingling. Things like zoning rights didn't matter to women like Haven unless they stood to profit from them. There was obviously more at stake for her in this deal than just honoring the memory of her late and very unlamented husband.

Nola heard a few mumbled protests from the anti-development crowd, but no one was crass enough to heckle the widow of a suicide. And then it happened!

It happened so fast there was no way to stop it. Half a dozen masked marauders dressed as superheroes burst through a back door shouting "Earth First, Fascists!" and "People Over Profits!" Armed with Super Soakers, Superman, Green Lantern, and the rest of the caped crusaders blasted commissioners and concerned citizens alike with a spray of red liquid from their powerful toy guns.

Tony and Nola rushed forward, shouting that they were police officers, but they got caught up in the tide of frightened people running back to get out of harm's way. As she pushed through the panicky crowd, Nola was nailed by a blast from Wonder Woman that turned her new silk blouse into a sticky Jackson Pollack. Tony bench-hopped his way to the dais, and the two of them took off after the retreating vandals, but by the time they reached the parking lot, the Justice League of America had already hopped into a white Ford Explorer and were hauling fuel-injected ass toward Carrillo-Street and the freeway.

Tony pulled out his phone. Catching his breath, he called out to Nola. "I got the last three plate numbers — you?"

"Same three, damn it, but Wonder Woman was wearing Ana Khouri gold cuffs."

"In English for the fashion-impaired, please?"

"Psycho-expensive designer gold bracelets. Not exactly your typical tree-hugger must-have accessory for winter."

Tony gave the three license plate numbers they had along with a description of the Ford to Kesha back at the station; CHP and black and whites would take it from there. Frustrated, he and Nola made their way back to the scene of the melee.

The room was still in a high state of anxiety. Bitchy Resting Face woman was cowering under a table and had to be coaxed out. For the second time in a week, Nola saw Haven soaked to the skin in red liquid. Dr. McDorable was showering her with concern. He should have been showering her with diamonds considering the solid she'd done him by reading Gus's speech favoring his development project with such pathos and dignity.

A faint cran-apple smell still hung in the air. Tony sniffed Nola's blouse, a "couldn't resist" impulse buy that had cost her an arm and a leg and part of a condo payment.

"Is that fruit punch?"

"Yes, and if there's rum in it, I'm gonna suck it dry," she replied, knowing the expensive silk would be DOA by the time it hit the dry cleaner.

While she was taking witness statements, she realized that, contrary to the culprits' intention, calling the commissioners greedy pigs and pelting them with fruit punch had actually fomented a sense of defiance among them. Even Bitchy Resting Face woman, finally coaxed out from under the table, was bravely asserting that she refused to be cowed. Gus's speech, citing the badly needed tax revenues the project would bring to the city, was starting to make sense to all of them. The tide was turning in Dr. McDorable's favor. The meeting, so abruptly adjourned, had morphed into a conversational referendum in support of the Wyatt project. Although circumstances necessitated that the final vote be postponed until the next meeting, it was practically a done deal.

Kesha called Tony back with a hit on the plates. The only white Ford Explorer in the Santa Barbara area with those last three numbers belonged to an Intrepid Rent-a-Car out by the airport. Nola looked down at her ruined blouse. The red punch had dried and was sticking to her skin in spots.

"Tony, sweetie, does this blouse make my boobs look bloody?"

Their next stop was Vandenberg and interviewing a post-traumatic-shock therapy group looking like an extra from a Tarantino movie wasn't going to cut it, so they formulated a new plan. Nola would go home and change out of her juicy couture while Tony checked out the rental place alone. Later he'd pick her up and they'd ride up to Vandenberg together. On her way out, Nola took a last look around the juice-splattered room and wondered what kind of song Charley would have made up about this high-fructose mess.

Twenty-Two

The Intrepid Rent-a-Car office was chronically overlit. Management thought the hyper-fluorescent glare helped snap exhausted travelers out of their stupors, making the lines move faster. Employees thought it was slowly giving them brain tumors. Tony thought it made Marisela, the lovely rental manager answering his questions, look like something out of a telenovela version of *Twilight*.

When he asked her about the Ford, she checked her computer and found it was still in inventory. In fact, it hadn't left the lot in a week. When he asked to see it for himself, she offered to walk him out to the appropriately numbered spot. Out in the sunlight, the vampire aura died away, leaving a lovely, middle-aged woman with midnight-black hair and sparkling dark eyes.

The Explorer was parked in its assigned spot just as Marisela had predicted. The last three numbers on the plates matched the ones Tony had seen. It had to be the same SUV. The gas tank was full and the odometer matched the computer printout, but gas tanks could be filled and odometers rolled back.

"Do all employees have access to the vehicles, Marisela?"

"Well, yes. The keys are kept right on the seat. But you'd have to show paperwork to drive one off the lot."

The beefy, middle-aged gatekeeper, Arlo, acted suitably

affronted when Tony asked if anyone could have driven the Ford past the gate without him knowing. He swore he hadn't been away from his post all morning, even to take a leak, and there was no way he'd let one of the punk kids who worked there take a vehicle out for a joyride. Tony outwardly took his word for it, but the way Arlo avoided eye contact, and the thin film of perspiration on his upper lip, suggested he probably had more cash in his wallet now than when he'd arrived at work that morning.

Marisela was apologetic as she accompanied Tony back across the lot. "I'm sorry you had to come all the way out here for the wrong car."

"Oh, it's the right car. How often do you run them through the wash?"

"Usually just once. When they're first returned to the lot."

"See, that's interesting, because that SUV didn't have a speck of dust on it, and the wheel wells were still wet."

The sparkling eyes sparkled a little brighter. It wasn't everyday Marisela got to play crime stopper. "I guess we're walking over to the car wash," she said with a grin.

"I guess we are." Tony grinned back.

The short list of suspects consisted of Kyle, a gangly kid with more tattoos than personality, who looked a little high, and Carlos, who had a gold decal embedded in his front tooth. It was the familiar silhouette of the naked woman that truckers sported on their mud flaps. Shrunk down to fit a tooth, it looked more like an errant sesame seed than bling. If you didn't look closely, you'd think the kid just needed a little face time with a toothbrush.

Carlos's shift had started at five-thirty — Kyle hadn't started until ten. Tony played neutral, but the timeline pointed to Kyle.

"Guys, a Ford Explorer from this lot was used this morning in the commission of a crime. I just checked the vehicle, and it appears to have been recently washed. Any thoughts?"

Carlos shot Kyle a look that as good as ratted him out. Kyle had no choice but to make up a story on the fly. "Ah, yeah, when I came into work, I saw the hood was all covered in bird shit so I ran it through, but it was just sitting on the lot, so no way anybody jacked it."

When Carlos threw in his two centavos, the naked woman on his tooth glinted in the sunshine. "How could anybody get it by that fat hot-dog burp at the gate?"

"Not to cast any aspersions on Arlo," Tony said, "but gatekeepers have been known to take bribes. Can anyone verify you've been here all morning, Carlos?"

"Yeah, when I wasn't running cars through the wash, I was shooting the shit with Jordy in the return garage."

Marisela confirmed this was true.

"How 'bout you, K?" Tony asked Kyle nonchalantly.

"I was hanging with a couple of my buds at their crib in Isla Vista."

"Right, I'll need their names."

"Why?"

"To check your alibi, genius." Carlos's glinty toothed interruptions were starting to get annoying.

"Carlos, I think I can take it alone from here," Tony said with a look to Marisela. She nodded at the young man to get back to work, and begrudgingly, he obeyed.

Kyle reluctantly gave up Malcolm's and Ian's names and address, but refused to elaborate on the specifics of "just hanging."

"You guys must have been doing something. Playing Halo? Bare-knuckle boxing? Braiding each others' hair?"

Tony's sarcasm was wasted on Kyle, who was too wasted

to respond. Sullen and pot-eyed, he stuck to his nonstory till Tony gave him leave to get back to work.

Back in the rental office, Marisela wrote her number down on a brochure. The way she blushed made Tony wonder if she wrestled with the same midlife fears that were currently giving Nola the yips. All women were desirable provided they weren't ball-breaking shrews. Why didn't they get that?

He was pondering this thought when he spotted a food truck parked across the road. What Marisela might or might not be feeling was instantly wiped from his mind by the exciting prospect of a breakfast burrito.

Food had been trumping women's feelings in men's minds ever since the first cavewoman sat fashioning shoes out of hides, wondering where the relationship was going while her boyfriend parked himself in front of the petroglyphs with a hot sabertooth sandwich, not caring in the least.

A few minutes later, Marisela was back at work and Tony was in high-caloric Mexican heaven.

Twenty-Three

Tony was still licking tomatillo sauce off his fingers when he pulled up outside Nola's condo. She was waiting for him in the parking lot, newly dressed in a periwinkle blue tank and a skirt that made her legs look killer but was easily two inches of bare thigh too short for police work.

"Not exactly dressed to arrest," he called out as she crossed to his driver's-side window. "Tackle some dirtbag in that skirt, and the bystanders won't be innocent for long."

"No way I'm taking a beautiful drive up the coast in office slacks. Besides, who would I have to tackle? I'm just going to interview a few soldiers."

"Well, you do look like you're looking for a few good men. Speaking of which, Sam called. The Coastal Commissioners are all over him to catch the terps who spewed 'em this morning."

"Terps?"

"Teen perps." Tony smiled proudly. "Just came to me."

"I like it." Nola said. "Any potential terps at the rent-a-car place?"

"I found my man, and I use the term loosely. Kid's just half a step smarter than *Dude, Where's My Car?* But the fat Cerberus at the gate is swearing the SUV was never off the lot, and the kid claims he was hanging with two of his bros in Isla Vista all morning."

"You check 'em out?"

"Not yet. He'd have texted them by the time I was off the lot anyway. Might as well let them sweat a little. I'll drop in when we get back from Vandenberg."

"Sam's good with us heading up there?"

"Yeah, I told him if we could find the soldier — who passed the secret — that prompted the headline —"

Nola picked up her cue: "— that came from the terps — who filled the Super Soakers — that sprayed the commissioners —"

"— that swallowed the cat — that ate the rat — that lived in the house that Jack built — we'd have his bad guys," Tony ended with a flourish.

"Nicely done. I love a good Jack story." A flock of pelicans gracefully traversed the violet-blue sky. It was the kind of lazy, sunny day where even mean old men smiled and waved at the noisy neighbor kids on their skateboards.

"Climb in, and I'll tell you a few more on the ride up."

"Tony, I was just thinking. You know what would make this a way cooler drive along the ocean?"

Half an hour later, they were cruising up the Gaviota Grade in Nola's T-bird with the top down and the music cranked up. Tony hated chick rock, and Nola hated sports talk, but he'd only agreed to take the convertible on condition that he drive, which left Nola free to get silly with her Sirius radio.

"*California girls, we're undeniable…Fine, fresh, fierce… We got it on lock! West coast represent, now put your hands up! Oh oh oh ohhhhhh!*"

Tony's face contorted in agony like the Nazi in *Raiders of the Lost Ark* who foolishly peeked into the Ark of the Covenant. Listening to Katy Perry was worse than waterboarding to any straight guy over the age of twelve. Nola decided she'd make it up to him by listening to "Jock Talk" on the ride home. There was always some sports opera going on about A-Rod or some other ego-balloon ballplayer. Once Tony got sucked into that drama, he'd forgive her this little bit of mindless afternoon fun.

Their plan, once they reached Vandenberg, was to try and ferret out who had slipped the classified SE40 log sheet to Dr. Waxman. Sounded simple enough, but when they arrived at the main gate of the third-largest military base in the nation, they had to navigate their way through a throng of reporters clamoring to get in.

Captain Taylor, the liaison officer Nola had liaised with over the phone, greeted them with hearty handshakes and handed them their ID tags. He had more sparkling teeth than a TV weatherman and a personality that was sunny all week with zero chance of gloom.

In spite of the holes it would leave in her tank top, Nola dutifully attached her ID and tried to ignore the admiring looks she was getting. She'd been regretting her wardrobe choice since they'd arrived. Tony had been right. Showing up to a military base in a short skirt was the equivalent of walking into church in crotchless panties. In another context, the attention would have been flattering, but at the moment, it was shaving molto points off her presumed IQ.

Tony shaded his eyes from the sun and surveyed the lowing herd of press assembled at the gate. "Looks like this morning's story in the *Reader*'s getting some traction, Captain Taylor."

"Not a word of truth to it, Detective. Air Force Munitions Account does daily reconciliations of all stockpiled weapons. Any mistakes would have raised a red flag on day one."

Nola tried not to sound accusatory. "Any chance those inventories could have been doctored?"

"No, ma'am. Anything hinky and Major Burnell would have been all over it. He's speaking at the press briefing today. Top brass wants complete transparency on this one. That reporter just got it wrong, plain and simple."

Nola hoped it was true, mostly because no missing weapons meant a safer world, but also for Nancy's sake. The image of a disgraced Ken in a bathtub full of Moët with no one to blow him would go a long way toward boosting her morale.

"Any objections if Detective MacIntire and I attend the briefing, Captain?" Tony asked.

"I assumed you'd be curious. I rescheduled your meeting with Dr. Waxman's therapy group for after the Major's talk. I'll drive you over to the parade grounds now."

Tony and Nola looked longingly at the kickass military jeeps and Humvees zipping by as they climbed into the back of the wussy little golf cart Captain Taylor had commandeered to escort them around base. Still, being chauffeured around in the back of a golf cart was better than being part of the press corps that was currently being force-marched to the briefing on foot.

Tony took advantage of the cart ride to ask a few background questions. "What exactly does SE40 stand for, Captain?"

"Forty is the percentage-per-milliliter of the active agent in the defoliant, and SE stands for scorched earth."

A group of soldiers whistled at Nola as the golf cart tootled by. She pretended not to notice. "Scorched earth? Sounds pretty nasty."

"Can't shock-and-awe the enemy with fuzzy sock puppets, Detective MacIntire. The code name for SE40's deployment was The Carthage Project."

Nola decided to inject a little smart to make up for her

miscalculation with the skirt. "As in the Romans salting the earth of Carthage at the end of the third Punic war in 146 BC, so it could never support life again?"

Captain Taylor's big weatherman smile lit up again. "Roger that, very impressive ma'am."

Nola inwardly cringed at the despised "ma'am," but was glad to have scored the points. Tony rolled his eyes and murmured, "Overcompensating."

"What's that, Detective Angellotti?" Captain Taylor apparently had the ears of a bat.

"The Romans, I mean," Tony lied. "Bunch of smarty-pants showoffs, don't you think?" He pointedly grinned at his showoff partner, who acknowledged his taunt by sticking out her tongue.

"Actually, they were some pretty tough hombres," Taylor replied, unaware of the goings-on in the back of his cart. "But I'm sure our team could give 'em a run for their money. Not that the Air Force is out to damage the earth. We're actually very pro-environment. The 30th Civil Engineer squadron's been installing solar panels here on base as part of a renewable-energy pilot program. Our voltaic fields generate sixteen kilowatts of sustainable power at peak daylight hours. That's enough energy to support all 18,000 military and civilian personnel on base and still put power back in the grid."

"That's very impressive, Captain," Tony said, then whispered sideways to Nola, "Rehearsed."

"Shh. Play nice. It's a great thing," Nola whispered back.

Having delivered his information payload, Captain Taylor pulled the golf cart to a stop on a big lawn in front of a viewing podium. As Tony and Nola climbed out, he promised to collect them at the end of the briefing. One last "sunny with a chance of afternoon breezes" smile, and he was on his way.

Tony and Nola staked out a good vantage point and watched the news cameras jockey for position while Barbie- and Ken-doll reporters did last-minute touchups to their hair and makeup. Nola scanned the crowd looking for one Ken doll in particular. If she'd remembered to be looking with the eyes of a young girl in love, she might have realized that the cute, dark-haired guy in the clichéd Abercrombie safari jacket was, in fact, the pedestal-worthy pinnacle of masculine perfection that Nancy had described — only perhaps using a few less Ps.

Ken was milling around the crowd, wishing there was some way to let everyone know that he was the one who broke the story that was the cause of all the excitement. Unfortunately, a byline in the *Santa Barbara Reader* didn't come with a picture, so until he got a chance to ask a question ("Major, Ken Levine from the *Reader*...according to my sources...blah blah blah..."), he was fated to remain in dull anonymity. All morning, he'd been emailing copies of his story to the managing editors of TV news stations across the country. A scoop like this was a career maker. No more small-town paper; his star would most certainly be on the rise in the blathersphere as the day wore on.

An Air Force major stepped up to the microphone; the assembled reporters went quiet with excitement. Positive that the next few moments would make him famous, Ken had to lower his clipboard just a little below his belt line as the briefing began.

Twenty-Four

In Nola's mind, the military was a few Great Santinis barking orders at a lot of progressively smaller Santinis, but like an ill-chosen shade of nail polish, a mind can easily be changed.

There were no camouflage fatigues capable of disguising the breathtaking sexiness of Major Bryan Burnell. Taut and tan and buff and gorgeous, he made every straight woman's libido snap to attention as he stepped up to the microphone and took command of the briefing. Even the military buzz cut couldn't diminish the effect he was having on the collective female pulse. He was the man Nola had been asking Santa to bring her for Christmas ever since she hit puberty. For a moment, she thought she might need a fainting couch.

"Holy smokes!"

"Have we finally found your type?" Tony asked with a twinkle.

"Well, I wouldn't kick him out of the foxhole for eating kale chips."

Mid to late forties, intense brown eyes, skin the color of warmed honey...it was practically a biological imperative that the Major mate with a *Sports Illustrated* swimsuit cover-babe to ensure the planet would never run out of supermodels. But still, a girl could dream. And then he started to speak...

"Afternoon, everybody, seems we have a situation here

that requires some clearing up."

It was starting to feel like a joke. Even his voice was handsome. It was that soothing, pilot-over-the-intercom voice that makes you feel like no matter how much turbulence you encounter, you'll arrive at your destination safe and on time.

"I know you all came out here for a story, but contrary to what was reported in the *Reader* this morning, there are no missing super-secret weapons. Twelve canisters of SE40 were sent to this base from the Lawrence Livermore National Laboratory, and that's still how many we've got. All of 'em scheduled to be neutralized today."

Nola hoped the future Mr. Nola MacIntire was telling the truth. She could never rescue and raise two shelter dogs in a weathered beach house with a bald-faced liar, no matter how GI grope-able he was.

In the center of the crowd of buzzing reporters, Ken was starting to feel his first pangs of self-doubt. Was this the opening salvo of a full-blown military cover-up, or was it possible his informant had been, ironically, misinformed? But he hadn't just taken the information on faith. The proof had been downloaded from a computer right here on base. Twelve canisters had left the Livermore Lab, but only ten had been logged in on the inventory roster, and military inventories, especially ones pertaining to secret biochemical weaponry, didn't lie.

Before Ken could throw out his first question, Rachel Palmer, Action News's lissome Lois Lane, beat him to the punch. "Major, according to the story in the *Reader*, twelve canisters of SE40 left Livermore, but only ten were logged in here at the base. How do you explain the sudden reappearance of the other two canisters?"

Major Burnell flashed a smile so bright it added a few degrees to global warming. "There was no sudden reappearance, Ms. Palmer. All twelve canisters were logged in, just not together. They were transported in a vehicle that contained other ordnance, so they were logged in as they were unloaded: first ten, then later two. Apparently, the reporter from the *Reader* only got half the paperwork. If he'd bothered to call us to verify his intel before he went to press, we'd have been happy to save him some well-earned embarrassment."

Nola whispered to Tony. "Question: If I say the thing in Dr. Waxman's smashed hand was a flash drive with the downloaded partial inventory, are you going to say, 'no shit, Sherlock'?"

"Yep."

"Good to know."

Having established a verbal beachhead, Major Burnell pressed his advance. "I know this comes as a pretty big disappointment to some of you. Let's face it, your jobs go well when things go wrong. But I'm afraid you're just gonna have to live with the fact that no threat levels are up and no lives are in danger."

There was panic-sweat in the folds of Ken's safari jacket. He'd been called out, and if he didn't answer, his reputation, and very likely his career, would take a ball-scalding hit. Ratcheting up his courage, he called out, "Major? Ken Levine from the *Reader*. Do you expect us to just take your word for it that there *are* twelve canisters here on base?"

Nola's head practically spun off her shoulders as she strained to get a better look at the cause of Nancy's broken heart and her own dwindling stash of Skinnygirl margaritas. Ken was a cutie, she'd give him that, but like every other guy in a hundred-mile radius, he suffered in comparison to the man at the podium who was about to have him for lunch.

"Well, no, Ken, I don't just expect you to take my word, any more than I'd expect you to do a better job of verifying your information before going off half-cocked and wasting everybody's time on a Whiskey, Tango, Foxtrot story."

"That means 'what the fuck' story," Nola translated for Tony.

"Again, no shit, Sherlock."

"Well how do I know if you speak Air Force?"

The Major continued, "The canisters are made of a high-grade protective alloy and are clearly marked for safety reasons. After we're finished talking here, I'm going to take you all out to the weapons depot so you can see 'em with your own eyes. We've even flown in the head honcho from Livermore to verify that they're the same twelve canisters that left his lab in the first place. You good with that, Ken?"

Nola felt a flash of guilty pleasure as she watched Nancy's tweet-dumping boyfriend squirming on the hook, unable to construct a meaningful response.

As Ken struggled to sputter out an answer, a helmet-haired anchor from a Los Angeles affiliate jumped in with a follow-up question. "Major, isn't using a defoliant like SE40 considered to be biochemical warfare? And if so, why was the military trying to develop it in the first place? After the recent *New York Times* story about chemical weapons in Iraq…"

The sixteen-megawatt smile vanished as Major Burnell cut him off. "Let me make something crystal clear here. SE40 was developed to aid our allies' efforts to destroy poppy and coca fields — crops our enemies use to buy weapons and fund terrorism. However, once tests showed it posed a residual ecological danger, the whole damn project was scrapped. That's why we're destroying the stuff. We're the good guys, remember?"

Nola looked on smugly as Ken lobbed a final Hail Mary. "But what proof do we have that the canisters you're going to show us actually contain the original compound? How do we know the material in at least two of the canisters wasn't replaced by another substance as part of a cover-up?"

Major Burnell's gentle chuckle made others want to laugh along with him. Half the press corps was doing just that without knowing why. "Well, Ken, I suppose someone could have pulled off the old switcheroo. Of course, they'd need the proper multimillion-dollar safety facilities to avoid killing themselves and God knows how many other people in the process. This isn't something Joe Terrorist can just siphon into a thermos and go out and destroy the great north woods. Your unnamed source should have explained that to you while they were feeding you all that half-assed information. By the way, I'd really like to have a talk with that individual."

Ken's solid jaw clenched tightly. "In good conscience, I can't reveal my source."

"I'm surprised you have a conscience, kid. You scared people half to death with a story you didn't bother to vet. I'm guessing because you saw it as a stepping stone to bigger things. Well, I'm afraid your dreams of being the next Anderson Cooper just fizzled out on the launch pad. It's a tough lesson, but you're young. Better you learn it now."

And with that, the briefing was over. Major Burnell had, as his pilot-on-the-intercom voice promised, brought them to their destination safely and on time. A line of Humvees pulled up to escort the reporters to the weapons storage depot.

Nola watched Ken feverishly texting someone as he waited his turn to board. But just as repeatedly pressing the button for an elevator doesn't make it arrive any faster, repeatedly texting doesn't ensure a quick response; for the moment, Ken Levine was Tango, Foxtrot, shit out of luck.

Nola and Tony decided to opt out of the weapons tour, knowing that all twelve canisters would be produced as promised, that the scientist from Livermore would attest to their authenticity, and that proper paperwork would be furnished to back it all up. The Air Force would have dotted their Is and crossed their Ts before escorting the press on any significant fact-finding mission. Of course, that didn't mean everything was as up-and-up as Major Burnell made it out to be. An Air Force major should be fairly adept at subterfuge. On the other hand, it was equally possible he was telling the absolute truth. Some gung-ho soldier, seeing a partial inventory list, might easily have jumped the gun, creating a daisy chain of bad evidence: soldier to Waxman — Waxman to ROTC70 — ROTC70 to Ken. If Nola and Tony's guess was right, that soldier was most likely a member of Dr. Waxman's therapy group. The prospect of interrogating soldiers suffering from PTSD had been making Nola uneasy all morning. Now that it might lead to one of them being court-martialed over a well-intentioned screw-up, she wondered if she wanted to go there at all. She decided to test the waters with Tony.

"I'm not sure I like the idea of getting a soldier with post-traumatic stress in trouble for leaking a faulty story. I mean, aside from getting the press riled up, it's pretty much no harm, no foul."

Tony was nodding before she finished her sentence. "Under the circumstances, I'm inclined to give it a pass myself."

"Whew! I was afraid you'd say I was being too soft because I'm a woman. So how do we conduct this interview under the prying eyes of Captain Taylor without landing some misguided whistle-blower in a crossfire hurricane?"

"Beats me." He shrugged. "Lots of rocket scientists around here. Maybe we should ask one of them."

"We haven't released the information about Waxman's smashed hand. If we keep it under our hats, the connection to the stolen intel will be a lot less obvious." Nola's voice trailed off as she watched the handsome major hop down off the podium.

Tony was watching her watch. "So what *do* we tell them?"

Nola's mind snapped back to the issue at hand. "We'll say we're just investigating a routine accident, keep our questions vague, and hand out our cards when we leave. You good with that?"

"As gold," he said, jealously eying the line of Humvees filling up with press. "All this high-level military intrigue feels like we're in a movie."

Nola spied Captain Taylor zipping his way across the parade ground to collect them. "Yeah, only if this were a movie, I'd be a twenty-year-old martial arts expert in a skin-tight catsuit hijacking one of those Humvees, instead of a fossilized blonde about to be picked up in my grandmother's golf cart."

Captain Taylor tooted the horn twice and waved.

"Geez, it's like showing up at Indy in a clown car," Tony winced. "How 'bout if *I* hijack a Humvee?"

"You can't. You're clearly the late-thirties heartthrob who plays by the rules."

"How come you're twenty and I'm my real age?"

"Because age doesn't matter for men in the movies any more than it does in real life."

"Really? Sweet."

Twenty-Five

When things went wrong for Nola growing up, her father, a veteran wounded in Grenada of all places, would smile and ask the same simple question: "Is anybody shooting at you?" She never got further than, "No, but..." before he'd kiss the top of her head and say, "Then it's fine. You're going to get through it."

The five young men and two women in Dr. Waxman's PTSD therapy group *had* been shot at. They'd been strafed by bullets, blown up by IEDs, and shipped home as hollow-eyed insomniacs with nerves as raw as sushi.

They were all in their twenties, but for once Nola wasn't jealous. Her crinkly eye, elbow-droop, westward-ho inner-thigh expansion was nothing compared to the nightmare memories these fractured kids were dealing with. Terrifying images popped up in their heads like whack-a-moles; reason one away and instantly a new one appeared to take its place.

Dr. Waxman had been trying to slay the Imagine Dragons in their heads using his own variation of Stolorow's phenomenological approach to the treatment of trauma, and according to at least one member of the group, a soft-spoken female airman from Oklahoma, it was helping. The mental scars that kept her alert as a cat 24/7, fearful of any change in the frequencies of the world around her, were starting to abate. The others nodded in agreement, but their expressions were anxious. Whatever progress Dr. Waxman had made in reducing their stress levels was slowly eroding due to the shock of his sudden death. Nola wished she could help them disarm and diffuse, but fear of saying the wrong thing in front of Captain Taylor had upped her own stress level to "situation critical, danger Will Robinson."

She and Tony stuck to their game plan, keeping their inquiries vague, with no mention of weapon inventories, SE40, or Dr. Waxman's smashed hand. If Captain Taylor had an inkling that they suspected a member of the group was the source of the press leak, he was doing a first-class job of playing Clueless Joe from Kokomo — no clouds in the forecast for the rest of the week.

No one in the group knew where Dr. Waxman was going after their last session. He hadn't mentioned a midnight nature hike, but they wouldn't put it past him. Thanks to his example, Tasha now carried a reusable water bottle, and Pooch recycled his Kentucky Fried Chicken bags. Nola tried not to look horrified as the cute African-American Airman First Class described his favorite comfort food: two deep-fried chicken breasts stuffed sandwich-style with mashed potatoes and cheese. She knew it would be cold comfort in his forties, when his back fat gave him lat boobs, but at twenty-two, still military fit, Pooch was far too innocent to see that freight train coming. Knowing what she was thinking, Tony shot her a sideways whisper. "Mention bad calories and I'll plunge my pen in your thigh."

As the group went on talking, Tony and Nola's cop-dar zeroed in on Rohit Kodical, a strikingly intelligent senior airman, as the person most likely to have been Max's co-conspirator. A survivor of a missile attack on his convoy in Afghanistan, Ro had undergone three surgeries to repair the physical damage hidden under his fatigues. He was a good-looking young man with warm cocoa skin and eyes to match. Nola wondered if self-consciousness over his scars made him too shy to flirt with women. It would be a tragic miscalculation, but he might not realize it at such a young age.

Ro hadn't been overly vocal or suspiciously quiet during the interview, and no obvious tells had given him away, but something about him hinted at Indian-American Boy Scout. The kind of guy who would risk his career and a court-martial to blow the whistle on two canisters of high-grade poison gone missing. Since he was their chief suspect, Nola and Tony actively avoided drawing any undue attention to him, lest it spike Captain Taylor's curiosity.

As they wrapped up the interview, Tony maneuvered Taylor into diversional chitchat so Nola could hand out her card with a promise that any information discussed privately would be kept in strict confidence.

On their ride back to the main gate, Captain Taylor played tour guide. "See that rocket up ahead? That's the Falcon Heavy Space X. She can lift fifty-three metric tons into orbit. Imagine your average jetliner full of passengers with a herd of hippos riding on its back."

Nola eyed the massive space-age phallic symbol gleaming on its launch pad and laughed. "Okay, boats I get, but why would you refer to a rocket as *she?*"

Tony volunteered a theory. "Maybe because they're sleek, complicated, and sometimes for reasons no man can understand, they suddenly go haywire and blow up in your face?"

"Thanks, but I was asking Captain Taylor. I mean, why call something *she* when it's so clearly shaped like a giant intergalactic space penis?"

Captain Taylor blushed like a schoolmarm.

"Sorry, Captain," Tony said cheerfully. "We try to make her act like a lady, but she just keeps getting worse."

"Oh, come on," Nola said, pressing her argument. "It's long, cylindrical, and thrusty. You wouldn't say, 'Oh, look, there's the Washington Monument, isn't she lovely?'"

Captain Taylor cast another look back at the big rocket. "I guess you've got a point at that, ma'am."

Tony grinned. "Happy now, *ma'am?*"

Captain Taylor's radio crackled. "Okay, roger that," he answered, and the little golf cart cut a wide left and headed toward a row of giant hangars. "Slight change of plan, Detectives. Before you leave, Major Burnell has requested a word."

For no logical reason, Nola's heart skipped a beat.

Twenty-Six

The golf cart pulled to a stop in front of Igloo 8. ROTC70, SE40, Igloo 8 — Nola was starting to wonder if the key to all the nefarious goings-on lately didn't lie in math, which, contrary to what Throwback Barbie once said, was actually pretty easy for girls. Captain Taylor took her arm as she stepped out of the golf cart and kept his hand lightly on her back as he escorted her inside. In spite of her earlier vulgarity, he remained the consummate military gentleman.

What the Air Force called an igloo was actually an enormous hangar stacked end to end with precision-guided weaponry. Nola gazed at the impressive array of munitions like a kid in a Delta Force candy store. When Captain Taylor stepped outside to speak to the duty guard, she picked up an M203 grenade launcher, hoisted it on her shoulder, and pointed it at Tony. "Quick, take a picture with your phone for my Facebook page."

"Yeah, not doing that," he replied. "Put it back, GI Jane."

"Afraid I'll blow my head off?"

"No, but that's how I'll make it look if you don't stop pointing it at my crotch. I'm guessing the military frowns on civilians in miniskirts playing with their anti-tank weapons."

"Relax, Grandma. If I break it, I'll buy it."

"Actually, Detective, if you break it, I get buried in a mess of piss-ass paperwork." The soothing airplane-pilot voice was unmistakable. Major Bryan Burnell was in the building.

FML, Nola thought. Already self-conscious about her short skirt, she'd hoped to make a serious first impression on the Major, but as usual, her curiosity had passed go without stopping to collect two hundred dollars. When she turned around, she was doubly surprised to see how close he was to her. The man must be half panther, she thought as she offered her lame apology.

"Sorry, Major, but barring any highly unlikely twists in my life story, this was probably going to be my one and only chance to even pretend to fire a weapon this powerful."

"That's a very disarming excuse, Detective, but I'm still going to have to ask you to put down my gun."

"I guess that makes us both disarming," she said with a smile.

The Major didn't smile back; he just waited.

"Right. I'll just put it back now," she said sheepishly.

She put the grenade launcher back where she found it, while Tony and Major Burnell shook hands.

"Detective Angellotti," Tony said, "and my gun-happy partner here is Detective MacIntire."

"I really am sorry I was shouldering your weapon, Major," she said, in her serious-as-a-heart-attack cop voice. "Normally I'm very safety conscious."

Stepping away from the grenade launchers, she bumped into a metal shelf stacked with machine guns and nearly lost her balance until Major Burnell reached out to steady her.

It's a funny thing about life. One minute, middle age is creeping up on you like a psycho killer at a slutty teen beach party, and you're comforting yourself by shooting alcohol-infused whipped cream straight into your mouth and focusing on work — then a man you've just met catches you in his arms and sets off a spark that dissolves the arthritic candy coating that's been building up around your nervous system, and a message goes rocketing axon over dendrite, telling your brain that you're sixteen again.

"You okay?" he asked.

"Fine. Great. Well, maybe just a little bruised around the ego."

She'd been tempted to say something more flirtatious, but what would be the point? Men like Burnell didn't fall for aging blondes whose Christmas accounts went straight to their dermatologists. They went for the golden girls, whippet thin with expert French manicures, who didn't swear or lose their shoes or play with grenade launchers in skirts that were two inches too short for their age group. Which was actually a good thing under the circumstances. This was no time to lose focus. Why would Burnell ask to speak to them, unless he thought they knew something about the leak? She was going to have to play it cool, Miss Frozen Foods Aisle. If he touched her again, he'd get freezer burn.

"So, why did you want to meet with us, Major?" Tony asked.

"Well, first to show you that all twelve canisters of SE40 are present and accounted for."

The Major led them around the machine-gun shelves, past a cache of stinger missiles, to a pallet in the far corner of the hangar. Two large steel crates held six canisters each. They were clearly marked and in plain sight. Nothing hinky, as Captain Taylor would say. Nola wondered if the canisters were, in fact, the same twelve that had originally been sent from Livermore, but she kept her doubts to herself. Tony lied and assured Major Burnell that they *had* no doubts, and that their presence on base that afternoon was purely coincidental, but Burnell wasn't buying it.

"Really?" he said, more amused than angry. "Because

I think we've all made the same connection between Dr. Waxman's therapy group and the false press leak, and that's *exactly* why you're here today."

Friendly, but direct. It was a sound tactical maneuver. He was deploying the same *I'm not mad but aren't we all above this silly pretense* smile that Nola used on recidivist criminals and her twin eight-year-old nieces. The criminals usually cracked, the twins rarely did. Like high cheekbones and ridiculously small pinky toes, the wide-eyed, "it wasn't me" look was encoded in the MacIntire family DNA. Nola held it in reserve for moments just like this one.

"Actually, Major, we were just doing a routine background check," she said, with a face as innocent as an Easter basket.

"Just needed a few facts to fill in the paperwork," Tony threw in casually.

The Major's handsome face stayed smooth as glass. "Uh-huh."

After a minute standoff that felt like an hour, Nola opted to call an audible. "Hypothetically, Major, if a soldier *had* discovered two of the canisters had gone missing, wouldn't it be his or her duty to bring it to the public's attention?"

"No, Detective MacIntire, their duty would be to report it to their superior officer so rapid-response measures could be implemented pronto."

"But, hypothetically again...what if their superior officer was in on the plot? Wouldn't they be putting their life in danger by reporting it?"

"Possibly. But by disregarding the chain of command they would be, *hypothetically*, giving whoever stole the weapon time to deploy it. Isn't that putting the lives of thousands of people in danger?"

Major Burnell was sexy enough when his argument was debatable, but devastating when his reasoning was sound.

"Well-intentioned or not," he continued, "whoever leaked the information made a serious and potentially disastrous miscalculation, so if you've got a suspect, I really do need to know who it is."

He had a valid point, but Nola and Tony only had a hunch that Rohit Kodical was the leak. More importantly, even if it was Ro, they felt sure he hadn't done it out of anger, sour grapes, or a cheap bid for fame. After three operations to get shrapnel-free, the guy deserved at least one shot at a do-over.

Nola felt bad about lying, but what she said was only half a lie — the second part she pretty much meant. "Honestly, Major, we don't suspect anyone of being your leak. Believe me, if I thought you had another Edward Snowden on your hands, I'd figure out how to fire that grenade launcher and frag him myself."

"You know, Detective, I believe you might." The six-teen-kilowatt smile lit up like an incendiary shell. If the guy got any hotter, he'd set off the stack of short-range air-to-airs, and they'd all go up in flames.

Tony made their apologies, saying they had two other cases that needed their attention back in Santa Barbara, and the interview was suspended.

Major Burnell ushered them out to the golf cart where Captain Taylor was ready at the wheel to whisk them away. Nola was sure he still thought they were lying, but with no leverage, he had no choice but to let them go and pursue his leak through other channels.

When they said goodbye, Burnell shook Nola's hand with the same heart-pounding result as when he'd caught her in his arms. As the cart pulled away, she felt like she was leaving the last glass of wine on the road to prohibition. But she kept her stoic poker face right up to the minute he called out after her.

"Hey, Detective MacIntire, if you're serious about wanting to learn how to fire that grenade launcher, give me a call, and I'll find us some time on the range."

Nola hoped Captain Taylor was too busy driving to notice the deep suck of breath she took in. The kind she usually reserved for squeezing into her skinny jeans. The involuntary surge of excitement that was scrambling her prefrontal cortex had to be shut off. It was dangerous to feel this excited, dangerous to feel this good. Burnell was flirting with her, but guys flirted with her all the time. There was no real intention behind it. To make herself calm down, she mentally repeated the saddest thing she could think of: *Sick kids, sick kids, sick kids.* It was a macabre trick she used whenever she became momentarily overwrought. She hated being overwrought; why couldn't she ever be just the right amount of wrought? For the thousandth time, she realized she really ought to forgo a few hot yoga sessions and put the money toward a good shrink, or at least some helpful pharmaceuticals.

Twenty-Seven

Major Burnell's tossed-off offer to meet Nola on the firing range had created a problem that, if not dealt with swiftly, would make the trip back to Santa Barbara a nightmare. All the way to the T-bird, Tony had sat beside her in the golf cart humming "Home on the Range." She had no intention of taking Major Burnell up on his offer to go shooting, so if she didn't want to hear a whole big harangue about it on the ride home, she'd have to resort to trickery.

She had the satellite radio tuned to SportsCenter before Tony's butt even hit the driver's seat. Two bobble-headed analysts were nattering on about the latest breaking-bad basketball news. Like a masculine moth to a testosterone flame, Tony was immediately absorbed in the burning saga of who was trash-talking whom, as if the future of the planet was riding on the outcome.

It was sneaky and sexist, but it was the only sure way she knew to keep him from pestering her with annoying questions, like: "Are you going to call him?" "Why not?" "Why don't you check under the sofa cushions — maybe your self-esteem got lost down there with the loose change?" Unfortunately, radio sports was only a temporary fix. When the jock-opera topic switched to soccer, Tony lost interest and turned his busybody best-friend attention her way.

"So are you going to call him?"

"Yes. Yes, I am," she lied.

"When?"

"I thought I'd wait till we hit the Lompoc tunnel. Then, when he tells me he was just having a laugh, I can wrest the steering wheel from your aging hands, and we can both go out in a fiery crash, instead of me just dying alone from embarrassment."

"Yeah. That's just the *no wine* talking. Ask him to dinner, drink a couple of appetizers, and you'll be fine."

"Right. Not happening. So, how 'bout that sports team you like? Or don't like? That guy who did that thing must have really made you mad. Let's talk about it in detail."

Tony wasn't in a mood to be amused. "I don't get it. You're wearing your 'do me' skirt, your dream guy says, 'Okay, I'm in,' and now you're pussying out. I would really like to know why?"

Nola stared up at the sky and sighed. "For starters, my dream guy isn't prettier than me, so Major Burnell is definitely *not* my dream guy. And second, he wasn't really asking me to call him. It's just something guys say."

"Yeah. When we want to get with girls."

"Yes. Girls. Not admittedly adorkable cops of a certain age."

"Okay, beautiful, I'm sorry, but that age you speak of is way too old to use words like 'adorkable.' You and I both know that was a serious invitation, so why are you making that skirt into a liar?"

"Hasn't it occurred to you that Major Burnell knows we were lying to him and that he thinks if he charms me a little, I'll go all weak in the knees and tell him who we suspect is the leak?"

"What occurs to me is that you're certifiable," he said. "But do what you want. I won't say another word."

"I wish."

"No. Seriously. I'm done trying to keep you from dying alone. I'm just going to bury you in a thong and high heels and hope some nice necrophiliac undertaker gives you a goodbye bang for the road."

Nola winced. "Bury me in a thong and you will feel my icy cold ghost breath on the back of your neck every time you try to swing a golf club. It's bad enough having to wear them while I'm alive. My idea of heaven is a fluffy cloud rave, where drop-dead gorgeous men go wild every time I flash a little comfortable granny panty."

"And on that disturbing image..."

"Fine," she said. "Subject changed. Now that we have a pretty good idea who passed the info to Waxman, and we've tacitly agreed not to follow up on it, how do you want to divide the rest of the day's workload?"

Tony turned up the radio. Still soccer. He turned it down. "Well, you could do some interviews, and I could take a nap."

Nola made a counteroffer. "Or, you could check out Kyle's alibi buddies in Isla Vista, while I pay a surprise visit to Ken at the *Reader*. Now that he's been caught with his Pulitzer-hopeful pants down, maybe he'll be more amenable to giving up his source."

"Or," came Tony's counter counteroffer, "while you stake out Ken, I could drop in on the widow Gillette and find out if Gus had any prior run-ins with ROTC70... if the juice came out of her blouse... if she's ready to start dating again... *then*, I could check on Kyle's buddies in Vista."

"Haven first, huh?"

"Hos before bros, right?"

"Ri-gh-t," Nola stretched out the word for full sarcastic effect. "In fact, maybe I should drive. That way when we get to her place, you can just combat tuck and roll out of the car to save time."

They cruised into the Lompoc tunnel; Tony's voice echoed in the dim concrete cylinder. "At least one of us isn't afraid to follow up on the sexier angles of the case."

"Because one of us hasn't read enough Raymond Chandler to know better," Nola echoed back. "Women like Haven eat guys like you for breakfast, then stick their fingers down their throats, so they won't gain weight."

"I'd still do her," he said cheerfully, as they emerged from the dark.

"So would I," Nola said with a smile. "Preferably, in the back of the head with a hatchet."

"Wow!"

"Too harsh?"

"Like dry-swallowing an elephant tranquilizer."

"Okay, forget the hatchet," she said, then added under her breath, "maybe just a small ball-peen hammer?"

They were back in sight of the ocean, by the cutoff for the Circle Bar-B Ranch, where Nola went horseback riding on her days off. She wished she was riding now. The smell of saddle soap and leather and the rush of galloping up the mountain might help clear the cobwebs out of her head. She was convinced that Haven had murdered Gus, but she had no idea how to prove it. "All kidding aside, Tony. I really believe she shot her husband, and it's killing me that she might get away with it."

"Look Nols," Tony said, placating, "I tried to see it your way, but the autopsy proved the gun was pressed right up against Gillette's temple. You think she just said, 'Honey, hold this gun to your head while I pull the trigger,' and he couldn't resist?"

"Why not? You probably couldn't," she said with a sideways smile. "Look, I admit, I don't know how she did it. Maybe he was asleep. Or maybe she wormholes through space and suddenly pops up behind people, like Burnell does. Seriously, how could a guy built like a concrete bunker catch us by surprise like that? It defies the laws of physics, right?"

"That was pretty stealthy," Tony laughed. "Check the backseat, maybe he's behind us now."

The sports bots on the radio finally stopped yammering about soccer and began yammering about baseball. It was nearly spring, when a young man's fancy lightly turns to thoughts of long balls hit out of the park. The longest committed relationship in Tony's life was with the Dodgers, which meant that for the remainder of the ride home, Nola was free to chase thoughts around in her head undisturbed. Gus and Max, Max and ROTC70, missing weapons and development deals...there was lots of connective tissue, but no substantial body of evidence. As they cruised down the Gaviota pass, motives and theories crashed and bounced off each other like bumper cars. Sadly, nothing stuck.

When Tony pulled into the parking lot outside her condo, she reclaimed her driver's seat and dialed the radio away from the Sweat Sock Diaries back to Icona Pop.

"On some level, you do know that music sucks, right?" he said, closing her car door for her.

"I don't care, *I love it!*" She sang to the tune of the song, knowing the double meaning would be lost, since his pop-music references had come to a gear-grinding halt somewhere back in the 1990s.

As Tony climbed into his Audi to go interview Haven, Nola called to him from the convertible: "Keep your ears open, I hear they rattle before they strike."

He threw her a thumbs-up, but Nola suspected that if Haven *was* in a cop-seducing mood, it was going to give a whole new meaning to the phrase, "Officer down."

Twenty-Eight

Haven's orgasm, like everything else in her single-pur-
pose-driven life, was right on the money. She rolled back onto
the bed and sighed. It was a mixed exhalation of pleasure and
relief. Sex with Gus had been an act: seven award-winning
performances a week. Even Broadway stars got Monday off.
Sometimes she'd switch his Viagra with her Valtrex just to
give her shock absorbers a rest. "Sorry, baby, must have been
a little blue dud."

The current man in her bed had come as a complete surprise, so to speak. Still not age-appropriate, but extremely
sexy, he hadn't slobbered all over her, twisted her nipples like
bottle caps, or shouted "bottoms up" to signal his prefer-
ence for back-door action. Even now, his breath on her neck
was sending ripples of pleasure down her legs, making her
wonder if she might not want this to be more than a little
one-time strange.

"Mind if I use the shower? My wife gets suspicious when
I come home smelling of sleek, tawny twenty-two-year-old."

Lawrence Wilson always mentioned his wife as soon as
possible after sex. It was his not-so-subtle way of keeping his
temporary playmates from getting any romantic ideas.

Fine, play it your way, Haven thought. She could get sex
from any man, but money to support a trophy-wife lifestyle
without the balding old fart that usually came with it was a

rare and beautiful thing. "Just leave the check on the Chippendale when you go," she replied without a hint of irritation.

"A hundred grand, as promised," Larry said, twirling her hair around in his fingers.

Haven pulled away and sat up against her pillow. "Made out to the dummy corporation?"

"As you wished, Milady."

"You also offered Gus a three-percent partnership."

"A silent partnership," he said, pointedly.

"Oh, don't worry, I can be very discreet."

"One of the many…" he said, kissing her breasts, "exciting reasons…" he continued, kissing her stomach, "…I'd like to do this again sometime."

"Well, you're definitely moving in the right direction," she said, sliding back down on the bed.

As his lips traveled lower, the intercom rang. Larry looked up and laughed. "I've been told I'm good, but I never made a girl chime before."

"There's someone at the gate," she said, annoyed at the interruption.

The ex–Dr. McDorable rolled over and hopped off the bed. "Lucky for us you have a very long driveway, and I take very short showers."

Tony had to wait a suspiciously long time before Haven's voice came back over the intercom, and even longer before the scrolled ironwork gates that separated her heavily mortgaged estate from the real world swung open. If he'd been checking out other cars on the street, he might have noticed a boy and girl, slouched low in a sporty Boxster, watching him disappear up the driveway. Just another amusing kink in their plan.

Twenty-Nine

Two bloody drains and a compression wrap.

Ken wasn't in his cubical at the *Reader*, but the newspaper's owner and chief editor, Jillian Crawford, agreed to spare Nola five minutes of her time. Normally people spend at least a week in isolation after a neck lift, but the day's journalistic tailspin had flushed Jillian from her post-op recovery room ahead of schedule. Nola, who sometimes thought about having a little nip-tuck herself, was definitely having second thoughts. The price of surgical youth apparently included a week or two looking like you'd been dating Chris Brown and forgot to duck.

As she waited for Jillian to finish up a call with her lawyers, Nola started playing fashion-show narrator, in her head.

Today's It Girl is Jillian Crawford. Seated at her distressed antique desk in a cream Alaia cling dress. Jillian's recent cosmetic surgery has made her a fashion-forward icon for women everywhere. Notice how the carpaccio-colored bruising on her swollen jaw is dramatically offset by the bold stitching on the sutures behind her ears. In counterpoint, the artful draping of her Hermès scarf is simplicity itself. The patterned silk delicately camouflaging the compression neck wrap that's currently keeping her head from falling off. Rounding off this breezy ensemble are a diamond Cartier pin bracelet and two bloody mucus drains. Elegantly dangling from behind each ear, mucus drains are truly the surgical fashion statement of the...

Jillian abruptly hung up the phone, bringing Nola's er-satz runway show to a screeching halt. "Sorry to make you wait, Detective MacIntire. Just gauging the legal fallout I'm in for if the Air Force decides to sue the paper for libel. So, what is it you'd like to ask me?"

The bloody drains behind Jillian's ears bobbled as she spoke. Nola answered in the compassionate voice she nor-mally reserved for assault victims. "Well, first, Ms. Crawford, based on your conversation with your lawyers, I'm getting the sense that Ken Levine's cover story this morning came as a complete surprise to you?"

Jillian's neck wrap made her swollen chin jut forward like she was daring someone to hit her again. "Surprise is putting it mildly," she said derisively.

Nola tried not to stare as she listened to Jillian's story. While she was away on surgery leave, Jillian had promoted her daughter to temporary managing editor of the *Reader* with the express understanding that nothing in the pre-determined layout be changed. Unfortunately, without so much as a text to run it by her, the girl had switched cover stories at the last minute, replacing the scheduled piece on the film festival with Ken's erroneous account of the missing bio-weapons. "Now, of course, I look like a complete fool," Jillian said angrily, mucus drains bobbing.

Nola imagined the scene behind the scenes. Ken romancing the girl into giving him the cover story. Prom-ising it would make the paper famous...make her mother proud...make the bathtub bubble with champagne sex...

"Next week's cover is going to be a giant fried egg," Jillian huffed. "Because that's what's all over my face at the moment."

Every time Jillian moved her neck, she winced in pain, and Nola automatically winced with her. "I understand you're in damage-control mode, Ms. Crawford, but should you really be out of bed right now?"

"I know I look repulsive, Detective, but I had the unfortunate fate of inheriting my mother's turkey wattle, and it wasn't a cross I was prepared to bear at forty-five. But perhaps you're one of those enlightened women who frown on cosmetic surgery."

"Actually, I totally get it. Gravity's a bitch," Nola said, remembering the nasal-labial landslide going on in her own traitorous face. "So, did Ken tell you who passed him the false information?"

Jillian started unwrapping an ice pack. "No. Of course I asked, but surprisingly, he went noble. Said he promised his source anonymity and he was a man of his word. Which, to be honest, isn't really like Ken. He always struck me as the 'give up his grandmother to get ahead' type. I rather doubt his interest in my daughter is entirely based on her charm."

"Are you thinking of firing him?"

"I fully intended to, but when I went out to the guest house to read my daughter the riot act this morning, she rightly pointed out that I couldn't really fire him without firing her, too. Ultimately, it was her call to print the damn story. She's lucky I like having her where I can keep an eye on her, or they'd both be out on their asses. But I assure you, in the future, Ken won't be covering anything bigger than cat-up-a-tree stories." Jillian pressed the ice pack under her bruised chin. "If you want to speak to him yourself, I suggest you try Long Boards in about an hour."

"Is that his usual haunt?" Nola asked.

"No. Just an educated guess. I sent him to do a story on the new tidepool exhibit on Stearn's Wharf. After the spanking his ego took today, I'm guessing he's going to want to drink, heavily. Long Boards is just across the pier from the aquarium."

"Thanks," Nola said, grateful for the tip. "Nice bit of deductive reasoning. Um, do you happen to have your doctor's number handy?"

"Dr. Benioff. His office is on Quinto. You'll love him. He's a genius with eyes."

Jillian's assumption caught Nola off guard. "Actually, I just thought you might want to give him a call. Your left drain is leaking."

Jillian put her hand behind her left ear and felt the thin trail of sticky, pink liquid oozing from the plastic drain. "Oh, for God's sakes! What else can go catastrophically wrong today?"

Jillian didn't hear Nola's goodbye. She was already calling the surgical center.

Out in the hallway, Nola pretended to read a plaque awarded to the paper by the Rotary Club so she could secretly check out her eyes in its mirrored surface. Why had Jillian just assumed she wanted them done? Had the hooding and the crow's feet finally hit critical mass? An even better question was: Why was she letting one little comment bug her so much? The looks she'd gotten at Vandenberg that morning had boosted her ego-rocket sky-high. Toss in breathtaking Major Burnell's offhand invitation to join him on the firing range and her compliment quota was filled for the year. Why couldn't she focus on all the good reviews instead of obsessing over the one bad one? It was one of those deep, philosophical questions that great minds had been pondering for ages. Right up there with: "What is the true meaning of existence?" and "Why doesn't he call?"

As she stared at her Rotarian reflection, she imagined her Pilates instructor Suzanne's calming voice saying: "Eyes are for seeing. You see perfectly, ergo your eyes are perfect just the way they are. Namaste."

Nola realized that what imaginary Suzanne was saying was true. Blind people only wished they could see their crow's feet in a Rotary plaque. Feeling grateful for her moment of spiritual clarity, she headed out to her car. Maybe getting older did make you wiser. Too bad it also made you older. Oh well, someday she'd be senile, and then she could relax. She grinned at the thought. It was nice to know that her hoody, wrinkled eyes could still look on the bright side.

Thirty

Tony's unexpected arrival was adding an extra bit of excitement to Haven and Larry's tryst. She'd had to playfully remove his hand from under her eleven-hundred-dollar peasant blouse to get up and answer the door. Having an affair with her mother's favorite television idol was proving to be just the little pick-me-up she'd been needing. How wonderful it was to have Dr. McDorable's autograph, especially on a big, fat check.

On her way to let Tony in, she'd resolved to use the first of her new windfall to re-hire the maids. Opening your own door was for ugly women and feminists, although when you got right down to it, weren't they really the same thing?

She led Tony to the great room and introduced him to Larry. She could have answered his questions at the door, but she liked the tension she created when there were two men in the room. She made the introductions with just enough soft flirtation in her voice to get Larry's antlers up. A little payback for the clumsy way he'd thrown his wife in her face while she was still bathing in the afterglow.

Tony had sensed the sexual vibe the moment he entered the room. The more nonchalant they tried to appear, the more obvious it was that they'd just been banging each other's brains out. Larry claimed he'd come over to thank Haven for reading Gus's speech and to make sure she was okay, but the faint whiff of girly shampoo in his wet hair said otherwise.

That Larry had been the next man on Haven's to-do list had actually come as a relief to Tony. Teasing Nola about sleeping with the spun-from-suntanned-sugar girl was fun, but if Haven had actually set her sights on him, he wasn't a hundred-percent sure he could withstand the assault.

"So, Detective, to what do I owe this unexpected pleasure?" Her voice had the warming effect of smoky scotch sipped by a fireplace.

Tony shook off the peat and came straight to the point. He explained about ROTC70 and asked if Gus had received any threats from them in the past. Haven claimed she'd never heard of them. Gus always got crank mail from conservation nuts before a big vote, but a stupid name like "Ro-whatever," she'd remember.

Larry hadn't heard of them either, but he had assistants who filtered his correspondence. Bomb threats, bogus paternity suits, stalker-grams, and voodoo dolls went straight to the private security company that he paid to protect him from his fans.

Haven openly flirted as she answered Tony's questions. Her body language was just short of Hamburg hooker on the Reeperbahn as she stretched and curled beside him on the big Fendi sofa. When Wilson put a proprietary hand on her shoulder, she deftly slipped out from under it and offered Tony a drink.

Larry's testosterone pawed the ground. "I appreciate that you're just trying to do your job, Detective, but Mrs. Gillette is going through a very difficult time right now. Couldn't you have just asked her these questions on the phone?"

"I don't mind, Larry," Haven cooed. "I appreciate Detective Angellotti coming all the way out to see me." She moistened her bottom lip with the tip of her tongue.

Her performance was so over the top, Tony couldn't believe Larry was falling for it. Nola's right, men are idiots, he thought as he answered Larry's question. "I could have called, Mr. Wilson, but I thought I might have better luck sparking Mrs. Gillette's memory in person."

"I wish I could be more help," Haven said, shifting again on the sofa. "The only person I ever heard threaten Gus was that dried-up grizzle-chicken he was married to before me. She was always threatening to put his balls in a bagel slicer, cut off his dick, and feed it to her Asian fish...blah blah blah. Stupid cow."

"Her name's Susan, Detective," Larry interjected. "Maybe you'd have better luck driving out to Montecito and trying to spark something with her." The inference couldn't have been plainer if Larry had written it in his own musk.

"If you do decide to see Susan, I should warn you, she bites," Haven said, rolling up her sleeve to reveal one perfect, sun-kissed arm with two small scars the size of teeth marks.

"She actually bit you?" Tony asked.

"At a charity gala for the Global Hunger Project. There were dozens of witnesses."

Before Tony could ask for more details, there was an urgent banging on the French doors. A spooked gardener was standing outside the glass.

"What is it, Rigoberto? What's wrong?" Haven asked.

"The pool!"

"What about it?"

"It's *el fuego*! On fire!"

Tony ran with Rigoberto to a cliff overlooking the ocean. Gus and Haven's infinity pool hung right on the edge. Just as Rigoberto had reported, the pool was lit up. A thin film of flammable liquid had been sprayed over the water and set ablaze. Haven and Larry arrived while Tony was calling the fire department. They gaped in horror at the firefall spilling into infinity over the cliff. Rigoberto handed Haven a note he'd found stuffed under a hurricane lamp, and she read it aloud: "Life's a bitch and then *you will die*, Bitch. ROTC70."

The skin under her spray tan turned two shades whiter than Larry's professionally bleached teeth. It was the kind of moment that called for a music sting. Or at least for Larry to make some appropriately heroic speech to calm Haven's fears. But without his writers, he appeared to be lost. Babbling a bland promise to "always be there for her," he hopped in his Aston Martin and got the hell out of Dodge.

Walking back to the house, Haven held Tony's hand. No more tricks, no more guile. She was genuinely scared.

Thirty-One

The bartender at Long Boards sized Nola up in less time than was flattering.

"Glass of white wine?"

"Sex on the Beach with a foofoo umbrella, cayenne on the rim, and two cherries," she said pertly.

"Sorry, I had you all wrong."

"No, just playing. Foxen chardonnay. You were right on the money."

Long Boards was a popular bipolar eatery out on the wharf. Downstairs was an elegant restaurant, but behind the hostess stand, a set of marine-themed mosaic steps led up to a surf bar with an open-air deck, barrels full of peanuts, and sawdust on the floor. The food was great, and the drinks were better.

The sun was getting low, and the last sailboats and kayaks were making their way back to the marina. The aquarium across the pier was closing its doors, meaning if Jillian had called it correctly, Ken should be dragging in any time now.

Nola put her phone back to her ear, so Tony could finish filling her in on the latest doings chez Gillette.

"Sorry, just had to order," she said into the phone.

"I heard. Should you be doing white wine on duty?"

"It's okay, I don't inhale. So, where are you now?"

"Still poolside with the fire department and the forensics

165

monkeys."

"Pool fire. That's one you don't hear every day. Is Wilson still there?"

"Nah, first hint of trouble he vanished like a magician's quarter. But I gotta say, his sex-stained presence is making me start to wonder again if maybe you were right."

"Go on," she coaxed, oozing mock self-satisfaction.

"Maybe Haven murdered Gus and staged the suicide so she could go with the hotter, richer guy."

"She could have accomplished that with a divorce." Nola reached for a bowl of peanuts on the bar. "Slip into this and take a twirl around the dressing room: I think Wilson bribed Gus to support his real estate deal, and Haven murdered him to keep the money for herself."

"Wilson's rich. She marries him, she's got all the money she wants," Tony countered.

"Maybe Wilson's not the marrying kind," she postulated. "Or maybe he's already married. Whatever's going on, you gotta figure a girl like Haven's going to make sure she has something other than her perfect, heart-shaped ass to fall back on." The amused bartender grinned as he placed her chardonnay on the bar in front of her. "Just office talk," she whispered with a wink, before turning her attention back to Tony on the phone.

"But why would a dying man need to take a bribe?" Tony asked. "Gus wasn't taking meds or looking for a miracle cure. In a couple weeks it was going to be '*Hasta la vista*, baby.'"

Tony was right. Nola's Jiffy Pop brain hit the stove again. A thousand thought-explosions went off in her head. If Gus didn't take the bribe, maybe he didn't write the speech. Maybe Haven did. Wait! Back up the motive truck. Haven told Sebastian she didn't know the password to Gus's laptop. Wouldn't she *want* him to find the speech if she'd written it? Unless…oh, crap, it was so obvious. Haven had played them. Give a man a fish, and he might get suspicious. Let him fish for himself…

"Christ, Tony, we as good as authenticated it for her!" Nola cried into the phone.

"What?" he replied, confused. "How many glasses of wine have you had?"

"I'm not drinking, I'm thinking. Sorry, sometimes I forget I'm not doing it out loud…Gus's speech wasn't written by Gus. Here's what I think happened…"

When she finished explaining her thought process, he had only one question.

"If Haven took Wilson's bribe to rewrite Gus's speech, how come there's no trace of communication between them? He didn't come up on her cell records or the landline, and no burner turned up when our crime-scene guys searched the house."

"It was two a.m., and our guys were convinced it was a suicide. How hard do you think they looked?" Nola said, cracking open a peanut, her first meal since breakfast.

"Fair play," Tony conceded. "Plus, the sight of those kittens in that see-through nightie was more than a little distracting."

Nola paused with the peanut halfway to her mouth. "Uck, Tony. Her boobs were covered in blood."

"Were they? I barely remember that part," he said, laughing.

"Amazing," she said. "Someday, I'm going to invent a silicone-implant sponge with a nipple on the tip. You know how much women would pay to see a man clean a bathroom?"

"Are we done with this conversation?" Tony asked. "The firemen just put out the pool, and I need to ask the arson investigator about our flammable material."

Nola popped the peanut in her mouth. "Yeah. Just don't leave without confiscating Gus's laptop. We need Sebastian to go through it again."

"You got a legal precedent handy? I left mine in my other jeans."

"Oh, right. I don't know. Tell Haven we're looking for more hate mail from the kids who left her the death threat."

"Better tell a judge first. If we spook her, she might 'accidentally' destroy the hard drive while we're waiting on a warrant. We can pick it up tomorrow when the house is empty."

"She's leaving?"

"Yeah. Personally, I think the R to the C brats blew their wad setting fire to the cement pond, but she's scared to death. She's checking into the Biltmore tonight."

"I thought she was broke," Nola said, cracking open another peanut. "Boy, those kittens are like bouncy ATM machines."

"Yep. Wilson makes the deposits, and she makes the withdrawals."

Before Nola could respond, she spotted a sallow, expressionless Ken Levine coming up the colorful tile steps. "I gotta go too. Levine just walked in looking like the weight somebody else lost."

"Poor guy's had a rough day. Go get him, killer."

Nola slipped her phone into her purse and carried her chardonnay to the far end of the bar, where Ken was dumping his satchel full of aquarium notes on the sawdust floor.

"Hi. Nola MacIntire. Buy you a drink?"

Ken's tired eyes gave her the once-over.

"Thanks, but my girlfriend's meeting me here."

"Not an issue," Nola said, flashing her badge. "I'm not a cougar, I'm a cop. I need to know where you got the information for the article you wrote today."

Ken scowled down at his satchel full of aquarium notes. "Why? Did a sea urchin knife a tourist?"

"Yeah, luckily we've got a starfish witness. Are we done playing now? 'Cause we both know the story I mean."

"Sorry, I don't give up names."

"Well, maybe we should talk about that."

"Or you could just blow me."

"In a tub of champagne?"

"What?"

"Look, don't give me that 'good reporters don't give up their sources' bullshit, because I'm not talking to a good reporter, I'm talking to you. Your pals aren't just playing Robin Hood anymore; they're starting to pile up felonies. If you cooperate with me now, you'll be saving yourself a whole lot of grief in the future."

"Yeah, I've still got nothing to say to you, and my girlfriend just walked in, so either arrest me for contempt of cop or get bent."

Curious, Nola turned to see what combination of alluring feminine attributes had stolen Ken from Nancy. The sultry brunette ascending the mosaic steps had lanky arms with thin wrists and Ana Khouri gold cuffs that spoke volumes.

Hello, Wonder Woman, Nola thought, as she stared into the face of the girl who had murdered her blouse. It was a sophisticated face: narrow and elegant, with straight hair brushed back from the forehead and dark brown eyes that were looking a little surprised at the moment.

Thirty-Two

Monica instantly recognized the cop she'd Super Soaked at the commission meeting, but it was too late to turn back. The tall blonde was standing at the bar with Ken, and they were both staring straight at her. There was nothing to do but continue walking over like everything was copacetic. Maybe it was. Ken had no idea she'd played Wonder Woman that morning, and all the cop had seen was a costumed girl in a mask. Momentary flash of fear abated, Monica assumed a breezy air of detachment as she walked to the bar to join them.

"Hey, Ken," she said, giving him a quick kiss on the cheek before turning her attention to the cop. "Hi. Monica Crawford. Am I interrupting something?"

"Actually, I was just leaving." Nola slipped a ten under her full glass of wine and walked out.

"Who was that?" Monica asked casually.

"Police," Ken said. "She wanted my source for the story that blew up in my fucking face this morning."

"Yeah, sorry, that was *très* brutal."

"Monica, you gotta tell me who gave you that flash drive."

"Ken, we agreed I'd let you write the story, but I wouldn't tell you where I got the information."

"I *agreed* because you told me it was a hundred-percent

reliable. Now that I've been royally fucked, the least you can do is tell me the name of the jerk who bent me over."

"Look, we all thought the information was solid. I have to show some loyalty."

"Jesus, you're my girlfriend. How 'bout showing some loyalty to me?"

"You know, you've got to stop calling me your girlfriend. I'm really not."

"What? What's that supposed to mean?!"

"We just had a little fun. That's all."

Ken's face was turning the color of the giant lobster he'd just left at the aquarium. "What the hell are you saying?"

"I'm saying I've decided not to fuck you anymore. Pass me her glass. No use letting good wine go to waste."

"Are you fucking kidding me?" he said, loudly enough to draw a warning look from the bartender.

"It's nothing personal." She tossed the words off lightly. "I just met someone else."

"You met someone? What the hell are you talking about?! My career's turned to shit because of you, now you hit me with this! Jesus, who is this guy? Have you fucked him already?"

"Well, obviously," Monica said.

"Fuck, fuck, lying bitch, fucking cunt!"

"Right back at ya. Let's not forget you were hooking up with me weeks before you dumped your crybaby girlfriend. We're both a couple of twats — get over it, hypocrite."

"At least I felt a little bad about it. You just announce it like some *Resident Evil* avatar."

"Yeah, it's a classic case of Narcissistic Personality Disorder."

"What's that supposed to mean?"

Monica shrugged. "I don't know, it's something my

shrink is always saying to me."

"Yeah? Okay. Fine." Ken glared at her with smoldering contempt before playing the only revenge card he had left. "I guess now I can go ahead and tell the police that it was you who brought me the story."

"Go ahead." She laughed. "I'll just say you're lying to try and save your career and get back at me for breaking up with you."

Ken kicked his satchel, and his notes went flying. "Fuck!"

The bartender held up two fingers, meaning "three and you're out on your ass."

"I don't know why you're so mad at me," Monica said, sipping Nola's wine. "You really should be thanking me. Who do you think talked my mom out of firing you?"

Thirty-Three

Haven couldn't wrap her mind around it. A death threat, just when things were going so well. Gus was dead, and no one could prove she'd murdered him. She had a sexy new married man in her life, and she'd secured a pristine beach for developers who were cutting her in on the profits.

It was so unfair. *What have I done to deserve this?* she thought as she lay on the Armani chaise in the solarium, waiting for her Xanax to kick in. It was taking forever, and she really needed to pack.

After Larry did his scared-rabbit run, she'd called him in his car and shamed him into paying for her to have an open-ended stay at the Biltmore Hotel. She'd be a prisoner at the fashionable resort until the cops arrested the lunatics who were threatening her life. She thought of her favorite movie heroine, Scarlett O'Hara, trapped at Tara, forced to pick cotton and make dresses out of drapes. Now she'd be trapped too. Holed up in a private bungalow, forced to live on room service and pay-per-view. There were tennis courts and a state-of-the-art spa, but what about her spinning classes? Oh well, she'd think about that tomorrow.

Tomorrow... First thing in the morning she'd have her sister's husband wire Larry's hundred-thousand-dollar check to the Caymans. For now, it was up in her bedroom, safely tucked into her latest copy of *Vogue*. A hundred thousand. It was all she'd have to live on till the development started paying dividends. It wasn't nearly enough. As the Xanax started to take hold, she remembered how Scarlett had squeezed every penny out of the tattered remains of Tara. The banks had paperwork for all the art, the jewelry, and most of the furniture at the estate, but there were plenty of small things she might be able to slip out and sell. As long as the cops and the fire department were still fanned out over the grounds searching for clues, she was safe enough inside to turn the whole house upside down. With the steely determination of her favorite movie heroine, she rolled up her eleven-hundred-dollar Michael Kors peasant sleeves and went to work.

She struck pay dirt in the library, where Gus had an extensive collection of signed first editions. If she used Larry's money and her sister's name to buy unsigned firsts, she could trace the signatures inside and the banks would never know the difference. Later, she could sell the originals at a tidy profit. Death threats aside, things were looking up. Another bit of good news was finding a signed copy of *Gone with the Wind*. Her favorite movie had started as a book. Who knew?

She was gathering up a first batch of books when she realized that in her excitement over her plan, she'd lost track of time. The pink and orange sunset over the ocean was melting into pools of dark, and the cops and firemen were packing up to leave. Afraid to spend one moment alone in the house once they'd gone, she hurried upstairs to pack.

Patrol car doors were closing outside as she squeezed her favorite Giambattista Valli cocktail dress into her already overstuffed Louis Vuitton garment bag and made a run for her Mercedes SL. Lights, discreetly hidden in the boxed hedges, cast an eerie green glow along the driveway as she followed the parade of police vehicles off the estate. Outside the gates, she sped ahead of the procession, anxious to reach the Biltmore, unaware that in her haste to pack she'd left behind one very important item.

The sound of metal on metal clanged in the darkness as the line of police cars disappeared down the road, and the big iron gates of the estate swung shut.

Alone under a stand of eucalyptus trees, a shadowy figure crouched, listening, waiting to make sure the house was really empty and no one would be coming back. Emerging from the trees, Angry Susan approached the code box on the gate. 40-23-40 — Gus hadn't even bothered to change the combination. Jessica Rabbit's body stats still worked. The metal gates creaked and started to swing open again. Susan was in.

Thirty-Four

The cute valet at Long Boards handed Monica the keys to her Boxster and mouthed "holy shit" to his buddies back at the stand as they watched her climb in and drive off down the bumpy pier. The sulky brunette was out of their league and out of their lives. Caught up in imagining all the pornographic things they'd like to do to her, they failed to notice the little black T-bird that was hot on her tail.

Nola had been waiting in the parking lot for a little over an hour. She'd expected Monica and Ken to leave together, but it didn't really matter. The telltale gold cuffs made Monica the one to follow. She tailed the Boxster up Garden Street onto the 101. Monica took the exit to Isla Vista and cruised to a stop in front of a faux-Hawaiian apartment building where Nola used to party back in the day.

Nola parked the T-bird a discreet distance down the block and watched Monica disappear inside the building. She'd give her enough time to get in the elevator or climb the stairs before going in herself to read the mailboxes and have a talk with the manager. She was reaching for her cell to call Tony when her passenger door swung open.

"Nice night for a stakeout," Tony said as he sank into the seat beside her.

"Jennifer Love Hewitt! You scared the hell out of me! You're lucky I was reaching for my phone and not my Glock.

What are you doing here?"

"I was about to go in and check on Kyle's alibi buddies when I saw you stealthily pull up. What are *you* doing here?"

"Ken wouldn't give up his source, and just as I'm running out of bluffs, his girlfriend Monica shows up wearing gold Ana Khouri cuffs."

"Seriously? I actually have to score one for the fashion police?"

"Yep. Her accessories prove she's an accessory."

"How long have you been working on that?"

"Most of the ride over, and yeah, not my best work," Nola said, scrunching up her nose, disdainful of her own joke.

"Handy that all of our suspects live in the same building," Tony said cheerfully.

"Actually, Jillian Crawford, Monica's mother, who, by the by, is also Ken's boss at the *Reader*, mentioned that Monica lives in her guest house, so she's probably just here to visit her crew."

"Okay. How 'bout we go do the same?"

"Guns drawn, kick in the door, Guy Ritchie–style?" she asked hopefully.

"Or we could just knock."

Thirty-Five

Ian opened the door on Tony's second knock. He was drinking a glass of OJ that reeked of cheap gin. Nola and Tony held up their badges and backed him into the room. Tony spotted Kyle on a stained futon on the floor, sipping his own gin and juice.

"Hey, Kyle. We were just in the neighborhood, so we thought we'd drop by. Love what your friends have done with the place — sort of early American tenement, am I right?"

The shock of seeing Tony made Kyle's G&J go down the wrong way, and he launched into a coughing fit.

"You okay there, buddy?" Tony said, picking up a glass-blown bong, still smoldering, on the cardboard box they were using as an end table.

Nola asked Ian his name and thought she heard "Ian," but he was so high and drunk, she couldn't be sure.

Alerted by the noise, Monica and Malcolm entered from the bedroom. Both of them were carrying beers and wearing the same shade of Bobbi Brown lip stain.

"Hey, Mon, sorry to spoil your hookup," Nola said before turning to the young Orlando Bloom at her side. "Ian's present and accounted for, so I'm guessing you must be Malcolm."

Malcolm sipped his beer like two cops in his living room weren't no thang and casually asked Monica, "You know her?"

"She was interviewing my ex lov-vah at Long Boards," Monica said, snarkily. "What's up, lady? Did he get mad that I dumped his sorry ass and send you out to find me?"

A large pizza box showed up at the open door in the hands of a scruffy Serbian man wearing a hat that said Sal's. "You the ones ordered the pizza?"

"Yeah," Tony said, taking the box from the delivery guy. "How much do we owe you?"

Tony paid the man with some cash lying out on the grubby kitchen counter, making sure to add a nice tip. The kids watched in sullen silence as he opened the box and grabbed a slice of sausage and peppers.

"Hope you don't mind me jumping in on this. I'm effin' starving. Anybody else? You might as well. You'll only get crappy vending-machine food down at the station."

Malcolm crossed his arms and puffed out his chin like a teenage Mussolini. "You're arresting us? For what?"

Tony answered through a mouthful of pizza. "Under-age drinking and whatever kush is in that bong. Oh, and for Ocean Spraying the Coastal Commission this morning."

Monica looked at Nola with mock sympathy. "Sorry about your top."

"I know you don't mean that, but thanks for the confession," Nola said with a wink.

"What confession? I'm talking about those little holes in your tank. Kinda tacky...don't ya think?"

"Yeah, I had to wear a name tag at Vandenberg today. And speaking of accessories, I'm going to need those Ana Khouri cuffs you're wearing. On your next crime spree, you might want to consider dressing down. Might be smarter...don't ya think?"

"I'm not giving you my jewelry," Monica replied, in the mistaken belief that she had a choice.

"Oh, c'mon," Nola cajoled. "If you give me your cuffs, I'll let you wear mine. Or we can all go down to the station peacefully. Felon's choice."

Ian and Kyle were too dazed and confused to put up an argument, but Malcolm's outrage came flying out of the gate. "This is bullshit! You can't just walk in here without a warrant."

"Sure we can." Tony held up the bong. "We had probable cause. I smelled a classic felony in the hallway outside your door. Probably why I'm so hungry."

He took another bite of pizza as the patrol cops Nola'd radioed for earlier arrived at the door. She waved them in and grinned at the terps. "Okay, kids. It's showtime. All of you have the right to remain silent…"

Thirty-Six

As usual, where Haven went, men's pulses beat faster. Wives and girlfriends heaved a collective sigh of relief when she finished her salad niçoise and Campari at the Biltmore's four-star restaurant and retreated down one of the lush garden paths to her private bungalow.

As she passed the croquet lawn, she realized that in her haste to leave the estate, she'd forgotten to pack Larry's check. It was alone and unguarded, tucked into the copy of *Vogue* on her nightstand. It was too risky to go back and retrieve it now. Her tormentors might be lying in wait for her to return. Or...they might have followed her to the hotel. They could be watching her now. Regretting her decision not to order room service, she stepped up her pace back to her bungalow. If anything happened to the check, Larry would just have to write her a new one. Thankfully, men would always be writing her checks. Women who had to earn their own money never had enough time for upkeep. It was comforting to know she'd never have to wear a hair-covering hat, hide her chipped fingernails, or go weeks without waxing. And even death threats were preferable to supermarket makeup.

As she was reaching for her key outside her bungalow door, another unpleasant thought occurred. What if her persecutors broke into the house just to trash it? If they stumbled onto the check, she'd be exposed. They could plaster it all over the internet or send it anonymously to the police. That cyanide-blonde cop would go straight to Larry, who was about as tough under pressure as an origami swan. If he confessed to the bribe and told them about her call to him the night Gus died, they'd know she'd rewritten Gus's speech *before* he died. Something that only made sense if she was already planning to kill him.

Haven stood frozen at her bungalow door. She'd rather cut her own bangs than return to the estate, but there was no way she could take a chance on orange being her new black. The stakes were too high. She had to go back.

Thirty-Seven

Angry Susan was sitting in Gus and Haven's great room desperately trying to think. She'd found out about the threat and the pool fire from her maid, Marta, who was married to Gus's gardener, Rigoberto. Thankfully, the servants were the one bit of property she and Gus had managed to divide equally in the divorce. When Susan heard from Marta that Haven was moving to the Biltmore, she'd been struck with an idea.

Getting into the mansion had been a piece of cake. Gus not only used the same gate code he and Susan had used back when they were married, but he'd also hidden a spare key in a cherub's mouth in the driveway fountain. *Could the man be any lazier?* she'd thought as she removed the key from the angel-baby's marble tongue.

The alarm system had been trickier. It wasn't their old code or a cartoon rabbit's measurements or Haven's minuscule BMI, which Gus had been happy to taunt Susan with at their first divorce hearing. Fortunately, when the alarm company called to check on the incorrect entries, Susan had been struck with a flash of divine clarity. When the operator asked for the password, Susan confidently said, "I got mine," and it worked like a charm. Alarm company satisfied, she'd had free run of the place ever since.

It hadn't taken long to locate most of the objects Gus had

ANNE FLETT-GIORDANO

cheated her out of in the divorce. One by one she'd loaded them into his rolling Gucci trunk: the Escher woodcut, the Cartier clock, the framed letter from Dorothy Parker to George S. Kaufman full of bitchy little comments about Helen Hayes. But she'd been unable to locate the real prize, the object she valued most in the world. She'd spent two hours going up and down the stairs, in and out of every room, and her failure to find it was making her frantic.

Gian Lorenzo Bernini was a child prodigy already setting the Baroque world atwitter when he'd sculpted the exquisite little bronze that had stolen Susan's heart.

Looted from a private collection by the Nazis, the lithe male nude had quietly passed from owner to owner under the oblivious nose of the stolen art division at Interpol. Susan had purchased it from a dealer in Zurich in a hush-hush transaction conducted in cash. Rather than show it off downstairs, she'd placed it on her bedside table. A beautiful man to say goodnight to as opposed to the braggart oaf she'd married. It had remained there till the night Gus presented her with divorce papers. Realizing it was gone, she'd confronted him, screaming, but he'd just laughed. He didn't even bother to deny he'd taken it. He didn't have to. She'd purchased it illegally, so he knew she was powerless to get it back. The thought of him smirking at his cleverness every time he looked at it had haunted her ever since. So why couldn't she find it? Gus would have wanted it someplace visible, a constant reminder of his triumph. He wouldn't have hidden it in a bank vault or lost track of it or sold it at any price.

Suddenly, it hit her. Gus would never have sold it when he was rich, but he wasn't rich when he died, he was bankrupt. Insurance companies would furnish his creditors with a list of his assets. But the looted Bernini couldn't be insured. It would have been the only piece of artwork the banks didn't know about. The only one Gus would have been free to sell.

For a moment, she thought she was going to be sick. Her hatred of the man was so powerful it was turning her blood to bile. But there was no outlet for her fury. The bastard was already dead. The portrait of Haven in pearls over the mantel stared down at her mockingly. Seething with anger, Susan grabbed the fire poker and slashed at the painting with all her might. She tore and ripped at it until, too exhausted to raise her arms, she collapsed on the sofa, spent.

Staring at the broken bits of canvas and wood, she tried to imagine Haven's reaction when she came home and found her oil-based doppelganger so viciously defiled. Of course, she'd assume it was the work of the same maniacs who'd left her the death threat. She'd be terrified that they'd so easily found their way into the house. She'd feel helpless and vulnerable. Then a new thought occurred. Wouldn't a second death threat really seal the deal? Nothing too elaborate, just menacing enough to ensure that the miserable little whore never felt safe again.

Choosing a medium for her message was a no-brainer. The mirror in Haven's bathroom made a perfect blank canvas. Susan stood on the granite sink counter and scrawled out the words, "PREPARE TO DIE BIT," but the lipstick snapped before she could add the "CH." She climbed down and rifled through Haven's vanity for another lipstick in the same color. There were a thousand shades of red, but Scarlet Letter had been too metaphorically delicious to pass up. Settling for Queen of Hearts, she was about to climb back up on the sink when her eye caught a reflection in the mirror that made her cry out. Behind her on the sunken bathtub amid a clutter of foot scrubs and pumice stones sat her precious Bernini, a loofah dangling from its gracefully outstretched arm.

It was too incredible. A breathtaking work of art reduced

to a bathtub caddy. Gus had truly cast Baroque pearls before swine. She rushed to examine it. Aside from some soap scum that had hardened around the base, it was safe and unharmed. She needed something soft to wrap it in, a blanket or, better yet, the cashmere throw she'd admired in the great room. She was gently untangling the loofah when she heard footsteps in the doorway.

"Put that down," Haven's voice was as wicked as a stepmother.

Susan looked up into the gorgeous face that had ruined her life.

Haven smirked at the message on the mirror. "There's a 'ch' in bitch. I'm surprised you don't know that, being it's a word that so perfectly describes you."

Having recovered from the initial shock of being caught, Susan cradled the Bernini protectively. "Gus stole this from me, and I'm taking it back, so get out of my way."

"Or what? You'll bite me again?"

"I would, but I'm afraid I'd catch chlamydia."

"Right, like anything could live in your dried up old cuze."

Years of pent-up rage exploded like a thermite bomb. Blind with hate, Susan rushed at Haven, who swung wildly with her Birkin bag. The heavy purse caught Susan smack in the face, and the clasp ripped a gash in her cheek. The searing pain of being Birkin bitch-slapped tore away any remaining vestiges of restraint. Susan swung back, and the bronze Bernini collided with Haven's skull with so much force that she was unconscious by the time her body hit the travertine floor. Adrenaline cresting, Susan stood triumphant over her fallen nemesis. There'd be hell to pay later, but for now she was victorious. And it wasn't like she'd actually killed the bitch. Not like she'd fantasized all those nights she'd spent alone. The perfect C cups were still rising and falling in rhythm. In a few minutes Haven would wake up, and the first thing she'd see would be the lipstick message scrawled on the mirror. All Susan had to do was add the missing "ch."

Thirty-Eight

The harsh lighting in Interrogation Room A was making Nola tired. She'd augmented her two-peanut dinner with a PowerBar, but her blood sugar had barely spiked. She needed a chopped chicken salad, a good night's sleep, and a confession from Monica, stat, but none of these were seeming likely at the moment.

Across the gray metal table, Monica was looking fresh, well fed, and fully aware of her constitutional rights. She hadn't even bothered asking for a lawyer. When Nola brought up the gold jewelry that tied her to the Super Soaker attack, Monica correctly pointed out that Ana Khouri cuffs were the rich gals' must-have status symbol for spring, ergo there was no way Nola could swear in court that Monica's pair and the pair worn by Wonder Woman were one and the same.

"Maybe your attacker was just some *Project Runway* fashionista offended by your Gap couture," she said with mock innocence.

Nola had never wanted to play bad cop, punch-the-suspect cop so badly in her life. The snarky smiles and sarcasm were so blatantly contemptuous, she almost wished the revolution *would* come, so this pretty little liar could be sent down to slave in the mines. When Nola asked about Ken's story in the *Reader*, Monica claimed she'd never heard of Dr. Waxman and that she didn't have a clue where Ken's information had come from.

"So you just took his word for it that the story was true? Isn't vetting stories pretty much a managing editor's only job?"

"Is it? Oh well. My bad."

This last bit of snarkasm pushed Nola over the edge. "Look, Ms. Crawford, it's pretty obvious that you consider yourself to be superior to me in every way. Well, I concede you are younger and cooler and far better dressed. But here's the thing. I am smarter than both you and your Barney's personal shopper put together. I've put lots of smart-ass brats behind bars, and believe me, you're next. So here's what I need you to do. Take a moment to count up all the things that make your life *sooo* much better than mine, then decide how long you're willing to go without them. Because if you're honest with me now about squirt guns and pool fires and all the other hinky things you and your various boyfriends have been up to, I *might* talk a judge into putting you on probation. On the other hand, if you keep shooting me those smug, rich-girl smiles, then trust, not only will I make sure you do max jail time: I will come and stand outside your crappy little cell with *my* smuggest of smiles. Then I'll go out and have a cocktail, get a facial, take a walk on the beach, and think about you in your prison coveralls porking up on mac and cheese — jaiil food's pretty much all carbs, I'm afraid — and I will *just be loving* how incredibly better my life is than yours. So you take a minute to count, then tell me what it's going to be."

It didn't take a minute. Monica's smile was smugger than ever. "I'd like to call my stepfather now."

Next door, in Interrogation Room B, Tony wasn't faring much better. Malcolm was sitting across from him like they were just two buds grabbing a microbrew at Freebirds. Every question Tony asked was answered by a quick lie followed by a longwinded dissertation from the student radical's handbook.

"Where were you between nine and ten this morning?"

"Hanging in my crib with Ian, Monica, and Kyle, talking about how the World Trade Organization is the surreptitious capitalist paradigm for…"

The rest was all just revolutionary white noise. The first couple of times Malcolm went on a tangent, Tony had sat back doodling potential lineups for the Dodgers, waiting for the kid to talk himself out. But Malcolm had the fiery zeal of a revivalist preacher and enough conspiracy theories to keep Oliver Stone in plot lines for life. Tony pitied Malcolm's future cellmate. Listening to this kid go on and on, he'd probably end up shivving himself.

Sam and Juan were interviewing Kyle and Ian respectively. The two stoners had emerged from their *Leaving Las Vegas* stupors and were exercising their right to take copious handfuls of Advil and remain silent. They mostly shrugged their way through the proceedings until the two-thousand-dollar-an-hour attorney, Malcolm's father, had rousted out of bed, arrived, and shut down the questioning.

Unfortunately, no discarded costumes, Super Soakers, or accelerants had been found in or around Malcolm and Ian's apartment. The kids had covered their tracks better than a Native American hunting party. With the lawyer standing watch, Sam didn't dare keep their skinny asses in jail overnight. After all the Sturm und Drang, they were issued a couple of tickets for the pot and the drinking and told they were free to go.

Monica strolled out of the interrogation room like it was just another Valentino trunk show. Her stepfather was waiting for her in the squad room. Nola guessed he'd be tired, angry, and very rich. There was no way Jillian could support her daughter's "gotta have" lifestyle on the profits she squeezed out of the *Reader*. What Nola hadn't figured on was coming face-to-face with Lawrence Wilson twice in one day. When Jillian said her husband was extremely attractive, she hadn't mentioned he was also a television star. Larry was standing by the front desk talking to Sam, and he was not a happy camper.

"You're saying my stepdaughter sabotaged my *own* hearing today?" Larry shot Monica a look that was tantamount to child abuse. She shrugged it off like a loose sweater and smiled at Tony, who was typing up interview notes at his desk.

Hearing Dr. McDorable's voice was almost surreal. Nola had only seen Larry's soapy hospital show once or twice, but when he spoke he sounded exactly like the concerned doctor he'd portrayed.

"*Is she going to live, Doctor?*"

"*It's too early to say, Nurse. Removing a spleen from an eye socket's a very delicate operation, but I've got to try — then later we can sleep together.*"

Fifty Shades of Grey's Anatomy, or whatever it was called, always managed to end on a sexy note.

Sam usually tread lightly with celebrities, but he wasn't holding anything back. "We also believe your daughter helped set Mrs. Gillette's pool on fire this afternoon."

Larry struggled to keep his composure. "But you're not officially charging her with anything?"

"Not at the moment, no. For now, she's free to go."

Nola gave Monica the nudge, and Stepfather and Daughter walked out of the station together in nerve-shattering silence.

Nola grinned at Tony and Sam. "Well, that promises to be an interesting ride home. I don't know about you gentlemen, but my ovaries just sent me a thank-you note for never having children."

Sam, who routinely peppered his language with words that would make Kanye blush, grimaced. "Do you have to say ovaries?"

"Sorry. Fallopian tubes? Uterus?"

"Yep, just keep digging that hole," Sam said. "I'm sure there's another sexual-harassment seminar down there somewhere."

"Oh please, I haven't had sex, inappropriate or otherwise, in so long, even identity thieves don't want to be me."

Sam laughed and went over to a credenza that contained a bottle of Courvoisier. Late-night protocol called for a nightcap.

"There is one plus to all this," he said, taking out the cognac. "Now that Wilson knows his own stepdaughter was involved in this morning's melee, he'll probably get the rest of the Coastal Commissioners off our backs."

Tony took a dimmer view of the situation. "Yeah, but we still have two unsolved murders: one with no suspects and one that, so far, we can't even prove *was* murder."

Nola fished three paper cups from the water cooler. "And we've got four miserable kids who think they're smarter than we are." She handed out the cups and hopped up on her desk, dangling her legs over the side.

"I'm sorry we couldn't hold the little bastards, but great work finding them, you two," Sam said as he started pouring. "Legs are looking good, by the way."

Tony pushed his chair back and swung his feet up on his desk. "Thanks, boss. Been killing some power squats down at the gym."

"I believe he meant mine, Tony."

"Nope. I meant his. Yours are too long for that skirt. I

can practically see up your ovaries."

"And on that note, gentlemen…" Nola raised her cup and made her favorite toast, borrowed from *The Maltese Falcon*: "Success to crime."

Thirty-Nine

It was after midnight when Nola finally pulled into her parking lot. The sight of the drunken couple walking arms around waists toward her condo was so discouraging that it was killing the pleasant, warming sensation left over from the cognac. Ken and Nancy were so wrapped up in each other that they didn't even notice She was there till their paths converged outside the front door. Even then, it took Ken's mojito-muddled brain a second to realize his bad luck.

"What? Are you following me?"

"Actually, I live here," Nola said sweetly. "Hi, Nancy."

Ken looked at Nancy accusingly. "You know her?"

Nancy opted to play dumb. "Ah, yeah, she loaned me a screwdriver the day I moved in. How do you guys know each other?"

Nola went along with the pretense. "Ken and I met earlier today. I had some questions for him. Now I have one more. How many girlfriends do you have in a night, Ken?"

The opportunistic little skunk didn't miss a beat. "Not that it's any of your business, but I asked Monica to meet me at the bar tonight so I could break up with her."

If you ate more moral fiber, you might not be such a lying shit, Nola thought, but for Nancy's sake she kept her response to a simple, monosyllabic, "Oh?"

So relieved to be back on the horse with her tarnished

knight, Nancy rushed to his defense. "It's true. He told Monica he'd made a mistake, then he called me. We've been talking all night down at Long Boards. We're good again."

Faced with the age-old dilemma: Do you tell your friend she's living in a fool's paradise, or do you wait and let the fool discover it for herself? Nola decided that ripping the bandage off fast would cause the least amount of pain.

"Nancy, Monica told me she went to Long Boards tonight to break up with *him*. And from the way she was sucking on her new guy when I arrested her, it's probably the only true thing she said to me all night."

Stunned, Nancy looked to Ken for a denial. Ken didn't bother to lie. He was sobering up quick. "You arrested Monica?"

"Yes, and I know she and her friends in ROTC70 were the mysterious source for your story this morning, so if you don't want to be named as a co-conspirator, I suggest you say goodnight to Nancy and start walking."

It was an idle threat. She'd arrested Monica and her crew for the pot and the booze, they were Teflon on the rest, but Ken didn't know that, and she suspected he'd had all the drama he could take for one night.

"Fuck," Ken said to no one. Rude, stewed, and no longer about to be screwed, he told Nancy he'd text her later and started toward his car.

"Not to your car," Nola called out. "You're too drunk to drive. You can call an Uber from the street."

Nancy's expression was a *Webster's First Edition* definition of agony as she watched him change course and walk away. Even faced with his latest set of lies, it was Nola she was mad at. "Why did you do that?"

"Because you're not that egomaniac's fallback girl. You're too good for that."

"Shouldn't that be up to me?" she said, eyes welling up.

"Absolutely, I'm just buying you a night to think it over."

"I don't need a night. He loves me, he realizes that now."

"Does he? Because I think he got emotional ass-kicked today, and all he *realizes* is that he needs someone to kiss it and make it better. If Monica hadn't dumped him, he'd be darkening her door tonight, not yours. I was with him at the bar when she came in, and trust me, he was not going to break up with her."

Ten minutes later, Nancy was back, curled up on Nola's rattan chair, a tiny sobbing mermaid in a sea of Kleenex. "I'm so stupid."

"You're not stupid. Every woman falls for a charming user at least once in her life. Take it from me, it's best to get it out of the way early."

Nancy's curiosity was instantly aroused, but Nola had no desire to satisfy it. Dredging up past bouts of bare-knuckle romance wasn't exactly her idea of fun. She tried to blow it off, but misery was way too anxious for company. Nancy kept pestering her with questions till the whole story of Josh spilled out.

"All eight years he cheated on you?"

"Or made sure I knew how much he wanted to. Check that, actually the first year was heaven, then the warranty ran out."

"Did he ever tell you he loved you?"

"All the time. Then he'd complain behind my back and flirt right in front of me. He used to whisper to his female friends that if it wasn't for me, they could be together."

"How do you know?"

"They told me. Look, talking about Josh still makes me feel like a fool, and it's too late to start Skinnygirl self-medicating." Even if it wasn't, Nola had no intention of activating her liquid escape pod tonight. Nancy was already tipsy and dehydrating at the speed of sixty Kleenexes a second.

"You couldn't have been a bigger fool than I've been," Nancy sniffled.

"Please, I should have worn a jester's cap with bells on. Josh always said that Valentine's Day was commercial schmuck bait. Then one year I get a box of chocolates to cover the fact he'd bought the same box for the French girl he'd been crushing on at work."

"At least you got to eat the chocolate. Ken left me tied to his bedposts, covered in Nutella, because the drunk girls across the hall banged on the door and begged him to hook up their new game console. And then he stayed to play with them!"

Nola's jaw dropped. "Seriously?"

"I know, it's insane! I'm lying there like some masochistic Mallomar while he's over playing *Walking Dead* with Hannah, Marnie, Jessa, and Shoshanna. Then he comes back home all happy 'cause he beat them."

"Wow, he might at least have had the good manners to lick you first."

For the first time, Nancy laughed. "I guess I really am a masochist. Just an emotional one."

Nola laughed too. "Join the club. Josh took me on a romantic tropical vacation, then told me over a candlelit dinner that he knew he'd break up with me someday. *Someday.* I cried all night."

"Oh, harsh. That's how you broke up?"

"I wish. If it was, my place in the *Guinness Book of Monumental Idiots* wouldn't be only one 'how dumb can a smart woman be?' step away from Hillary Clinton's. The next day on the beach, when I asked him if he meant it, he started spouting all this philosophical bullshit that basically added up to, 'I want to hump every girl I see,' so I walked back to the hotel, packed my bag, and flew home sobbing. When he got back to our room and realized I was gone, he searched the island in a panic. When I finally answered my phone, he said I'd done the perfect thing to make him realize how much he really loved me. We stayed together another three years."

"Three years?"

"Yep. Even when the schoolteacher he 'hung out with' after I flew home got flustered and disappointed when I answered his phone. Even when he called at five in the morning from the French girl's bed and I'd been up all night freaking out, afraid that he'd been killed in a car accident. Hear my harlequin bells jingling now? Don't be me, okay? Be better than me."

"How did you finally end it?"

"Eventually, my self-esteem crashed so hard that there was no way to reboot, so I cheated, too, and in a didn't-see-that-coming turn of events, suddenly I became the evil villainess in our tale."

"Did he try and get back together?"

"Yeah. When the usual 'now I know I really love you' didn't work, he parked outside my apartment and threatened to shoot himself. When that didn't work, he even offered to marry me. Marrying me was apparently the only fate he could think of that was worse than suicide. It was deeply flattering."

A glimmer of hope sparked in Nancy's eyes. "He asked you to marry him?"

Nola's heart sank. "That's what you're taking from my pathetic recap? You're hoping that if you go through enough hell with a guy who keeps telling you he loves you, but doesn't — eventually, in a panic, he might ask you to marry him?" The spark in Nancy's eyes died, but Nola had lost the stomach for her fool's errand. Broken hearts and Kleenex had to fall where they may. "Look, you've got Ken on speed dial, and I've run out of cautionary tales, so if you decide to take him back, I hope it turns out right for you."

Still holding out hope for Ken, Nancy couldn't help but ask, "Do you ever think maybe Josh did love you, at least a little bit?"

"Nope. He doesn't even remember me now unless he reads about me in his journal. You don't have to read that you loved someone. If you did, it never leaves you. Run Lola run."

The smile was losing out to the tears again. Nola wondered how such a tiny girl could hold so much water. She must have hidden humps, like a camel.

"Oh honey, I promise someday Ken'll be just so many clouds in your coffee."

"I don't know what that means."

"It's from an old Carly Simon record. My mother used to play it into the ground. You'll be up all night anyway, so iTune it. While you're at it, check out 'Tired of Being Blonde.' The woman actually had some very insightful things to sing. Oh, but avoid 'Jessie.'"

"What's that one about?"

"Sadly, tonight it's about you."

Forty

Up until the time of Descartes, the Western world generally accepted the idea that physical pain was a mystical experience, a reflection of God's displeasure that emanated from the human heart. But René had other ideas. His PowerPoint presentation consisted of the image of a hammer striking a human hand, which sent a message through a tube to a bell in the brain. The greater the pain, the louder the bell would ring.

The bells of Saint Mary's, Mark's, Luke's, and John's, together with those on Santa's sleigh, were ringing in Haven's ears as she lay sprawled, legs akimbo, on the cold bathroom tile. She had gradually come to, but she was still too weak to move. Memories of how this incongruous situation had come about were lost in the hot-poker-through-shattered-bone sensation that gripped the bloody side of her head. She desperately needed it to stop. Thankfully, it began to dawn on her that she wasn't alone. Xochile was starting the spray-tan compressor. It must be Tuesday morning, but surely she could see Haven wasn't ready; she wasn't even naked yet.

"Xochile, I need help," Haven whimpered. "Help me."

Xochile was wheeling the compressor toward her, the spray nozzle in her hand.

"No, help, I need help. I was attacked."

Xochile was bending down now, but instead of helping

her, she was climbing onto her chest. More pain.

"Stop, it hurts! Xochile, get off!"

The face was fuzzy. It was fuzzy, but now she saw it wasn't Xochile. It was someone else, and the pain, they were hurting her. She wanted to fight, to scratch at the eyes glaring down at her, but the weight of the knees pinned her arms. And the compressor kept humming and the pain kept crushing her. When she tried to scream, her attacker shoved the spray-tan nozzle so far into her mouth that it choked off the sound. Gooey brown liquid poured down her throat. Vomit came up, clogging her larynx, but the spray kept coming till her arms stopped shaking, and her body stopped moving, and her heart stopped beating. Beautiful golden girl Haven Gillette was dead.

Forty-One

The weather had finally caught up with the season. Coats and sweaters were appearing on State Street, and iced lattes had given way to espressos with biscotti at the Coffee Cat. Nola was walking past the restaurants, past the shops, past the theaters, when up ahead she saw him, the same old guitar with the feather on the strap slung over his shoulder. He was singing to the crowd in front of the Fiesta Five. Charley Beaufort was alive!

For a moment, she couldn't believe her eyes. She stopped walking and started jogging. Ignoring the blinking Don't Walk sign at the corner, she dodged cars and broke into a run. He was singing about the people going by, what they looked like, what they were wearing, what they talked and laughed and frowned about as they passed, but she couldn't quite make out his words, just the general tenor of his voice.

"Charley, Charley, who tried to kill you?"

Charley flashed his big, warm smile and kept singing and strumming the guitar.

"Please. Tell me!"

The guitar was getting louder, too loud to hear over. When she reached out to stop his hands, stop the music, she woke up.

Nancy had stayed until around two-thirty. Now it was nearly a quarter to four, too late to take a pill and too early to get up.

Charley was the only straight-up murder on Nola's plate, and she was about as close to solving it as she was to growing fins. The poor little junkie Sam had indicted was ducking flying monkeys and itching up a storm now, but they still couldn't get anything more cogent out of him than, "Dude just shot him, click, click, click."

Three clicks, but two bullets. The ones Alex dug out of Charley's chest. It was the kind of inconsistency that kept her awake nights, and tonight or, more precisely, this very early morning, was no exception.

Forty-Two

"Hello, hello, hello." When the sun came up, Nola threw open her balcony doors and blasted old Nirvana down to the homeschool kids on the beach learning evolution-free ocean-ography from their moms. Poor kids. They deserved at least one true-blue, angst-filled smell of teen spirit.

The bad dreams and frustrated ambitions of the previous day and night had been Etch A Sketched away when Tony called to say he'd conjured up enough probable cause to get Judge Peña to issue a warrant for Gus's laptop. If Baz could lock on to anything suspicious about Gus's speech to the commission, things would finally start to pop.

In celebration, she was treating herself to the rare luxury of basking in the skin-aging sun while she sipped her Obama Blend. It was a whimsical mix of Hawaiian and Indonesian beans from Vices and Spices. She'd been unable to resist the Commander in Chief's smiling face above the slogan: "Yes, you can have a good cup of coffee."

Tony was on his way to pick her up. They'd decided to drive to the Gillette estate together to confiscate the laptop and get in whatever other snooping they could.

One of the kids on the beach, grateful for the music, braved a judge-y look from his homeschooling mom and smiled up at Nola just as the refrain kicked in.

"Hello, hello, hello, hello..."

Forty-Three

Nola was sitting outside on her condo steps when Tony came to pick her up.

"Hey, you're on time. Did hell freeze over while I was sleeping?"

"I skipped the lather, rinse, and repeat this morning and went with dry shampoo in a can," she said as she walked to the car. "Did you call ahead to see if Haven was back from the Biltmore?"

"And let her know we're on our way over?" he scoffed. "Do ya think I'm new at this?"

Nola removed an empty Taco Bell bag, a golf tee, and a softball jersey from Tony's passenger seat and hopped in. "I hope she's not home. It's so much easier confiscating evidence when the owners aren't swearing and threatening to sic lawyers on you."

"Don't worry, sweetheart, trouble is my business."

"Thanks, Roland."

"Nice. See?" he said. "If you were twenty, you wouldn't know *which* iconic literary detective I was plagiarizing."

"Yeah, and my knees wouldn't creak like a haunted house every time I do a plié in barre class."

"You know what'll stop that?"

"Stop taking barre class?"

"Unless you're still hoping for that shot with the National

Ballet." He swung the Audi back toward the road. "Do female swans even live to be forty?"

"I assume they live just as long as male swans, only with more pain," she said, popping on her Ray-Bans and settling back in her seat.

As they swung onto Cabrillo, he sniffed the air. "Your dry shampoo smells like baby powder."

"I know, it totally gives away the fact that I was too lazy to hoist a blow dryer. It's the smell of shame, baby."

Pajamas straight out of the dryer had been one of Nola's favorite feelings as a kid. With a workable theory of Gus's murder and a warrant on the dashboard for his computer, everything was feeling warm jammies as they pulled up in front of the Gillette estate.

No one answered when Tony buzzed the intercom outside the big gates, but this time he had the combination. Haven had pressed the crinkled piece of paper into his hand before taking off for the Biltmore in the hot little SL. The same SL that was currently parked halfway up the driveway to the house.

"Why would she park there?" Tony wondered aloud.

"And if she's home, why didn't she answer when you buzzed at the gate?" Nola's warm-jammies feeling was quickly turning to soggy flannel. "Something is feeling very wrong here," she said as they climbed out of the car.

When Tony rang the bell, it echoed inside, then silence. When the same thing happened the second time, Nola looked back toward the yard. "Maybe she's out roasting marshmallows over the pool."

"No, you were right the first time," he said. "Something's not right here."

"Well, you're the guy. Start breaking some glass."

Tony picked up an antique doorstopper and smashed a

hole in the stained glass panel that ran the length of the big, wooden doors. The alarm they were expecting didn't go off. The house remained silent.

"Uh-oh. Guns-drawn time?" Nola asked.

"Looks like it," Tony replied, unholstering his Beretta. Gun in hand, he reached through broken glass and opened the door.

They announced themselves loudly in the foyer. When there was no answer, Nola pointed her Glock toward the stairs and whispered, "I'm up, you're down."

Tony nodded and crossed toward the great room as Nola started up the stairs. When he found the brutalized remains of Haven's oil painting on the floor, he guessed what they were going to find next.

He'd finished searching the media room and was headed into the wine cellar when Nola came back downstairs. "No point looking in there, you're ice cold," she said. "And you're not the only one."

"Dead how?" Tony asked as they walked back to the car to get crime-scene gloves and booties out of the trunk.

"Beauty-product poisoned? Suntan strangled? Bludgeoned? It's impossible to tell what actually killed her till we call Alex to come examine the body. I think you better see for yourself."

Nola hadn't wanted to report the murder till Tony got a look at Haven's body and they had a chance to talk. Crimescene guys measuring and taking photos sometimes got in the way of clear thinking. As they climbed the stairs back to Haven's bathroom, Nola's Fitbit beeped. Four thousand steps and it wasn't even noon yet. If she searched the house from top to bottom a couple more times, she could have an extra glass of wine that night.

Tony stopped at the bathroom door and stared in at

the gruesome tableau. Haven's body was lying face up in a Savansana relaxation pose, arms open to the sky. It didn't look staged, it looked like she just fell that way. The spray-tan splatter suggested she was already lying down when the nozzle was forced down her throat. The blood from the gash in her skull had pooled with the sticky brown tanning liquid on the tile, but a few tiny droplets leading from the door to the body looked clean. Tony read the lipstick message on the mirror out loud. " 'Prepare to die, bitch.' Seems kind of prosaic for such a poetic crime."

"Agreed," Nola said. "Death by spray tan is the sort of thing that lands on Nancy Grace, or at least Greta Van Susteren. Sam's dream of a crime-free Santa Barbara till after the film festival is about to burst like a sebaceous cyst."

"Can't you say 'shit-filled balloon' like a normal person?"

"Oh yeah, that's so much nicer."

Tony pulled out his phone. "I'll call the crime-scene unit."

"Tell 'em to pack overnight bags. Murder in this house seems to be trending."

"You see anything in here that might have made that gash in her head?"

"No, but the night Gillette died, there was a small bronze sculpture sitting on the tub by the foot scrubs that could have done the trick." Nola indicated the empty spot where the Bernini had played loofah caddy. "It seemed oddly out of place in a bathroom. It looked more like it belonged in a museum, but the rich be nuts, so I didn't think much about it at the time."

"Expensive piece of art. Could explain why the killer didn't leave it behind. I noticed an Escher in the hallway is missing, too," Tony said, before turning his attention to the call.

While Tony spoke to dispatch, Nola checked out the expensive cosmetics display on the granite sink. La Prairie Cellular Gold Serum ran around seven hundred dollars an ounce. Seven hundred dollars that could have been donated to a food bank, she thought. Then again, if it really worked...

Resisting the urge to see what a couple of hundred-dollar dabs of genuine liquid gold might do for her eye creases, she moved on to the lipsticks. She found a broken Scarlet Letter in the sink and a Queen of Hearts on the granite counter. The colors matched the ones the killer, or killers, had used to write the two-toned message on the mirror. They'd have to wait till the equipment van arrived to see if there were prints on the tubes, but they didn't look as if they'd been wiped clean.

Nola looked down at Haven's bloody, matted hair and silently apologized to the universe for saying she'd like to hit her in the head with a hatchet. *Be careful what you wish for,* she thought, *and call your mother more often,* she threw in for good measure.

Tony clicked off his phone and ran his cop's trained eye over the corpse. "I suppose it's possible the kids we arrested last night could have come back after we released them, killed her, and then burgled the place. But it seems pretty ballsy for that limp crew. Vandalizing pools and ripping up oil paintings is one thing, but you'd really have to hate her guts to be this brutal."

"Well," Nola said. "I know one person who'll be thrilled to see her rocking a body bag."

"You think Angry Susan could get *this* angry?" he asked.

"Please. If that woman were any more toxic, she could shrink a tumor."

"So after Alex gets here, let's grab some hazmat suits and go interview her."

"Just like watching the detectives..."

As usual, Nola had to rummage around in her purse to find her phone. When she finally dug it out, the ringtone was on its last downbeat, and she didn't recognize the caller ID. "MacIntire."

"Hello, Detective. Major Burnell, ah, Bryan. Hope you don't mind, your station gave me your number."

Temporarily gob-smacked, Nola waved to get Tony's attention and pointed to her phone. "Hello, Major...Bryan. No, it's fine they gave you my number. Do you have some new information about Dr. Waxman?"

"Actually, this is a personal call. I'll be in Santa Barbara tonight, and I was wondering if you'd like to have dinner?"

"Dinner?" Her voice quivered like a teenager's. Tony was already aggressively nodding yes.

"Well, I'm standing next to a bloody corpse right now."

Tony threw up his hands to God, the standard Italian reaction to lost causes, but Bryan just laughed. "Well, I'll give you credit, that's the most inventive blow-off I've ever received."

"No, it's true," Nola said. "I'm knee-deep in a murder investigation, and well..."

Even cell-phone proximity to a man she was too attracted to for her own good was making her fumble for words. Past experience had proven that the best thing for everyone involved was for her to say, "Thanks, but no thanks" and ring off as quickly as possible.

"...I wouldn't be finished tonight till at least eight-thirty or nine."

What the hell was she saying? *Please say it's too late. Please say it's too late...*

"No problem," he said. "I eat late."

She needed another excuse, anything to get out of it. But her mind was a terrified blank. "Oh, well, great, then," she said, regretting the words as quickly as they came out of her mouth.

"What's your address?" Bryan asked, like a normal human being.

"Ah, maybe we should just meet at the restaurant, so if I'm stuck at work, you can wait at the bar, or not at the bar, if you were thinking of someplace, you know, more casual."

"No, something tells me you're going to need a drink. How 'bout you finish with your bloody corpse, and then tonight I'll take you to Paradise?"

Well, someone thinks a lot of himself, she thought, before she remembered... "Ohhh, the Paradise Cafe. Sorry, took me a minute. Crime scene. Confusion. Great. I'd love to go to Paradise with you. To eat dinner...there."

"Okay, see you between eight-thirty and nine," Bryan said, still normal.

"Great," she squeaked. "Bye."

Tony watched in a state of stupefied amazement as she clicked off.

"I know, I know," she said hanging her head. "How many times could I say 'great' in one conversation?"

"Forget the 'greats,' let's talk about 'I'm with a bloody corpse, but okay.' You know I'm no longer baffled that you don't date more. I'm genuinely shocked you go out at all."

"He's just too perfect. I should cancel."

"No, you should marry this guy and stay married till the day you die. Dating is clearly *not* your thing anymore."

"Be fair. You know this only happens with guys I'm *way* too attracted to. Why does a guy like that want to have dinner with me anyway?"

"A pretty cop rocking a skirt above the legal limit who's all hot to fire his anti-tank weapons — do I really have to spell it out for you?"

"Thanks for the pretty, but guys like Bryan date women like her." Nola indicated Haven's lifeless body on the floor.

Shocked at her momentary lack of situational awareness, she quickly backpedaled. "Please forget I just used a murdered girl's corpse as a dating example. In fact, let's just table this whole conversation until after Alex liver-probes the body. Way, way after."

The crime-scene unit pored over the house with their usual ham-fisted, fine-toothed comb. A male fingerprint expert dusted the *Vogue* on the nightstand for prints. Not possessing the right set of chromosomes, he wasn't tempted to flip through it, or he surely would have been drawn to the cardamom trumpet skirt on page thirty-four and the hundred-thousand-dollar check tucked neatly into the seam beside it.

Forty-Four

The crime-scene unit was still processing Haven's bathroom when Nola and Tony left to question Angry Susan. The killer, or killers, had wiped the spray tanner down. There were trace fibers on the nozzle from one of Haven's monogrammed hand towels, but no fingerprints. Strangely, however, they'd neglected to wipe down the lipstick cases, which sported a thumb and two partials in mint condition.

"Why wipe down the spray tanner and leave prints on the Queen of Hearts?" Tony wondered aloud as they drove to Montecito.

Nola had no idea, but Queen of Hearts was totally apropos. She'd been feeling like Alice in Wonderland all week. Nothing was making any sense, starting with their meth-smoking caterpillar hearing Charley's killer fire three gunshots, "click, click, click," when they'd only found two bullets at the scene. Throw in bio-weapons magically disappearing down rabbit holes, messages in the looking glass, and a major who didn't mind if she was late to a very important date. It was getting a little surreal.

As they pulled into Susan's driveway, she warned Tony what to expect. "Believe it or not, the devil actually does wear Prada."

"As long as she has a big, bloody scrape somewhere visible," he said with a heart full of hope.

They'd found blood on the clasp of Havens's Birkin bag, and it wasn't her blood type. If she'd hit her assailant with the pricey purse, they could match the clasp to the wound and test the DNA. Juries ate that stuff up.

Marta left them standing on the doorstep while she went to tell "Mrs. Susan" that the police would like a word. A moment later she ushered them into Susan's opulent living room and politely asked them to wait. They'd been cooling their heels for twenty minutes on an overstuffed sofa even your average storybook giant would find a scooch too deep when Susan finally made her entrance. She hadn't bothered to bandage the gash on her cheek. It was raw and red, and it practically screamed, "Arrest me!"

So that's what a fifty-thousand-dollar cut looks like, Nola thought, imagining Haven's gorgeous bag being evidence-raped back in the lab.

The soft, mossy greens Susan had worn when Nola met her in the garden had given way to mossy browns with just a hint of ecru. The woman was a study in earth tones. Decidedly an autumn.

"I see you didn't come alone this time, Detective," Susan said, casting a bored glance at Tony. "Must be a slow police day. No parking disputes at Whole Foods or slap fights over the last zucchini blossom at the farmers' market?"

Ignoring the caustic greeting, Nola made introductions. Tony didn't bother getting up. There was nothing about the woman that engendered politeness, but the cut on her face was doing wonders for his morale. When Nola politely inquired about it, Susan laughed.

"I'll save you the trouble of trying to be cagey, Ms. MacIntire. I know why you're here, and I freely admit I did it. What's more, I enjoyed every minute of it. Most fun I've had in years."

Tony kick-started himself up from the cavernous sofa. "Awesome confession, lady. And here I'd heard you were difficult."

"Difficult?" She laughed. "I'm sure Ms. MacIntire used more colorful language than that. Even my friends call me a first-class cuntessa."

Class, first or otherwise, was the last word Nola would ever use in a sentence describing Susan, but she held her tongue. Why poke the suspect in the middle of a confession?

Susan didn't seem to give a fig if they stayed silent as stones. She went blithely on like it was just another murder-mystery game night at the yacht club. "Arrest me if you like, but you'll be wasting your time. I have a phalanx of lawyers already working to prove everything I took from that house was mine."

Nola and Tony exchanged a look. Susan was copping to the theft, but not the murder. Prints on the lipstick cases but not on the tanning machine. Curiouser and curiouser.

"Even the life you took?" Nola asked to gauge her reaction. Susan froze like a snapshot. "She's dead?"

"As disco," Tony replied. "What exactly did you hit her with anyway?"

"My Bernini. But it wasn't my fault. She attacked me first," Susan cried, pointing to the cut on her cheek. "I only hit her back in self-defense!"

Tony played along. "Uh-huh. So you cracked her in the head for hitting you, then you poisoned her in self-defense?"

A fly zapped out of the air by the tongue of a toad couldn't have looked more surprised. Susan's haughty attitude deserted her. Insisting she knew nothing of poison, she related her story from beginning to end without a hint of nastiness. "Would I have bothered to finish writing 'bitch' in the mirror if she was dead?" she argued. "She was unconscious on the floor when I left, but I know she was still breathing. I checked."

"Exactly what time was that?" Tony asked.

"Around ten. She hit me, and I hit her back. Then I took my Bernini and some other things that the banks have no right to — an Escher, a Dalí, a Cartier clock — and I drove home."

Back at the crime scene, Alex had guesstimated that Haven had died sometime around midnight. The damage to her skull had been significant, but choking on the poisonous tanning solution had been the ultimate cause of death. If Susan had a witness to corroborate her timeline, she'd still be guilty of assault but she might be off the hook for murder.

"Can anyone confirm what time you came in?" Nola asked, hoping the answer might be 'no.'"

"Yes," she said, vastly relieved. "Marta helped me unload the car. She's polishing ramekins; I'll go get her."

Tony took hold of Susan's arm. "You'll stay here. *I'll* go get Marta."

He started toward the hall, then looked back at Nola in utter confusion.

"Kitchen," Nola said.

"Right, of course, ramekins." He continued out, no closer to understanding but at least headed in the right direction.

"Polishing the silver, sounds like a dinner party," Nola said, marveling at Susan's cold-blooded ability to segue from bashing in heads to throwing a fête.

"I've invited a few friends over to celebrate getting my Bernini back. I suppose now I'll have to cancel."

Nola nodded. "It's probably wise, you know, in case we have to book you for murder."

In a flash, Susan's anger was back. Even dead, Haven was still vexing her. "Everything would have been fine if that little twat had just stayed at the Biltmore like she was supposed to. Tell me again, I forget, what kind of rat poison did I shove down her throat?"

"How did you know the poison was forced down her throat?" Nola asked.

"Because the only things that anorexic little whore swallowed willingly were Vicodin and old man cum."

"Holy smokes!" Nola said with a jolt. "I get where all this righteous anger is coming from, but take it down a notch, okay? There is *one* lady in the room."

"You don't *get* anything," Susan hissed. "You're not half smart enough to know shit about my life."

"Wow. Thank you for that, because it's going to make this sooo much more fun." Nola pulled out her cuffs and spun Susan around. "Susan Gillette, you're under arrest. Anything you say can and will be used against you in a court of law."

Susan was angrier than Nola had ever seen her, and that was saying something. "What the hell do you think you're doing?! Your partner's getting my alibi from my maid."

"It's your alibi for murder. I'm arresting you for the assault and burglary, which you've already confessed to. Of course, later we may still tack on murder; meanwhile, you have the right to an attorney, if you can't afford one... Oh, but why bother with that? It's a pretty moot point, right girlfriend?"

Tony came back with Marta, who had to hide a smile when she saw her snooty boss in handcuffs. She confirmed the time Susan had arrived home with the stolen loot. "I know because I had to turn off Jon Stewart to help her carry all her things inside," Marta said, simultaneously confirming Jon's universal appeal.

"There. You see?!" Susan spat out.

Susan would have to spend at least one night in county jail while she waited to get a hearing in front of a judge. Nola pitied the poor matrons who'd have to pat her down and coax her into a jumpsuit. While her boss was locked up, Nola hoped Marta would eat her dinner party food, try on her clothes, and sleep in her presumably sumptuous bed. Whatever she was getting paid, it couldn't be enough.

Being that it was wealthy Montecito, a patrol car arrived about thirty seconds after Tony called. Shoving Susan in the back of the cherry top made Nola feel good all over. The days were finally turning crisp, the birds were singing in the trees, and aside from three unsolved murders and having a date that night with a too-perfect man, everything was feeling very warm jammies.

Forty-Five

In spite of Bryan being too handsome, sexy, and smart, Nola wasn't totally nauseous at the thought of having dinner with him, but getting dressed for the date was proving problematic. Every dress, skirt, and sweater in her closet had a prior bad-date association. There was finger-guns guy, obnoxious vanity-license-plate guy, magic-penis guy... (David Isaacs's magic penis was like a phallic skeleton key, effortlessly opening up every female he bedded with awesome result. But then, over breakfast, he'd chatter endlessly about his exciting life in dentistry, and like a faulty porcelain crown, the spell would be broken.)

Nola was trying to ignore all the past date associations and focus on which outfit best displayed her assets while simultaneously hiding her liabilities when the doorbell rang. Throwing on a robe with no romantic history at all, she went out to the living room to answer it.

Nancy looked like she'd been rolling a Ken-size boulder uphill all day, but somehow she managed a smile.

"Hi. Sorry if I'm bothering you again."

"No. Not at all," Nola said. "You okay?"

"Working on it. I just wanted you to know I almost called him this morning, then I saw my bookcase still in pieces and remembered his breakup tweet, and I knew you were right. He's not really in love with me, and he never will be."

"Sorry, Nance."

"He wanted to see me when he came to get his car, but I wouldn't let him up."

"Oh, that's tough, I know."

"He tried to make a joke about me being his 'tweetheart.' The sad thing is...a week ago, I would have laughed at it."

"Well," Nola said with a sigh, "on the bright side, not laughing at his not-funny jokes is the first step to recovery, so congratulations."

"Thanks," Nancy said. "You look great — are you lip plumping?"

"That obvious, huh? Nothing like slathering a little bee venom on your lips to show a guy you're trying too hard."

"A new guy?"

"Yep. He's a way-too-handsome-for-me soldier I met up at Vandenberg yesterday. I have no idea what to wear. Come and help me stare down the closet of indecision."

She was shimmying into her Calvin Klein with the fitted bodice that only had slight guy-who-insisted-they-sing-the-Mariah-Carey/Ol'-Dirty-Bastard-"Fantasy"-remix-during-the-karaoke-portion-of-his-cousin's-wedding associations when the doorbell rang again.

Nancy was a ball of curiosity. "Is that him?"

"No, we're meeting at the restaurant. Would you mind going to see who it is and, if possible, get rid of them?"

"I'm on it."

Nola was already having second thoughts about the dress when Nancy returned with a breathless announcement. "It's him!"

"What!"

"He must have misunderstood you or something, 'cause he's here, and even with the soldier haircut, he's super-cute. Oh, and he's wearing a green army T-shirt and camouflage pants."

"Camouflage pants?"

"Yeah, you're a little overdressed."

"A little? I'm wearing more mascara than Lady Gaga."

"Who cares what he's wearing? He's hot. And I'm totes loving the age thing."

Nola was so busy slipping out of her dress that it almost blew by her...almost. "What age thing?"

"Um, nothing, you know, I just think it's cool."

"Nancy, what are you talking about?"

"He just seems a little younger than you...it's no big deal, younger guys date older women all the time now."

Nola saw a woman in a lilac bra and matching thong gaping at her in horror and realized she was staring at her own reflection in the closet mirror. "You think he looks younger than me?"

Finally, she had it. Definitive proof that all the creams and peels and concealers and exfoliations were just worthless charges on her credit card. Bryan was at least seven or eight years older than she was, but to Nancy's objective eye, she was practically robbing the cradle. It no longer mattered if she moisturized at night or maintained a proper thigh gap, she was showing her age like overhead lighting. The battle was over; the wrinkles had won.

"Exactly how old, and please be honest, do I look to you?" Nola asked.

"Around thirty-five...I guess...Oh God, are you like twenty-nine or something?"

"No, you're right — well, close enough. But he still looks younger to you? By how much?"

"I don't know...ten years maybe?"

"Holy crap, Nancy, who did you let into my house?"

"A really cute soldier who said he was here to see you."

"Did he say his name?"

"It's Indian, Ro something."

Early twenties Ro Kodical. Nola was so relieved she could have cried. "Oh, thank God."

"I'm so sorry, you said a cute soldier."

"No, no. You didn't do anything wrong. Ro's not my date, but I do need to talk to him. Would you mind keeping him company while I jump into some jeans?"

"Sure."

"He was pretty badly wounded in an attack in Afghanistan, so you might want to avoid asking if he's ever been in combat, stuff like that."

"Oh gosh, that's horrible. And here I am crying about my stupid boyfriend shit."

"Well, your stupid boyfriend was a shit, it's allowed."

Nancy started out, then turned back. "Does he have a girlfriend?"

"I don't know. Why, ready to rebound?"

"He just seems kind of sweet."

"I only met him yesterday, but I got the distinct impression he is. You better get out there, I don't want him to bolt."

"Don't worry, I won't let him out of my sight," Nancy said as she hurried out to play hostess.

Nola slipped into pants and a sweater as quickly as she could, fearing Ro might have a change of heart and take off. But her fears were groundless. When she came into the living room, he was deeply engrossed in a conversation with Nancy about their shared love of *Game of Thrones*.

"Hi. Sorry to keep you waiting."

Ro leapt to his feet as though she was his commanding officer making a surprise inspection. "I'm sorry to just drop by, ma'am. I should have called. I was down on the beach trying to make up my mind and…"

"Relax. At ease. It's fine, really. Sit down. Can I get you something to drink?"

Nancy popped off the sofa. "I just offered him a Coke."

"Oh, sorry," Nola apologized. "I don't have Coke."

"I do." Nancy chirped. "I'll just run to my apartment and get it." Ro tried to protest, but Nancy assured him it wasn't any trouble, she was happy to do it. Judging by the smile on her face, she meant it.

Like any red-blooded American girl who works out and survives on vegetable fumes and toothpaste, Nancy's ass looked great in tight jeans. And like any straight, red-blooded American male worth his salt, Ro couldn't help but watch her walk away.

When she was out the door, he turned back and saw Nola was watching him watch. People caught standing naked by a window were less embarrassed.

"It's okay, she thinks you're cute too," she reassured him. "She told me so back in the bedroom after she let you in."

Surprised by Nola's candor, Ro was lost for a response. Nola helped him out by filling in the silence. "I'm not trying to set you up or anything. She's just been through a bad breakup, so it's probably too soon. I just thought you might enjoy the compliment."

Ro's eyes swept the floor. "Thank you," he said shyly.

Now that Nancy was gone, his nervousness was more evident. Clearly, it had been a tough decision for him to come. He was clenching his fists so tightly his biceps were twitching. Nola wanted to put him at ease, but there was something she was curious about. Her address wasn't on the card she'd handed out at the interview. So how had he tracked her down?

"I really appreciate you coming to talk to me, but, just out of curiosity, how did you find me?"

"I Googled you, then I Google-mapped you," he said in a worried voice. "I hope that's okay?"

"Of course," Nola smiled. "Sometimes I forget that Google almighty is up in the clouds looking down on us twenty-four-seven."

The biceps twitched again. "I really hope *no one* is looking down on us right now, ma'am."

"I promise, Ro, whatever you've come to tell me will remain just between us," she said, in her most comforting voice. "Oh, and it's *really* okay not to call me ma'am."

She waited for him to begin, but he was taking a long time to buffer, so she gave him a little prod. "So, what *have* you come to tell me?"

"I could tell during the interview that you and your partner thought I was the leak. Even though you didn't say so, it kept eating at me that you thought I was some kind of traitor. I guess I just wanted to explain myself."

"Okay, first, I don't think you're a traitor," she said. "So let's take that off the table. But you're right about one thing, we did peg you as the leak. So, tell me what happened."

As Nola and Tony suspected, Ro had downloaded the portion of the weapons log that showed only ten canisters of SE40 arriving on base and passed it to Dr. Waxman on a flash drive. He'd chosen to go public rather than report the discrepancy to his superior officers because he wasn't sure who was responsible or whom he could trust. Nola's heart beat a smidge faster as she asked the obvious question.

"So, was Major Burnell lying yesterday?"

"I honestly don't know," he said. "I might have missed the second log entry like he said, or once the discrepancy became public, the canisters could have been returned, and the log could have been doctored. That kind of operation would be way above my pay grade."

The idea that the Air Force might have purposely way-laid two of the canisters for reasons of their own hadn't occurred to her before. If they had, surely the man in charge of weapons security at the base would have had to be at least tacitly involved. For all Nola knew, she was on her way to have dinner with a member of a military conspiracy, and she had *no idea* how to dress for that.

"So if it *was* some kind of operation, wouldn't Major Burnell have needed to be in on it?" she asked.

Ro shook his head. "Not necessarily. It could have all been planned at Livermore. Major Burnell might not have been NTK."

"NTK?"

"Need to know."

"Well, I wish I knew, because I'm having dinner with him tonight."

If Ro were a cat, he'd have darted under the bed. "You know the Major?" he said, knuckles whitening.

"Don't worry, okay. It has nothing to do with the investigation."

She had no idea if she was telling the truth. She still suspected Bryan's real reason for asking her out was to use his sexy manfluence to get her to reveal the name of the soldier who was currently sitting across from her. She also knew that was never gonna happen.

"One more question," she said. "Do you know if Dr. Waxman passed the information straight to Ken Levine, or was there an intermediary of some kind?"

"I don't know. All Dr. Waxman told me was that he would get it to the press."

Nancy knocked quickly before letting herself back in. She had a frosty Coke on ice, a new coat of lipstick, and her cheekbones looked slightly more pronounced than when she'd left. When she handed Ro the glass, the sweet spark between them was like something out of a Hallmark movie.

"Thanks, you shouldn't have gone to so much trouble," he said, with a shyness that made Nola ache.

"No trouble," Nancy said. "It's just Coke. It was nice meeting you." Clearly she was regretting that this was goodbye.

"Wait," Nola interjected. "Ro, before we let Nancy go, how are you with Swedish diagrams?"

"Not following, ma'am."

"You see, Nancy has this bookcase…"

Forty-Six

Nola stood at the door of the Paradise Cafe, paralyzed with indecision. She could see Bryan inside at the bar. The Major was having a scotch, and she was having major misgivings about joining him. For all she knew, he might be part of a military cover-up. Or he might be trying to trick her into revealing a press leak. He might even be the next guy she fell head over heels in love with. It was a lot of pressure for a first date.

Any way she looked at it, there was more trouble in Paradise than she was up for. She was about to leave and call him with some work-related excuse, then follow it up with a text to Tony using some lame play on the words "Major indecision," when he spotted her and stood up. For better or worse, the date was on.

As she crossed to join him, it occurred to her that he looked even better in civilian clothes. Not too drab, not too flashy; it had probably taken him less than two minutes to get dressed. Meanwhile, her own closet looked like a clothes bomb had scored a direct hit.

He casually kissed her cheek like they'd been dating for months and getting together for dinner was the most natural thing in the world. She ordered a no-sugar gimlet, hoping one part vodka, one part lime juice would get the butterflies in her stomach hammered enough to pass out.

"I hope I didn't keep you waiting long," she lied.

"Just long enough to wonder if there was some secret reason that you wanted to meet me here instead of letting me pick you up at your place." He looked down at her hand. "You're not married, are you?"

"Nope, no wedding-ring tan line." She smiled. "But, as long as we're on the topic of ulterior motives, any covert reason for this dinner invitation that I should know about?" Whew! It was kinda bald, but at least she'd put it out there.

"Such as?"

"Such as, you still think I know who leaked the story and maybe getting a couple of drinks *in* me will make it easier to get a name *out of* me."

"*Do* you know who leaked the story?" he asked.

"Nope."

"Fine. Now that's out of the way — you like trout? They do great trout here. Wood-fire grilled."

"I love trout. So I have your word of honor as an officer and a gentleman that inviting me to dinner tonight isn't just part of some military black op?"

"Black op?"

"Did I use that wrong?" Nola shot the bartender a grateful look as he returned with her sugar-free cocktail.

"Seems a bit dramatic," Bryan said. "Now I'm starting to wonder if the only reason you accepted my invitation was because you think I have some dark secret to hide."

"Do you?" she asked.

"Nope. So where does that leave us?"

"Both liking trout and both still pretty suspicious of each other," she said, sipping her drink.

"I'm good with that," he said, smiling. "Most couples have to be married for years before they reach this level of mutual distrust. I think we're making excellent progress here."

Bryan's smile was like Joshua's trumpet; Nola's walls didn't stand a chance. She hated herself a little for being so easy, but the guy could have the Taliban at hello.

Even the pretty hostess who escorted them to a twinkle-lit table on the patio couldn't take her eyes off him. She was obvious to the point of being rude, but Nola forgave her. His face was like a gorgeous traffic accident; people couldn't help but look.

When the waiter came, they both ordered the trout. When their salads arrived, Bryan put his napkin in his lap and his cards on the table.

"I know it's customary to save the big stuff till at least after your second drink, but since you're the forthright type, what do you say we do it now, and get it out of the way?"

"Okay. Provided you go first," Nola said, wondering what was coming next.

"Married twice, no kids, one big, old, slobbery black lab named Jackson. How 'bout you?"

"Never married, no kids, currently no pets, but my biological puppy clock *is* ticking. I definitely see a little shelter mutt in my future."

"Bigger is better."

"Only guys think that," Nola said, smiling. "So tell me, what did you like most about each of your ex-wives?"

Bryan raised an eyebrow. "Strange request."

Nola shrugged. "Just being pragmatic. If you say it was how serene and self-possessed they were or mention their love of all things domestic and the way they always woke up looking beautiful in the morning, I'll know I'm not the girl for you, and we can finish our salads, cancel the fish, and call it a night."

"Is that what you're hoping for?"

"Don't deflect. You must have loved something about

them. You married them."

"Okay. Well, I guess I loved Kate because she was feisty and athletic, crazy competitive, and she didn't care how she looked in the morning, although I have to say she always looked pretty great."

"All good, but *very* not me. Next."

"Okay, next was Sally." He smiled, remembering. "She was always happy. Whatever we were doing, she found a way to make it fun. We'd probably still be together, but she couldn't deal with the stress of my occupation, and the fact that I was away half the time. Oh, best thing about her, she didn't care where I dropped my stuff, or if the bed was made, and she was only woman I ever met who didn't own a coaster. It was like living with a sexy, female guy."

"Yeah, I think you might want to ask for the check about now."

"Hang on, what's your story? You said you've never been married, but a woman like you hasn't spent her life in a monastery."

"No, but what can you really say about rentals?" she said, sipping her drink and hoping to avoid what she knew was coming next.

Bryan eyed her dubiously. "Must have been a couple you kicked the tires and thought about buying."

"One. But it was long ago and far away. On cold nights, the elders sometimes gather the children and tell the legend around the fire."

"Stop kidding and spill. What rare qualities did you love about him?"

"Okay, I suppose fair is fair. I think mostly it was his boundless curiosity. His excitement just swept me along in its wake. Also, and the importance of this can't be stressed enough, in spite of being hella smart, he could be incredibly silly without being childish or annoying. He'd hide drawings of super villains for me to find in the toilet paper and drive me through sprinklers in his beat-up convertible to make me laugh. He was pretty magical when he was manic."

"And when he was 'depressive'?"

"Ah, then the world went dark." She sighed. "He'd get so close to what he wanted, then he'd shoot himself in the foot by worrying that it might not be what he wanted after all. Of course, that made him vulnerable, which made him sweet, and it made me feel needed. Until I wasn't. Sound anything like you?"

"Not even in a *neighboring* ballpark. Emotionally, I'm on an even keel, this conversation is about as silly as I get, and the Air Force really doesn't do vulnerable."

"Yikes," she said. "Shall we quit now and just split the check down the middle?"

"Nah, let's give it a shot. Luckily, the quality I like best in a woman is an abiding love for mesquite-grilled trout."

By the time they'd passed on coffee to finish their wine, they were laughing like old friends. In spite of possibly having tried to steal a weapon that could put whole ecosystems at risk, Bryan was turning out to be a great date. Of course, Nola knew part of what she was feeling was just a biological predisposition to be attracted to his perfectly symmetrical features. Any ape would feel the same. Then there was her self-imposed chastity over the last few months. A libido can only be suppressed for so long. How else could she explain why, after a single piece of fish, she was ready to ride him like a stripper pole? Thankfully, she was far too old to be having sex on a first date. She resolved to take things slow. A small after-dinner kiss, say goodnight, and go.

"You up for a walk to the Coffee Cat?" he asked. "We could grab some dessert and take it over to the park. It's too nice to be inside tonight."

"Love to." It wasn't the quickest turn on a dime and break your resolution she'd ever made, but it was close.

They strolled up Anacapa, grabbed coffees, and skipped the park in favor of the courthouse. Sitting with Bryan on the low, stone fence by the sunken garden with one manly black coffee, one girly nonfat café au lait, and a brownie to share felt as warm and comfortable as the tattered old sweater she only wore when she was alone. When he kissed her this time, it was for real. So real and so good she had to resist the impulse to curl up in his lap and purr. Purrable kisses made her nervous. First dates going this well made her nervous. And feeling nervous made her prone to say exactly the wrong thing.

"What are you thinking about?" he asked.

"A dead body."

Oh, my God, she thought. Tony was right. It was amazing she ever got a second date. After they'd kissed, her eyes had lit on the spot where she'd first seen Charley's body, and when Bryan asked, she'd just blurted it out.

"You're a very unusual girl, Ms. MacIntire."

"I'm sorry I said that. The kiss was perfect. Honest. It's just that I caught a murder here a few mornings ago. The body was right over there in the grass. He was a street singer, sweet guy. There was no rhyme or reason to the killing, and I'm fresh out of suspects. You're never going to kiss me again, are you? I don't blame you. Really, it's better you know I'm an idiot now while there's still time to save yourself."

Yep. She was definitely a candidate for shock therapy. If Bryan had half a brain, he'd gulp down his coffee and start saying his goodnights. Surprisingly, he didn't.

"I read about that in the paper," he said. "I forgot they... I mean you... found the body here. Maybe you should email me a list of your current crime scenes, so I'll know where *not* to try and kiss you in the future." His laugh was everything good in the world, and the way he'd deftly slipped the word "future" into the conversation was the stuff that fairytales were made of.

"It's my fault," Nola said. "I should have said something when you suggested we walk over here."

"No worries. I skipped the park because I saw a big party tent set up over there. Probably some gala thing for the film festival."

"I saw it, too. You a movie guy?"

"Depends on the movie. How about you?"

"Love 'em. Unless they're based on a true story, because they always change the truth for dramatic effect, which presumes a level of stupidity on the part of the audience that I find really insulting, she said pedantically."

Nola and Tony frequently referred to themselves in the third person for fun. She hoped Bryan would get the joke and not think it was just another personality quirk that was coming off weird. Bryan broke the brownie in two and handed her half. "I just don't get all the fuss people make over them, cameras, press conferences. They're just movies. I never go near that festival hoopla, he said with a sly note of superiority."

"Oh, my God!"

"What? Did I do the 'he said' thing wrong? Maybe I should just kiss you again."

"No, you're brilliant. The night Charley was shot, he was coming from the Arlington. He was singing to the crowd waiting for the *Batman* movie. Some news crew might have footage of him with whoever killed him, or at least with the last people to see him alive. It's a long shot, but it's something. Okay, now you can kiss me. And by that I mean...yay!"

The next kiss started the kind of chain reaction that makes a woman smile in her dotage because when she remembers it, it still feels like yesterday.

Forty-Seven

The sex that night was baby-bear's-bed good. Not too hard, not too soft, just blissfully, wondrously, incredibly just right. Nola was so lost in it she never once fell into her usual habit of thinking about all the other women who'd come before her or all the ones who'd surely come after. Bryan's body was the best ride at Disneyland on the best destination-birthday any girl ever had.

The sex the next morning was even better. She had to struggle to keep her happy-exhausted cowgirl legs from going rag doll as she kissed him goodbye at her door.

Fortunately, Bryan's back was to the hall, so he was unaware of Nancy and Ro stumbling out of Nancy's front door in a matching state of bliss. Nola kissed Bryan again while she signaled for them to get back inside quick. Nancy gave a conspiratorial little thumbs-up as she shut the door behind them. Love, even the rebound kind, was conquering all that morning.

When the coast was clear, Nola let Bryan catch his breath.

"Wow," he said. "I will definitely call you."

"And I will definitely answer."

By the time she shut the door, grabbed a Pellegrino, and went out on the balcony to watch him drive away, her phone was ringing. "Hello?"

"Hi." It was Bryan calling from his car.

"What's up? Did you forget something?"

"No, I said I'd call, so I'm calling. You free this weekend?"

"Maybe, what have you got in mind?"

"Astronomy. Sounds sexy, right?"

"Mmm... *All of us are in the gutter, but some of us are looking at the stars.* Pretenders via Oscar Wilde, and yes, I would love to make out in a planetarium."

"I'm talking real stars. How are you at camping in the wilderness?"

"I'm better at wrestling alligators. Don't suppose we could start in the backyard and work our way up to wilderness?"

"*A good plan violently executed now is better than a perfect plan executed next week.* George Patton via the German army."

"See, it's the violently executed part that worries me. Will there be bears?"

"No fun if there isn't."

"Okay, I'm in."

"Really? 'Cause my backup plan was a trip to Paris."

"Wait—"

"Sorry, too late. I'll call you later to plot course and plan strategy."

"Roger that, over and out," she said, happy as a champagne pop. "PS, I had a really nice time last night."

"Yeah, me too. I'm going to call all my buddies now to tell them I got laid."

"What a coincidence. Me too."

A sexy guy she could talk nonsense to. It was the romantic jackpot. So he had a thing for telescopes in the forest with the dirt and snakes and poison oak. There'd be plenty of time for theater dates later. She had the "new boy bounce," and it felt so good. A thousand aerobics classes' worth of endorphins were pumping up her endocrine system. Unable to stop grinning, she called Tony to spread the glad tidings.

"Angellotti," he answered.

"Hi. Hope I didn't wake you. Just calling to see who *didn't* get laid last night."

"Thank God. I can finally stop lighting candles for you up at the mission."

"*And*, not only was he a great lay, he gave me a great lead."

"Good, 'cause I need an excuse to get out of here."

"Uh-oh, Chelsea?"

"Yeah, she's moving way too fast. She showed up uninvited last night, naked under her coat."

"Actually, that sounds like something you'd like."

"Normally I'd love it, but she said it was my early Christmas present. Christmas is eleven freaking months away! That's girl-speak for 'she thinks we're still going to be together then,' right?"

"'Fraid so."

"Chelsea's great and all, but I don't know if I still want to be together in December. I'm not sure I still want to be together tomorrow."

"Then why didn't you tell her to keep her coat on and go home?"

"'Cause she's got a banging body, and hello? I'm a guy."

"So you let yourself be date-relationship-raped? How dumb is that?"

"I know. Now she's making me pancakes. What do I do?"

"Use your non-penis-centered voice and say, 'no means no,' then send her over here. I'm starving. And yeah, he was that good. He was carbs-for-breakfast good."

"Oh Christ, she's squeezing fresh orange juice. I'm in

domestic hell."

"You got yourself into this pulp-fiction romance — just man up and get yourself out."

"Yeah, I think I'd rather man up later over the phone. I can meet you anywhere in five minutes. What's the lead Burnell gave you? I'll need facts to back up my 'gotta go' story."

"The last place Charley sang was outside the film festival. If we're lucky, some news crew caught a shot of him with his killer. I'm going to call around for footage and get Sebastian to put it together and screen it for us this afternoon."

"Okay, I'm on my way to the station now."

"Relax. It'll take at least a couple hours. Just come over here, I'll make coffee and burn you some toast."

"Yeah, Sam, I'll be there ASAP."

"Ohhh. I take it she's in the room with you. Is she giving you the 'I went to all this trouble to make you breakfast and now you're leaving' look?"

"You got it."

"Either say goodbye or put a ring on it, dude. You've already lost your window of opportunity for in-betweens. And lend her some sweats. The naked-under-the-coat thing is fun when you're doing it, but it feels really stupid on the ride home the next morning."

Forty-Eight

Monica and Malcolm lay entwined in her sleigh bed. They were upstairs in her bedroom in Larry and Jillian's two-story guest house. A long night of light beer and heavy sex had begotten a lazy early morning that was quickly morphing into a late one.

Rancho Perdido ("Lost Ranch"), named for its hidden location in the hills, had almost quadrupled in value since Larry bought it. Oprah had purchased the estate next door, and having property abutting the pop-culture goddess was tantamount to hitting the real estate lotto. The heavenly scent from her mimosa trees alone added an extra hundred grand to the asking price, should he ever desire to sell.

"What's that smell?" Malcolm asked as he rolled over to check the time.

Monica pulled the bed throw up around her shoulders. "It's the mimosa trees next door at Oprah's place."

"Really? You didn't tell me you were squatting next to Montecito royalty."

"Didn't think you'd care."

"Oh hells yes, shawty."

"Wow," Monica teased. "Like, when you do dated urban slang, you're like still sooo Bev Hills. But, whatevs."

"And when you do Kardashian, I want to bang you like Kim and strangle you stupid like the rest of them, but it's time to start the play clock." Malcolm threw off the throw and launched himself out of bed.

Monica's nipples perked up in response to his rough energy, the sudden blast of cold air, and the sight of his tight glutes as he stood bare-assed at the window.

"Not a very imposing fence between you and the big O," he said. "Maybe we should hit her place one night."

"One atrocity at a time, sugar." Monica yawned and pulled the cover back over her. "Speaking of which, be careful getting the stuff out of the stable this morning."

"Afraid your pops might decide to go for a ride?"

"Hardly. The horses are all for show. He probably gets saddle sores just riding my mother. But there are always workers around, so just be cool."

Their conversation was interrupted by a knock downstairs. The knocker didn't hang around for an answer; he just walked right in.

Larry never waited for his stepdaughter to invite him in. Monica lived in the guest house, but he owned it. As far as he was concerned, it was his to enter and exit as he pleased. He walked to the bottom of the short stairway and called up to her.

"Hey, Mon, you up there?"

"Yes. Go away, I've got company."

"I need to talk to you."

"Oh, all right." After a long, silent spell, her voice came back again. "Well? Go ahead."

"I'm not going to keep shouting — I want to talk to you alone!"

Larry heard rustling and footsteps, then a very

unpleasant surprise came jogging down the stairs. Larry was lost-luggage, stuck-in-traffic, dingo-ate-my-baby mad when he recognized his stepdaughter's latest boy toy. He was well aware that Monica had a perverse streak, but banging the enemy was one bit of twisted evil too far.

"Yo, man, nice pile of adobe you got here," Malcolm said by way of a greeting.

Larry answered his pleasantry with a heavy-lidded glare. Malcolm grabbed his jacket and boots off the floor and headed out the door. "Nice talking to you, Dad. Looking forward to us having another enlivening debate real soon."

Larry was considering whether to call his security guys to kick the smart-mouthed kid's ass when Monica came padding downstairs in a cashmere robe and slippers. Barely acknowledging his presence, she went into the kitchen and grabbed some kefir from the fridge.

"So? What's so urgent, Daddio?"

"Are you clinically insane, sleeping with that kid?"

"Since when do you care who I bounce with? Besides, it was your idea that I get with him and his pals in the first place. So far, it's all been working out just the way you planned, *n'est-ce pas?*"

"Christ, Monica, this isn't just a real estate game anymore. Haven Gillette is dead!"

"So I heard. Did you do it?"

"What?!" he shouted, taken aback by her hubris. "No, of course not. Did your boyfriend?"

"Not a chance. The note by the pool was my idea. Just adding to the drama."

"We don't need any more drama! I told you to quit the group after the squirt-gun stunt. You did your job; the commissioners are on my side. It's crazy to keep seeing that boy, especially now that the police are involved."

"But that's what makes it so exciting."

"Hey, I'm not about to see a two-hundred-million-dollar deal go south because you like playing Bonnie and Clyde."

"If I did my job so well, why haven't you paid me yet?"

"Drop the kid, and I will."

"Mmm, don't think so. Under those culturally stereotypical T-shirts he's got some sweet abs, and he's so passionate about saving the planet. It's really kind of noble."

She offered him the kefir bottle, and he pushed it away. "Don't tell me you're actually buying into that anti–Wall Street environmentalist crap?"

"With my mink-collared jacket and crocodile boots?" She laughed. "I like the world order just the way it is, thank you. Playing warrior princess with Malcolm just adds a little juice to my dull day-to-day. I get so bored being bored, and Snapchat's just not doing it for me anymore. Of course, once I have my own money…"

"Well, if you want your money, you'll break it off with him today."

"Excuse me. How 'bout, if you don't want certain people to find out you were banging Haven Gillette, you pay me today."

"Blackmail. Very nice. The cops already know I was with her. That Italian detective's no fool."

"The cops know, but does Mom?" she asked with a venomous grin.

"You *would* make your mother's life hell just to get what you want, wouldn't you?" He scowled.

"Look who's talking. I didn't screw Haven. You did. You started this train rolling. You want to blame someone now that it's coming off the tracks, look in the mirror."

Forty-Nine

When Tony arrived at Nola's condo, she was on the phone with Sebastian. The eager-to-please kid had forgone his usual Sunday-morning game of disc golf up at Lake Casitas to do the forensic inspection of Gus's laptop, and quicker than you can say Usain Bolt, he'd found their smoking cyber gun.

There were two versions of Gus's speech on the hard drive. The first version, against the Wyatt Development, had been deleted and replaced by the pro version that Haven read aloud at the commission meeting. Most damning of all was the time stamp. The speech had been rewritten right before Gus died. Even the most anal-retentive nerd in the world wouldn't spend his last moments on earth finishing up a boring real estate report. They were no longer dealing with a suicide. Gus Gillette's cause of death had just officially been upgraded to murder.

Sebastian rang off to begin his second task of the morning, collecting and compiling video from the *Batman* premiere. While Tony had been extracting himself from pancake-making Chelsea, Nola had been calling every news outlet she could think of, asking for footage from that night, hoping to find anything that might shine a light-bomb on who killed Charley. For the first time in his imaginary existence, Batman might actually help solve a crime.

When she hung up with Sebastian, Nola presented

Tony with his toast and cappuccino. "Breakfast with no implied commitment, as promised."

"I asked Chelsea out twice," he said, as he slathered on jam. "Twice isn't an automatic invitation to be my girlfriend, right?"

Nola sipped her cappuccino. "Absolutely not. You think Bryan could feel the skin crease from my thong?"

"Probably. So what's the easiest way to let her know I'm not ready to do the breakfast/girlfriend thing?"

"Don't sleep with her when she shows up on your doorstep naked."

"Okay. Second-easiest way?"

"Tony, breaking up is like losing weight, there *is* no easy way. Hey, you think if I give up protein, carbs, and fat, I can lose ten pounds by next weekend?"

"Sure, if you swap that nonfat cap for liquid meth. You guys have another date lined up?"

"He's taking me camping in the wilderness to look at the stars."

"An away date already?"

"Some men aren't afraid of relationships."

"Yeah, and some serial killers do their best work in the woods."

"I'll leave you a trail of breadcrumbs."

"You'll leave me a monitor for your GPS tracking device."

"Don't be paranoid." She laughed. "Hey, now that we have proof that there were two speeches on Gillette's laptop, you think we can get a warrant for Wilson's financials?"

"Way ahead of you. I called Judge Peña's clerk while you were busy frothing the milk. It's in the works as we speak. So, how do I break it off with her without hurting her feelings?"

"Hmm...if I pretend to be your ex-girlfriend, you could say you were never really over me, and we've decided to get back together?"

"You think she'd buy that?"

"Of course she will. 'Cause you just lovvve me so much. Because I'm sooo unforgettable...like Nat King and Natalie Cole unforgettable."

"Yeah, it has to be at least a little bit believable. I'll just say you drunk-dialed me begging me to take you back, and I felt sorry for you, so I caved."

"Fine. So what do you think is the best diet meth? Amp? Blue Ice?"

"Well, they'll both make you lose a little tooth weight. Relax, okay? You're skinny enough to be dismembered in the woods. Any homicidal maniac would be lucky to have you."

"Then how come I had to drunk-dial you and beg you to take me back?"

"Obviously because you lost all your self-esteem when I broke up with you in the first place."

"I envy Chelsea. She's really dodging a bullet."

Nola finished her coffee, scooped a little nonfat foam off the rim of her cup, and licked it off her finger.

"Very ladylike," Tony said. "Did you do that in front of the Major last night, or are you saving it for your third date, when he takes you to the old abandoned saw mill?"

Fifty

When Nola and Tony arrived at the station there was a message from the lab. The blood droplets leading away from Haven's body were AB positive, but more extensive DNA results were still a ways away.

Angry Susan was Type O, same as the blood on the Birkin clasp. Marta's statement that Susan had returned home at eleven on the night of the murder and the unexplained AB blood at the scene were enough for any half-decent defense attorney to raise the specter of reasonable doubt. They decided to hold off on arresting Susan for Haven's murder. She was free to post bail on the two lesser charges of B&E and assault and return home to her ramekins.

There were a few anomalies in the rest of the evidence they'd collected, but working out exactly what they were was going to take time. On CSI, or "Completely Suspend Intelligence" as Tony condescendingly referred to it, lab techs were constantly pulling forensic rabbits out of their hats, but that wasn't how it worked in real life.

When Sebastian finished compiling all the news and publicity footage from the film festival, Nola asked him to set up his computer for a screening in Interrogation Room A. The hard metal chairs were hell on your ass, but the interrogation rooms were the only private, soundproofed rooms in the building. When she walked in to meet him, she caught a glimpse of herself in the one-way perp mirror. Under the harsh lights, her reflection was muy no bueno.

Bryan's night date in the wilderness was seeming better and better. At least starlight was flattering. Starlight and dim restaurants would probably get her through the next couple of years, but what would she do after that? Invite any guy she liked to go spelunking?

"Hey, instead of lunch on the beach, how 'bout we visit Carlsbad Caverns?"

Betty White, she remembered, as she sat down on one of the hard metal chairs and presented Sebastian with a pastry box.

As a thank-you for giving up his day of disc golf, she'd brought him twelve red velvet cupcakes. Two minutes later, there were only four left. Young men's stomachs were where calories went to die.

She was texting Tony to hurry up when he wheeled his cushy desk chair through the door and squeezed it in next to the computer.

"You're such a comfort hound," Nola complained. "If you'd sit on a torture chair, we wouldn't be so squished."

"Yeah, you'll be begging me to switch when your butt goes numb." Tony tapped Sebastian on the shoulder. "Ready when you are, SJ."

Sebastian hit play. The first video was from an L.A. channel, and it mostly focused on the movie stars. Ben Affleck and Jennifer Garner looked like a perfectly nice Santa Barbara couple, slightly embarrassed by all the attention they were getting. Jennifer Lawrence was glowing like a sky full of stars, and Russell Brand was so obviously in love with himself that Nola thought Russell and Russell might be one of the few Hollywood romances to last. Unfortunately, all the shots were tight, and Charley and his guitar were nowhere to be seen.

The next video was from a local channel, so the Arlington Theater and the hometown crowd played a much bigger role. The camera moved through the glittering throng outside the theater picking up B-roll — atmospheric footage to be edited around shots of the movie stars later. Tony was the first to spot Charley. He was standing on the periphery of the forecourt with his battered guitar case open on the sidewalk. He was singing about two teenage girls who'd just gone wild at the sight of Ryan Gosling climbing out of his limo.

"See these gals are all aflutter…
'Bout the movie star just came.
Their hearts done melt like butter…
And they're shouting out his name.
'Cause they got the blues…
The Santa Barbara International Film Festival blues, blues,
blues…"

The rest of the song was unintelligible over the shouting of the crowd. The camera operator swung away from Charley and raced to get a close-up of Ryan signing autographs. Nola hadn't spotted anyone staring at Charley with murderous intent, but there was a lot more footage to look at.

They were on video number five when Tony got a call from the fire department. The flammable liquid that had started Haven's pool fire wasn't something your average sicko could just add to his cart on Arson.com. It was a complex chemical compound that had been made by someone who knew how. Nola's mind went to Ian.

"Tony, the night we interrogated the kids — didn't that gangly one with the goat scruff whine that he had a chem final in the morning?"

"Ian Stark," Tony said. "Baz, we need to take a movie break to find out the name of Ian's chemistry professor and what chemicals the kid has access to."

It was Sunday, so the UCSB student records office was closed. Nola hated to ask Sebastian to break the law, but he was so damn good at it. Sebastian hacked the university database and came up with Ian's professor's name and contact number in less time than it took Nola to log on to POPSUGAR in the mornings to find out the best way to cook salmon, what Kate Middleton was up to, and what ten things you should never put near your vagina. Spoiler alert: One of them was fire.

Tony called the contact number, and the professor's boyfriend, Bob, answered. Professor Ranberg was spearfishing for yellowtail off the Channel Islands. His cell phone was out of range, but Bob promised to have him return Tony's call as soon as possible.

"Oh, Baz," Nola said. "Why does your generation want to blow everything up? In my day, science geeks were content just making new club drugs out of old cold medicines."

"In your day?" Tony teased.

"I know, I heard it. If I ever say it again, zap me with a cattle prod. Next video please."

The next batch of footage had been commissioned by the festival publicity department. "Pretty cool of those dudes to take the time to send this over," Sebastian said, grabbing another cupcake. "It's the grand finale tonight. They're premiering *The Euclidian Variation*. It's got to be hella crazy over there."

Nola stood up to get some blood flowing back into her glutes. "I read about that movie on Buzzfeed. Sounds like just another galaxy wars nap-inducer to me. Apparently the only thing *not* floating around in the space-time continuum is an original idea."

Like a stripper's boobs at a surgery center, Sebastian's eyes grew ten times their size. "I'm sorry, but did you read

The Euclidian Variation? Because it's mind-blowing! I camped on the street all night to get tickets, but there were so many people ahead of me I got shafted."

Tony rocked back in his cushy chair. "Ignore her, Baz. *In her day*, CGI was just a glint in some Pixar animator's eye. Plus she's obviously suffering from Numb Butt Syndrome, the crankiest syndrome of all."

"I'm not cranky. Sci-fi has just gotten lazy lately. I mean, how many armageddon movies can there be? We're at war with the aliens. We're making love with the aliens. We're annoyed because the aliens' kids are getting early acceptance to all the best schools, even though our kids are *supposed* to be legacies. Enough already. And yes, that did come out crankier than I meant it to, but it's still true."

Sebastian looked even more exasperated with her than when she'd mistaken his Vulcan Halloween accessories for cute elf ears. "*The Euclidian Variation* is brilliant. This math savant decodes an old text that survived the destruction of the library at Alexandria, and using a Euclidian theorem, he's able to enter an alternate reality where the Davilloyds, they're, like, the Seal Team Six of the galaxy, they have to..."

Tony signaled time like a referee. "Ah, Baz, maybe save the synopsis for later, we've got a lot of footage to get through."

The publicity video turned out to be a game changer. Larry and Jillian popped up in the crowd almost immediately. Jillian hadn't been lying about her pre-op turkey neck. Her hair and makeup were Tracie Martyn perfection, but from her chin to her cleavage there was some serious gobble-gobble going on. Her dress was haute-okay, but the shoes...

"Oh, my God!" Nola said. "Freeze the video."

Surprisingly, Tony was on the same wavelength. "Yeah, I see them, too."

"They're gorgeous, right?"

"What? What are you talking about?"

"Jillian's Louboutin bow-in-the-back pearl-gray stilettos that cost about a million policewomen's salaries and change. What are you talking about?"

"Oh, nothing as important as shoes, just a little side note pertaining to our case."

"Those aren't just shoes, Tony, they're magic shoes. See how you barely notice Jillian's turkey neck because the beauty of the shoes draws your eyes to her feet? David Copperfield on his best day couldn't pull off a better illusion."

Tony sighed the husband sigh, slightly under the breath and indicative of long suffering. "If you're done giving the Dr. Scholl's report, check out Wilson," he said. "See how he's staring off into the crowd? Follow his sight line."

Nola followed Larry's gaze across the forecourt to Haven Gillette, who was gazing back at him with a look that implied an ongoing flirtation. Nola wasn't surprised. Handsome, wealthy, and an ex-television star, Larry was probably a charter member of the Affair of the Month club. Jillian could tighten her neck till she looked like a lollipop, she was still going to need a good divorce lawyer someday.

"Nice catch," Nola said, sitting down again to get a better look. "So Haven and Larry *were* having a little something-something before Gus died. I wonder what kind of prenup Jillian signed."

Tony guessed it was an airtight one. Wilson was no fool. When they asked Sebastian to start the tape again, he didn't respond. Nola looked and saw his diencephalons had frozen on Haven's gorgeous body playing peep show under her evening gown. She gently patted his shoulder. "Baz, honey, your sex brain's stalled your motor — close your eyes and try to breathe through it."

"Sorry, that girl's just so...perfect," he said, still in awe. "She's like comic-book perfect."

Tony nodded in agreement. "Yeah, Plastic Man would do some serious stretching in that issue."

"I know, right? Even the Flash would take his time." Sebastian's head was nodding, too.

Nola had noticed the same phenomenon during her interviews at the yacht club. Men talking about Haven morphing into bobblehead dolls.

"Ah, gentlemen...the woman drank spray tan and forgot to say when, so maybe you could sound just a little less rape-y when you're talking about her. Oh, Julia Louis-Dreyfus! Stop the tape."

"What?" Tony asked. "Are we back to shoes? When you twist the heels, do they transform into vibrators? 'Cause that's the only explanation for all the fuss women make over them."

"It's not shoes. On your ten. By the velvet rope."

There was no mistaking him. Even in a throng of professionally handsome faces, Bryan Burnell stood out in a crowd. The same Bryan Burnell who'd told Nola just the night before that he wouldn't be caught dead at the film festival, had been caught on video not dead, but whispering intimately with an exotic woman with dark skin, fierce cheekbones, and a body borrowed from Zoe Saldana. Nola was outwardly calm, but inside, a great tornado of emotions was starting to swirl. Feeling the falling barometer, Tony took a shot at damage control. "Hang on, Nols, before you arrest, try, and hang the guy in absentia, maybe try to keep an open mind."

Sebastian was scanning the frozen computer screen. "Who are we talking about?"

"The liar liar pants on fire whispering to his lover, whose girl-delts are way too muscled up to pull off that strapless little cocktail number," Nola replied.

"There's that open mind I was talking about," Tony said.

"I don't need an open mind. I have open eyes."

"Maybe she's just a friend he bumped into," Tony suggested. "Or a woman he stopped seeing before he met you. Or maybe he *was* seeing her, but after last night he called her and said he'd just gone out with the most irresistibly insane woman on the planet, so, '*Hasta la vista*, sexy muscled ho.'"

Sebastian zoomed in on Bryan's gal pal. "I can tell you one thing about her. She's either a writer, a producer, or a director. See that white badge she's wearing? They only give those to people who have films in competition. If you want, I can isolate her image and email it to the submissions committee. Once I have her name, I can hack her driver's license, credit card statements, whatever you like."

"Thanks, Baz, but turning cyber-stalker over a guy is just a notch below baking Ebola muffins on my crazy-girl bucket list," Nola said sourly. "It doesn't matter who she is. I'm mad because he lied. He steered us away from the park last night because a film event was going on. He said he never went near all the festival hoopla, but obviously he was just afraid we'd run into his girlfriend."

"Or..." Tony paused to think of a logical explanation. When none appeared, he gave up. "Yeah, I got nothing. He's toast."

Nola scooped some frosting off the last cupcake and licked it off her finger. "Oh, he's beyond toast. He's those burnt little pieces that fall off and make creepy crumbs at the bottom of the toaster. The irony is...mentioning how much he hated all the cameras and the hoopla is what made me think to look through all this footage in the first place. Wow, he must have thrown up a little in his mouth when he realized he gave me that bright idea."

"Well, upside, at least I don't have to worry about him dismembering you in the woods." Tony popped Nola's icing-scraped cupcake in his mouth. Thanks to Tony, waiters all over Santa Barbara were under the mistaken impression that Nola always cleaned her plate.

Nola wiped her frosting finger with a napkin. Pissed that the last pristine dress in her closet now had *guy-who-had-a-hot-girlfriend* associations, she tapped Sebastian on the shoulder. "Baz, please fast-forward to the next scene, like I intend to do with my life."

Half an hour later, they were still watching video. The harder Nola tried *not* to scan the crowd to see more of Bryan and his mystery date, the more she was aching to do it.

"You're prettier than she is," Tony said, out of the blue.

"Why would you say that? I'm not even thinking about her. Or him. And why do men think telling a woman she's pretty is the solution to everything?"

She hadn't meant to sound so petulant, but it was really maddening. Friends always said you were prettier and smarter and funnier, even if you weren't. It was like putting a Band-Aid on a heart attack. Thank you for thinking I'm so vain that comparing me favorably to the other girl will make me feel better. Still, people had to say something, and it was nice of Tony to try, so why was she being such a Quaker Instant Bitch?

"And by, 'Why would you say that?' I mean, 'thank you,'" she added.

They kept fast-forwarding. There were two more videos showing Charley interacting with the crowd. In the first, he was singing about a young guy with a skinny tie and pancake butt who was dropping him some change. The second showed a woman in old-school Versace handing him a dollar. Both skinny-tie guy and Versace woman gave and received big warm smiles. They were hardly America's Most Wanted.

The next video was an interview with Ben Affleck. Charley was visible in the background, but nobody was paying any particular attention to him. They were about to fast-forward again when a couple swept in from the street and stopped right in front of Charley's open guitar case. Gus Gillette and Monica Crawford-Wilson were engaged in a heated argument. It was impossible to make out what they were saying over the crowd noise, but their animosity was visceral. Tony and Nola raced to shout, "Stop the tape!"

Sebastian hit pause, and the image froze. Monica's right hand was clutching Gus's arm to stop his forward progress, and her left was holding something. "Can you zoom in on her left hand for me?" Nola asked.

Sebastian zoomed in till the grainy object became clear enough to make out. It was an Evian bottle. Monica's glamorous, Samurai leather chic and bottled water were making it harder and harder to believe that her preferred social group was the Camelbak-and-bandana crowd.

Zooming in revealed something else unexpected. Monica was wearing the same badge as Bryan's girlfriend, only instead of white, Monica's was blue.

"Blue badges are for festival volunteers," Sebastian explained. "They take tickets, pass out programs. It's cool 'cause they get to see all the movies for free."

Monica didn't strike Nola as the volunteer type, but there were bigger issues at hand. They started the tape again and watched in slow motion. Gus and Monica shared a few more angry words, then he pulled away and stormed out of frame. When Charley started to sing, Monica shot him a look that served as a restraining order. He immediately stopped playing and made a small bow of apology. Contemptuous, she strode off and disappeared into the crowd.

Tony turned to Nola. "How are you at reading lips?"

"Better than I am at reading men, obviously, but I didn't catch a word. We'll have to get a good sound tech to filter out the crowd noise and bump up the background."

In spite of not knowing exactly what had been said, Nola was feeling a surge of excitement. They had video of Monica and Gus having a fight and poor Charley having had the bad luck to sing about it.

"Why would they be fighting?" Tony wondered as they watched the scene a second time. "Gus wanted to kill Larry's project as much as Monica did."

Nola considered Monica's glamorous Japanese garb and Evian bottle again. "Maybe our Glamourai terrorist is a double agent."

"Say what now?"

"I know it's weird, but go with me. If Monica and Larry are secretly working together, appearing to be anti-development puts her above suspicion, which makes her the perfect go-between to approach Gus with a bribe."

Tony picked up the thread. "Okay, so, following your logic trajectory, Monica makes the offer, but Gus is dying so he doesn't need the money, and maybe he's seen Larry and Haven sharing that look we saw earlier, so he turns it down. Probably tells her he's already written a speech against the deal, which leads to a fight."

"Exactly!" Nola said beaming. "Then Monica tells Larry she and Gus fought, and Charley made up a song about it and bang! Both Gus and Charley turn up dead."

Tony smiled. "Dude just shot him, click, click, click…"

"So, are you guys saying Larry killed both of them?" Sebastian was still playing catch-up.

"Or had somebody do it for him," Nola replied. "But, hang on, I've got more. With Gus dead, Larry gets Haven to rewrite the speech, then, rather than pay her off, he kills her too. It's a *threefer*. Ta da!"

Tony shook his head. "Sorry, you lose me there. You saw how Larry was looking at Haven. The only way he *didn't* want her was dead. When I interviewed them together, he was practically spraying the furniture to scent-mark his territory."

"So?" Nola shrugged. "He got over it. Show me a beautiful woman, and I'll show you a man who is tired of fucking her."

Sebastian looked up from his computer screen. "I don't think that's true."

Honestly, he was so adorably naïve she just wanted to eat him up. "Sorry, Baz, you're probably right."

"There's something else bugging me," Tony said. "If Monica's working with Larry, wasn't it a little counterintuitive for her to Ocean Spray the Coastal Commission?"

Nola shrugged. "They took a calculated risk. The attack turned all the commissioners in Larry's favor, right? I think Monica's been head puppeteer since she joined that group, and those boys are just too full of themselves to realize she's pulling the strings."

"Clever girl," Tony said admiringly.

"Me or her?"

"Both."

"Thanks. For the record, I still think Larry killed Haven."

Tony didn't agree, but you couldn't have everything. And there was always a chance Larry had paid Monica and her crew, or some other outside party, to do the job for him. Nola needed to find out if either Larry or Monica was AB positive. She promised Sebastian another dozen cupcakes if he'd hack Jillian's surgery files. Dr. Benioff would only have Jillian's blood type, but if she was an O, Monica couldn't be AB. At least that would rule her out. Before Sebastian could get started, Juan entered from the squad room with big news.

"ROTC70 just posted a communiqué on the UCSB message board."

Sebastian pulled it up on his computer. The words were culled from the lyrics of an old Phil Collins song: *"I can hear it coming in the air, hold on. Can't you feel it coming in the air? Hold on. Hold on."*

"Coming in the air." Tony didn't remember the song, but the hint was obvious.

"Hope that doesn't mean Ian's moved from flammable liquid to gas."

"I was thinking *air*waves," Juan said. "Like they're planning to cut in on the local news or something."

Nola stared at the lyrics on the screen. "Wait. There's a word missing. *I can feel it coming in the air...tonight.* They purposely left out the word 'tonight.' What's going on tonight?"

"*The Euclidian Variation!*" Sebastian shouted. "Holy shit, they're going to hit the premiere!"

Nola, Tony, and Juan exchanged a look. The kid was right. High-profile, loaded with press, the premiere made a sweet target, and Monica was a volunteer, which gave them someone on the inside. An attack coming in the air. It was unlikely they'd be swooping in on helos blasting "The Flight of the Valkyries" à la *Apocalypse Now*, so what else could it be?

"The theater ventilation system," Tony said. "Ian might have made some kind of gas bomb."

A random thought popped into Nola's head. "Christ, Tony, what if it isn't something Ian's cooking up in the bathtub? What if it's two canisters worth of deadly military poison?"

"You mean those weapons that were missing up at Vandenberg?" Juan asked, eyes wide. "Holy crap!"

Tony raised his arms to calm the alarm. "Hey, let's tamp it down for a second. Nols and I both saw all twelve canisters present and accounted for yesterday, and Burnell gave us his word they were never missing."

"Yeah, and now we know what that's worth," Nola replied, acidly.

The premiere was still hours away; there was plenty of time to mobilize. A tad neurotic when it came to romance, Nola was a Jedi George Washington when it came to her job. In a matter of minutes, she'd formulated a plan of attack and was calmly handing out assignments. She'd call Vandenberg and double check that all twelve canisters of SE40 were still safe, then turn her attention to tracking down Monica. Tony would head out with a team to search Malcolm and Ian's apartment. Ancillary teams would search Kyle's apartment and the car wash. Sebastian would try to trace the Phil Collins post back to its source, then do whatever he could to find Larry and Monica's blood types. Juan would check the national gun database to see if Larry had a permit for a .38 and get the video to a sound lab. Of course, Sam would want to alert the theater and the festival directors himself.

"Sam is going to have puppies when I walk in with this. You want to come with, Tony?"

"Behind you in a minute," he said, waving her on.

When Nola and Juan were out the door, Tony turned to Sebastian. "Listen, kid, obviously tracking that message has first priority, but when you're done with that, do me a favor. Email the image of the woman with Burnell over to the festival publicity department. MacIntire might not care who she is, but I've got an inquiring mind."

Fifty-One

Nola's grandmother Catherine religiously watched the morning news shows. On particularly crazy days, she'd text to let Nola know that "hells-a-popping." It was hells-a-popping and then some at the Santa Barbara Police Department as Nola, Tony, and Sam rushed to get ahead of the situation.

Ian's professor had surfaced on his Channel Islands dive boat. He called Tony back, but the news wasn't good. There were dozens of dangerous recipes for nasty gasses that any half-smart chemistry student could access online, and Ian was more than half smart. The scraggly little fart was on the Dean's List. The university chem lab had all the building blocks to make any number of gas bombs, and what Ian couldn't steal from school he could easily procure from a plethora of websites.

In light of the impending threat, Sam easily convinced Judge Peña to issue warrants for every area they needed to search for signs of chemical-bomb making.

As arranged, Tony took a team to Malcolm and Ian's apartment while Nola and Juan headed out to Larry's ranch. Monica's easy access to ten secluded acres and various outbuildings made Rancho Perdido a likely staging area for whatever ROTC70 was planning.

When Nola and Juan arrived at the gatehouse, they flashed their warrant at Larry's security team, warning them not to alert anyone on the premises that the police were on their way. Jeeps in communication with a search helicopter fanned out to cover the ten-acre spread. Nola and Juan took a small group of officers to search the house. A maid let them in. They were already spreading out downstairs when Jillian came storming down from her bedroom, fit to be sedated. The reddish-brown bruises around the compression wrap had turned a healing yellow-green that was barely visible under a thick layer of creamy beige foundation. With the mucus drains gone, she looked furious but healthy.

Monica and Larry were both away, so Nola presented Jillian with the search warrant, saying they were looking for anything that might tie Monica to ROTC70. She kept it vague, with no mention of Larry's guns or things that might be coming in the night. If Jillian didn't bother to actually read the document, it was her bad.

Juan's firearm check revealed that Larry had permits for a .38 Colt automatic, an authentic Nazi Lugar, and the .44 Magnum that Clint Eastwood had wielded in the first *Dirty Harry* movie. He'd bought the .44 at a charity auction for a children's hospital and presented it to Jillian on her fortieth birthday.

Nola thought giving a gun to a woman turning forty bordered on insanity. Even letting her hold a knife to cut the birthday cake seemed risky. But perhaps that was just her own psychosis.

Juan had also uncovered Larry's membership at the Montecito Gun Club. It was a private shooting range with a chic French restaurant and a steam room. Members, worn out from unloading a torrent of bullets into dummy targets, could relax over dinner or a schvitz. Unless Larry just went for the asparagus millefeuille and the pore-opening steam, he was most likely a pretty good shot. Sam had talked Peña into including the .38 in the warrant, but Nola didn't want to spook Larry or Monica by mentioning it to Jillian.

Out-of-her-mind angry, Jillian phoned and got Larry out of a meeting with his architects. Nola could hear him yelling over the phone. He demanded to speak to Nola, but she wasn't about to waste precious time listening to him rant. As she went room to room searching for signs of aerosol-bomb making, Jillian trailed behind her, holding the cell phone in the air so Larry could ream her out via speaker. When he finally went hoarse from shouting, he hung up, and Jillian dialed Monica. Eerily, Monica's ever-present cell went unanswered.

When Jillian saw Juan literally going through her dirty laundry, she stormed off, calling to the maid to help her find her Vicodin. Nola took advantage of Jillian's temporary absence to grab the .38 from Larry's library and hustle it out to Juan's car.

A thorough search of the main house failed to uncover any suspicious gas containers or aerosol-diffusing apparatus. The police chopper and the jeeps covered the ranch from end to end with the same result. Tennis court, stables, pool area: all clean. And aside from a near-empty bottle of Oxycontin and some Diet Coke, Monica's guest house was chemical-free. Glancing out the guest-house window, Nola thought she saw Oprah Winfrey watching all the activity from a hilltop cabaña on the next property. *Boy*, she thought, *I must really need sleep.*

Searching Monica's closets, she wondered again why a girl with so much expensive silk underwear would ally herself with the "property is theft" crowd. Sure, Malcolm was rock-star sexy, but so were the boys at the Montecito Country Club.

If Monica *was* a double agent working for Larry, as Nola

suspected, maybe she wasn't taking part in tonight's activity at all. All this searching might be just a waste of valuable time and resources. On the other hand, she could have jumped sides at some point and put in with the bad boys just for fun. It was impossible to know.

"...*watching the detectives...*"

It was Sam calling from Dave Hackel's office. Dave was one of the festival directors in charge of tonight's premiere, and he was fully cooperating with the investigation. According to his records, Monica wasn't slated to volunteer that night, and there was no credit card record of her having purchased a ticket. Of course, she might have slept outside on the sidewalk like Sebastian and paid cash, but Nola thought it was highly unlikely. Sidewalk sleeping wasn't for girls who walked in La Perla like the night.

It occurred to her that if Monica wasn't going to be inside the theater, maybe the attack wasn't either. The trust-fund anarchists could be planning to red-carpet-bomb the forecourt while the celebrities were doing interviews. When she broached the idea with Sam on the phone, he jumped at the suggestion. "Makes sense, there'll be a lot more press outside than in."

"Yes, but anything they release in the air would diffuse quicker," Nola said. "There's no way to be sure what they're planning. It's like packing for a spring vacation. One bikini, two heavy sweaters...we have to be ready for anything."

Across town in Isla Vista, Tony's team had found Malcolm and Ian's apartment as deserted as Monica's guest house. It was teenage-boy filthy, but the only thing that could be considered deadly was some rancid bean dip in the fridge. Kyle's apartment was similarly deserted, and Marisela confirmed he hadn't shown up for work today.

Sebastian had been trying to track all four kids via a

GPS trace, but ROTC70 was maintaining electrical silence, systems shut down, batteries removed. Malcolm, Ian, Monica, and Kyle all being AWOL and maintaining a cell-phone blackout pretty much confirmed that something was up.

The clock was running out. In a few hours, people would start arriving at the Arlington for the premiere. Sam called in every available officer to cover the doors in and out of the theater and to man watch patrols on the surrounding streets. The ventilation system was inspected, and metal detectors and bomb-sniffing dogs swept the Arlington from top to bottom.

Nola was en route from Larry's ranch to the theater when Sebastian called her in the car. The lab had been able to boost the audio from the publicity video. The lyrics to Charley's song about Gus and Monica's fight were just what she suspected.

"Thanks, Baz. Why don't you come down and meet us at the theater?"

"Seriously, dude? I get to see the movie?"

"Let's hope everyone does."

Juan was rushing Larry's gun to ballistics. If it came back a match, combined with Charley's damning song, they'd have a hell of a circumstantial case. But circumstantial cases, especially when it came to the rich and famous, had a tendency to fall apart in front of autograph-hungry juries. They needed more solid evidence. And that's when it hit her.

Her next call went straight to Tony's voicemail, so she pulled over and texted him instead. "I no R Killer! J"

Fifty-Two

After Nola texted Tony from the car, she called Sam with her killer good news. The evidence she'd need to prove her case was still being processed in the lab and might not pan out, so they tentatively whispered, "*Whoopee!*" and agreed to postpone any showdowns until tomorrow. This time they were in full agreement: *The Euclidian Variation* premiere was top priority.

When she arrived at the Arlington Theater, it was bustling with police and pre-premiere activity. She found Sam and Tony at Sam's makeshift command center behind the concessions stand in the lobby. His plan was basically to have every possible spot in the theater monitored by plainclothes cops who'd memorized Malcolm, Ian, Monica, and Kyle's recent mug shots. Plainclothes officers would be taking tickets, searching bags, and monitoring the restrooms. Even the guys selling bonbons had Berettas. *Step away from the popcorn and no one will get fat*, Nola thought as Sam filled her in.

Without a doubt, Sam's most creative use of undercover personnel was the twelve cops he'd had costumed up for the occasion. *The Euclidian Variation*'s production costs fell somewhere between *you gotta be kidding me!* and *no, seriously, you're kidding, right?* Anxious to recoup their sizable investment, the studio publicity department had gone all out for the premiere. Not only would the director and stars be on hand, but they'd hired a dozen extras to dress as Davilloyds and Cyducanes, the battling forces that made up the crux of the story. The Cyducanes wore dark cloaks and Klingon-esque makeup; the Davilloyds were basically snake-scaled humanoids in long silver robes with hoods. In less time than it took a disgraced politician to "find God" and run again, Sam had the extras out of their costumes and a dozen of Santa Barbara's finest in them. The costumed cops were currently patrolling the theater armed with neon tridents and hover swords.

The cops in costume were Bluetooth-equipped and tagged with reflective Xs in case ROTC70 had stumbled upon the same idea. Anyone in costume without an X would be immediately culled from the crowd and questioned.

As it got closer to show time, Nola and Tony circulated in and around the perimeter of the theater, checking and positioning personnel and keeping their eyes open for trouble, but as night fell and the klieg lights lit up the sky, none had materialized.

The crowd arrived, the press arrived, the movie stars arrived, tickets were taken, bags were scrutinized, a thousand handshakes, a thousand photos...there was tinsel and glamour and plenty of excitement to go around. The only thing missing were the spoilers.

Standing watch outside the theater, Nola was starting to wonder if they'd guessed wrong, and the kids had chosen another target altogether. Either way, it was going to be a tense night.

Fifty-Three

The inside of the Arlington Theater was magical. Trompe l'oeil painting, elegant balconies, and a thousand little stars shimmering in the ceiling created the impression of a lovely Spanish paseo at sunset.

The movie stars, VIPs, and average movie fans lucky enough to have tickets were sitting comfortably in their seats under the stars when Tony and Nola met up by a velvet-draped side door to compare notes. Nola was grateful for the calm but a little afraid of being branded as the cop who cried wolf. "How bad is Sam gonna kill me if I'm wrong about the hidden meaning in the website post and nothing goes down tonight?" She asked, only half kidding.

"You'll probably get off with just a small garroting," Tony said, scanning the well-behaved crowd. "I'm choosing to think of us as a law enforcement condom, better safe than sorry. You're sure the word *'tonight'* is in that song?"

"Positive. Maybe it's happening tonight, but we guessed the wrong target."

"Come on, you think they're gonna hit the Dunkin' Donuts on Milpas and ignore a star-studded gala full of press?"

There was a burst of applause as the festival's executive director walked up on stage to address the audience. A smart man adept at multitasking, he kept a watchful eye for dangerous activity as he introduced *The Euclidian Variation*'s two young stars, Christopher Marcil and Laura Solon, and its distinguished director, Jameson Lyons.

Chris, Laura, and Jameson had asked to be seated center aisle in the orchestra section. After the film, they'd be brought up on stage for a question-and-answer session. They were surrounded by VIPs to buffer them from overzealous fans, but seating them so prominently in the center of the crowd was a little too high profile for Nola's liking. Had the stars known there was a threat, they most likely would have agreed.

Sam and the festival organizers had decided to keep the celebrities in the dark along with the public. The threat was only a guess, the theater was blanketed with cops, and a dozen famous names hopping the next stretch limo back to L.A. would be a public relations disaster. One the beautiful little city could ill afford now that it seemed to be morphing into the murder capital of the world.

Tony nudged Nola and pointed to Sebastian on the other side of the theater. He was gazing at Chris, Laura, and Jameson with mad-fervent sci-fi devotion. "That's exactly how my mom looks at statues of Jesus," Tony whispered.

"We'd be smart to keep our eyes on them, too," Nola whispered back. "As juicy targets go, they're a terrorist's wet dream."

⏣ 👄 ⬤

On the surface, Chris, Laura, and Jameson appeared to be delighting in each others' company, but in *E! True Hollywood* fashion, things weren't quite as rosy as they seemed.

The fact that Jameson Lyons was one of the most hated men in Hollywood was a testament to his success. His winning streak equaled that of James Cameron and Martin

Scorsese, which put him in that stratum of Hollywood-director nobility so rare that if Spielberg pulled a hammy, they'd have trouble finding a fourth for tennis.

In addition to money and fame, Jameson had stockpiled an extraordinary string of hits, which had earned him the right to choose his leading ladies without studio approval. High on his list of hirable qualities were eye-catching beauty and an enthusiastic willingness to sleep with him on location — an enthusiasm so complete, you'd think the actress's job depended on it, which of course it did.

For Jameson, bedding rights to the next Keira Knightly or Scarlett Johansson was the only thing that made being on location with a bunch of cranky actors and even crankier screenwriters bearable. He'd chosen Laura over a host of other young starlets, not only because she was beautiful, but also because her wide, blue eyes and cupid-pink lips radiated such sincere innocence that it was easy to believe she was sitting on his face because she was actually in love with him and not just to further her career. It was a choice he had come to regret.

Actors also like to feel loved, and Chris Marcil was no exception. The only way Laura could extract herself from Jameson was if Chris claimed her for himself, and that's exactly what he did. The male star was top of the pecker order on a movie set, and Jameson had had no choice but to suck it up and make do with various wardrobe women and editing assistants until principal shooting wrapped and he was free to go home.

Chris's sexual usurpation of Laura had made six months on location in Tunisia and Alberta, Canada, feel like six months on location in Tunisia and Alberta, Canada, and Jameson was burning to get even.

Jameson wasn't alone in his jealousy of Chris. Most any

man in the world would have gladly traded places with him. As an actor, he had everything women and the camera loved: rugged good looks, boyish confidence, and the ability to make any character he played one-hundred-percent believable.

In *The Euclidian Variation* he played a math savant who discovers an equation that projects him into an alternate universe. The nerd-genius becomes a freedom fighter who battles the forces of evil with the help of a waifish girl warrior and enough awe-inspiring special effects to gloss over about a zillion gaping sinkholes in the plot.

Chris's sexual allure, killer on film, was even more devastating in person, and there were only two straight women in the theater that night not lusting over his HGH muscles and contacts-enhanced sable-brown eyes. The first was Nola, who was too busy watching for trouble to feel any movie-star contact high. The second was a frumpy redhead who had been inexplicably seated next to Jameson in the VIP section.

When an announcement came over the PA system reminding the audience to mute their cell phones so everyone could enjoy the film, the frumpy redhead bent over and reached under her seat. If Jameson hadn't been prickling over Laura running her perfect little hand over Chris's movie-star crotch, he might have noticed Monica Crawford-Wilson activating the timer on one of the aerosol bombs that Malcolm had taped underneath it that morning.

Wearing Monica's blue volunteer badge, Malcolm had breezed into the theater unnoticed with four of Ian's improvised devices in his backpack. Weeks before, Monica had slipped into the festival office, left cash for four VIP seats, and assigned fake names to them on the seating chart.

Attaching the bombs under the seats with black tape had been a piece of cake. Malcolm was already comfortably ensconced in a barber's chair when Kyle posted the cryptic Phil Collins message on the university website using a cell phone he'd lifted off a drunk sorority girl at the James Joyce. "*Can't you feel it coming in the air...hold on...hold on?*" A few fellow travelers who listened to wrinkle-rock would notice the missing "tonight" and realize an attack was imminent. Everyone else would have to be impressed in hindsight when ROTC70 posted again to claim credit for its success.

The plastic distribution devices Ian had created were simple. Flipping a lever triggered a timer that popped a pellet and released the gas. There was no explosive material to alert bomb-sniffing dogs, and the nano wires in the timing mechanisms were too thin to set off any pesky metal detectors. Malcolm, Monica, Ian, and Kyle had less than five minutes to leave the theater once they'd triggered the devices, but the risk only amped up the high.

They'd arrived separately at the theater at staggered intervals and gone straight to their seats. To avoid detection, their hair was either freshly shorn, bleached, or dyed, and they all wore glasses or colored contacts. They'd bought clothes they normally wouldn't be caught dead in, removed all body piercings, and covered their extensive tattoos with body makeup. Disguised as "normals," they had easily passed under the wary eyes of the police.

Their cue to trigger their timers was the ubiquitous announcement to please shut off cell phones so everyone could enjoy the film. The announcement had the added advantage of providing an excuse for each of them to get up and go to the lobby under the pretext of needing to send one last text or life-altering tweet.

Malcolm felt a power surge as he triggered his timer.

Thanks to his deviant brilliance, even with their cell phones off, none of the rich and famous would be enjoying the show tonight.

Always a bit twitchy, Kyle was the first to get up from his assigned seat and make his way toward the lobby. To Tony, he looked like just another self-absorbed millennial in a Hugo Boss sportcoat who couldn't resist taking one more call before the movie began. The short white hair and wire-rim glasses were a far cry from the dark, greasy-haired kid he'd arrested only a few nights before. There was no telltale viper-dripping-blood tattoo on Kyle's clean-shaven neck or skull-themed jewelry to give him away. All the same, any anomaly like someone getting up just as the title for the movie of the year started flickering on screen was cause for concern. Tony instinctively turned a watchful eye his way and whispered to Nola, "Think I should follow that guy?"

"If you don't, I will," she whispered back.

As Tony started up the side aisle to intercept the white-haired preppy, Nola noticed another young guy in a VIP seat standing up. He had a shaved head and a Paramount show jacket, and he also seemed to have gotten a call he couldn't refuse. He was apologizing to the people around him as he made his way to the outer aisle. One guy walking out just as the movie was starting was odd; two was downright suspicious.

Then a frumpy redhead sitting next to Jameson Lyons got up. The orangy-red hair and oversize cable-knit sweater didn't ring a bell, but there was something in the way she moved that poked Nola's memory. Something in the curve of her neck and in the thin, tapered fingers. *Oh, Sarah Jessica*

Parker, it's Monica! Nola practically shouted it out loud. The shock of recognition was as visceral as running into an ex-boyfriend on the one stupid morning you dared to run a quick errand without makeup. She alerted Tony over her headset as she ran down the aisle. "Tony, it's them! They've gone mainstream to blend in!"

Malcolm and Kyle were halfway to the lobby. Tony radioed for the cops disguised as Davilloyds and Cyducanes to stop them as he ran toward Ian, who had just stood up and was straightening his classic-fit chinos.

"Stop those two guys and anyone else trying to leave the theater," he shouted into his headset. "And check their empty seats!"

Monica was attempting to push by Jameson and Laura when she spotted Nola charging down the outer aisle to intercept her. She quickly reversed direction, pushing back down the row the way she came.

The credits for the movie were rolling, but the audience was fixated on the excitement in the aisles. The murmuring was gaining steam. Nola prayed they could avoid a stampede.

A Cyducane cop called for Kyle to freeze. When Kyle started running instead, he got slapped with a hover sword and tackled to the ground. Trapped between a Cyducane with a trident and a Davilloyde with a hover sword, Malcolm was running up and down the center aisle like a baseball player caught in a rundown between bases.

Thinking it was a publicity stunt, the audience broke into pockets of laughter and applause. Only Chris, Laura, and Jameson knew the melee must be real. No way would the studio authorize a stunt like this without warning them in advance.

Malcolm darted down a row of people, stomping on feet and springboarding off heads in his attempt to evade capture. When people started screaming, the audience stopped laughing, and the applause turned to confusion.

Tony caught Ian by the collar of his Tommy Hilfiger red, white, and blue polo shirt and drove him to the ground. A Davilloyd swooped in for the assist. Tony passed Ian off, then dropped to his knees to frisk Ian's vacant seat. When he reached back deep underneath the seat his fingers felt the tape. Wrenching the device lose, he pulled it free and shouted into his headset: "The bombs are taped under the seats. They're on timers. Shut them off!"

Monica was trying to escape by climbing over seats and people toward the stage. Nola didn't bother following her — she had to get to the bomb under Monica's vacated seat. Unfortunately, that meant running by Chris, who'd been fearful of an attack by a deranged fan ever since his neighbor Sandy Bullock found a stalker in her living room. For all he knew, the tall blonde barreling toward him was a crazed misfit like Hinckley or Chapman trying to parlay his death into her fifteen minutes of fame. He could see the headlines. "*People*'s Sexiest Man of the Year Murdered at Gala Premiere. Millions Mourn. Super Bowl Canceled."

Nola saw the look of abject panic in Chris's eyes as she ran down the row toward him, but she didn't have time for long-winded explanations. "Stay in your seat — just let me by!"

Adrenaline pumping overtime, Chris, who'd never liked taking direction, as Jameson could attest, took her admonition to remain still as his cue to cut and run. In his desperation to get away, he plowed over delicate Laura, knocking her back in her seat and leaving python-leather footprints on the train of her lovely Lanvin gown. Escaping by trampling his waifish costar/girlfriend might come back to bite him in the ass on YouTube, but this was freaking life and death.

Accustomed to keeping his head when all around him were losing theirs, Jameson Lyons saw his chance for revenge. As Chris pushed past him, a strategically aimed kick to the back of the knee sent the handsome movie star crashing to the floor in front of Monica's empty seat. Sure, there'd be bad blood between them, but Chris would have to suck it up if he didn't want Jameson spreading the story of his co-star-crushing cowardliness until it became the main topic of every agent-client lunch meeting at the Grill.

Seeing Chris tumble to the ground, Nola shouted that she was police and to get out of the way. Stunned by his fall and deafened by the crowd noise and the movie, he rolled over and started kicking and punching at her instead. Fending off his blows, Nola dove on top of him and thrust her arm under the seat to try to reach the bomb. She felt the tape and was about to pull it loose when Chris's fist connected with her eye, and she lost her grip. Slamming a forearm over his throat to choke some of the fight out of him, she reached under the seat again. This time she was able to wrench the device loose, but it was too late. She could already smell gas. As she tried to wrestle the valve shut, Nola MacIntire and Christopher Marcil slid down together into a dense black hole of Euclidian proportions.

Fifty-Four

When Nola started coming to, she was lying outside the theater by the fountain: Charley's favorite spot on hot summer days to chill and smoke a fatty. The commotion had abated, and aside from a few cuts and bruises, no one had been seriously hurt. Only Nola and Chris had succumbed to the gas, and Chris was already awake in an ambulance on his way to Cottage Hospital.

The gas wasn't deadly, just a highly vaporized knockout drop. Its purpose had been to send a few movie stars and VIPs into death-mimicking sleep, causing mass panic in the theater and a lot of national publicity for ROTC70. On that last score, the plot had been a resounding success. In the back seat of a patrol car, Malcolm was already rehearsing his prison interviews. Nothing local — he'd hold out for Sawyer, maybe Blitzer if he landed a choice time slot.

As the cobwebs-in-Jell-O feeling started to lift, Nola became aware of Tony kneeling by her side. "Am I dead?"

"Nope. But your right eye is turning a wicked shade of purple."

"Heliotrope or aubergine?"

"You must still be groggy," he said. "You're saying words that have no meaning."

The deadness in her limbs was turning to pins and needles. It wasn't an improvement. "Did we catch 'em?"

"Yep. The three stooges are on their way in to be booked, and Monica's in the theater office catching hell from Mom and Dad. You feel up to making some arrests?"

"Sure, I'm in mint condition," she replied, making a herculean effort to raise herself up into a sitting position. She made it as far as her elbows before she had to stop and lean back on them for support.

"Yeah, if the mint's been crushed in a mojito," Tony said, putting his hands on her back to steady her.

"No, I'm really okay," she lied. "I'm ready to stand up."

"Okay," he said. "But lean on me."

"Always do," she replied, smiling.

With Tony's help she struggled to her feet. She was stumbling like a newborn colt after a couple of martinis, but at least she was upright. The pins-and-needles sensation was agony, but she could feel life seeping back into her nervous system. "Thanks for not confronting the suspects without me," she said, genuinely grateful not to have missed the fun.

"Agatha Christie summations are your thing. If it were up to me, we'd just read them their rights and let the lawyers sort it out," he said, taking hold of her waist to make sure she didn't fall. "Once we're past this protective ring of cops, we're going to have to battle our way through reporters to get to the theater office. You ready?"

"Sure, I've always wanted a picture of me with a big purple eye plastered all over the news."

"How about on the front page of tomorrow's *L.A. Times* unconscious on top of Chris Marcil?"

"Oh no! Why didn't you confiscate the camera?!"

"No grounds. And before you ask — yes, your butt does look big lying on top of a movie star."

"Where's that gas bomb?" she said wearily. "I want another sniff."

Fifty-Five

Nola and Tony fought their way through a throng of reporters who were all shouting at once and angling for video. There were police officers posted outside the office door to keep the press away, but there was more shouting going on inside. Larry and Jillian were letting Monica know, in very loud terms, exactly what they thought of her insane behavior.

"Your boyfriend was five seats away from your mom and me! Were you *trying* to kill us?! Was that the plan?!" Larry shouted.

"Please. Do you see anybody dead?" Monica answered airily. "It was just a little guerrilla theater. Protest art."

"And that was worth dying your hair *poor-person red?*" Jillian screeched, seeming to have missed the bigger picture. "You can't just dye it back, you know — it'll ruin the texture!"

"The press is already dragging me into this with you," Larry said. "'Dr. McDorable's Dangerous Daughter.' My fan sites are blowing up!"

"Oh, Larry, you love it," Monica scoffed. "Your whole life's a selfie."

"You think this is funny?" Jillian scolded. "You think that hair growing out in prison will be funny? It could take months, maybe years!" Once again, she was sidestepping the deeper issue.

"Christ," Larry barked. "TMZ's using that *Enquirer* shot

where my robe's half open and my junk's hanging out!"

Nola was incredulous as she stood outside the door with Tony. "Seriously, what is wrong with this family?"

"Maybe we'll get lucky and they'll invoke their right to remain silent." He grinned. "So, ready to go shoot some angry birds?"

Nola was still shaky, and her eye was throbbing, but climbing into bed and slipping away to the enchanted lake house in her imagination would have to wait. Getting to the end of an investigation and skipping the fun bit where you hit the suspects with the evidence bomb was like getting to the last round of *American Idol* and leaving the stage without opening your mouth.

"Locked and loaded," she replied with a smile.

Tony pushed open the door and stood back to let her go in first. She was still a little wobbly, but she tried to make a strong entrance. "Hi, everybody, I'm fine, in case you were wondering."

The sight of Nola up and mobile with her swollen and decidedly aubergine eye brought the family squabbling to an abrupt halt.

The tiny office was packed with boxes of movie tickets, posters, and binders full of schedules. Redheaded Monica was sitting straight-backed and defiant on an ancient rolling office chair. Larry and Jillian flanked her on either side. Jillian's surgical neck wrap was camouflaged by a pashmina. Larry's angry face was the color of chum. If Monica had been wearing the pashmina, Nola was pretty sure Larry would have strangled her with it by now.

Tony followed Nola in and shut the door behind him. "Sorry to interrupt, but you know how it is, things to do, arrests to make, so we'd kinda like to move things along."

"Then let's cut to the chase," Larry said, bluntly. "Obviously my stepdaughter is part of this stupidity. What do we need to do to make as much of this as possible go away?"

Jillian took the opportunity to show off her knowledge of TV law. "If she turns state's evidence or whatever you call it on the boys who planned this, can you promise us she won't go to jail?"

"Okay, I know you people are new to this," Tony said, "but it's a bust, not a negotiation. And I'm not sure my partner here's in much of a forgiving mood." He moved a stack of folders off a filing cabinet so Nola could sit down. She shot him a wink of gratitude as she plopped her still-rubbery bones down on the anachronistic filing system.

Monica stared at Nola's eye. "Hurt much?"

"No more than your average cavity search," Nola answered, dripping honey.

Monica sighed. "Is that your not-so-clever way of saying I'm going to jail?"

"Does a kitten look cute in a bow tie?" Nola didn't care how snarky Monica got this time around. The fight was in the bag, and Monica was going down.

"Shut up, Monica," Larry snapped.

Jillian turned desperately to Tony. "Please, Detective, Monica isn't an anarchist. She isn't even a Democrat. She's just a very foolish girl who fell in with the wrong boy."

"Must run in the family," Tony said flippantly.

"What's that supposed to mean?" Larry growled.

"It means we know you had Monica offer Gus Gillette a bribe to push your real estate deal through," Tony answered matter-of-factly.

Jillian turned her neck around to look at Larry and winced in pain. "Larry...?" The rest of her question hung in the air unspoken.

"Oh, for Christ's sake, Jillian, he's fishing." Hackles up,

Larry turned to Tony. "It's absurd on the face of it. Monica and her jackass friends are against my project. They attacked my damn commission hearing."

Tony mimed hitting a tennis ball over to Nola's court. This was the part she loved, and he knew it. She took the imaginary ball and ran with it.

"Well, the whole eco-girl-terrorist thing was really just a cover, wasn't it? Plausible deniability in case a situation arose strikingly similar to this one. As an avowed environmentalist, Monica could be seen talking to Gillette, and no one would suspect she was your emissary. And getting her grunge band of brothers to attack the commission meeting actually swung the vote your way. Am I right?"

Larry was slick as wet pavement. "Not even close."

"Come on, Lar," she said, growing tired of his bullshit. "We have video of Monica arguing with Gillette when he refused your offer at the *Batman* premiere. You can even hear poor Charley making up a song about it in the background. Monica got real mad about that, didn't you, Mon?"

"Who's Charley?" Monica replied like the petulant brat she was.

"You remember the sweet street singer with the beautiful smile," Nola said. "We pulled two slugs out of him that match your stepdad's .38 Colt auto."

Nola counted two Mississippis in her head. It was the standard length of stunned silence before a suspect would come back with an outraged response, usually in the form of a question.

"*My* gun? What the hell are you talking about?!" Larry said, looking genuinely surprised.

"I'm talking about murder, Mr. Wilson," Nola snapped back. "Charley overheard the fight about the bribe, made a song up about it, and ended up dead on the courthouse lawn.

Our ballistics lab matched the slugs in his chest to the gun we took from your home today."

Larry had the same stunned look on his face that Dr. McDorable had worn in his season-five cliffhanger when, in the middle of a delicate brain surgery, his sexy nurse announced she was pregnant with his baby.

"Are you seriously trying to say that the homeless man they found dead the other morning was shot with my gun?!" he asked, incredulous.

Jillian looked like she was about to faint. She pushed her hair back from her head in a gesture of disbelief, inadvertently exposing her surgery stitches. It was a move the Frankenstein ladies who lunched at Intermezzo knew all too well to avoid. "This is crazy," she said. "Larry didn't shoot anyone. He's a TV star for God's sake!"

Monica grimaced at her mother's exposed sutures. "Don't look now, Mom, but your stitches are showing."

Tony grabbed Monica's arm and lifted her up off her chair. "I think your mom needs to sit down," he said sharply.

He wasn't lying. Jillian's face, under her thick layer of foundation, was turning the color of raw squid. She sank into the vacant chair without a word.

"Putting poor Charley aside for a moment," Nola continued, "we need to know where each of you were after midnight on the night Haven Gillette was killed."

Nola didn't even get to one Mississippi before Larry lost it. "Look," he snarled, "I don't know what tricks you're trying to play with my gun, or if this is just your clumsy attempt at a bluff, but I didn't kill the homeless guy and I sure as hell wouldn't have killed Haven!" The last bit he said with just a little too much emphasis for Jillian's liking. Nola saw a flicker of jealousy in her eyes, but she remained mute.

Tony turned to Monica and Jillian. "Can either of you

verify that Larry was in bed like he says?"

"I was in the guest house with Malcolm," Monica piped up. "The maid brought us grilled brie sandwiches, so I've got two alibi witnesses."

"Not what I asked," Tony said. "But okay."

"How 'bout you, Jillian?" Nola asked. "Were you in bed with Larry at that time?"

"Yes," Jillian said defiantly.

Nola shook her head no. "I asked your servants the same question this afternoon. Any chance you might want to re-think that answer?"

A heavy sigh escaped Larry's lips as he sensed his alibi slipping away.

"Yes, all right, I was sleeping alone on the other side of the house," Jillian admitted. "I was still bruised and bloody from the surgery and I didn't want anyone to see me."

"Right," Nola said. "So *you* don't have an alibi witness either?"

"Why on earth would *I* need an alibi?" Jillian sputtered.

Quicker than you can say spoiler alert, Tony jumped to the denouement. "Because you killed Haven Gillette."

The words hit Jillian like the jab of a collagen needle; her whole body flinched.

Nola threw up her arms, amazed. "What the hell, Tone? I had a whole build going!"

"Sorry, knee-jerk reaction. She just lobbed it up and I slammed it back."

Monica and Larry couldn't have looked more shocked if *The Euclidian Variation* had suddenly dropped them on their ass in an alternate universe.

"Now you're accusing me?" Jillian said contemptuously. "Tell me, Detective MacIntire, is there anyone in this town our family didn't shoot?"

"Well, there's Gus," Nola said. "Haven shot him. And just for the record, you didn't shoot Haven, you shoved a spray-tan nozzle down her throat. Your blood type's AB, just like the blood drops we found by the body. Sadly for you, those bloody mucus drains never quite stopped leaking. Juries just love biological evidence."

Tony held up his phone. "Shall I call the lab guys to swab your mouth and match the DNA, or would you rather just confess and save us all the trouble?"

"Oh, for God's sake. Yes, I admit I was there," Jillian said, her hands starting to tremble. "Monica told me Haven and Larry were having an affair, so I went over to confront her."

"That's ridiculous," Larry objected. "Why didn't you come to me? I would have told you it's a lie."

"Of course you would," she said dryly. "That's exactly why I *didn't* come to you. Anyway, when I got to the estate, the gates were open, and Susan Gillette was leaving in her car. The gates didn't close after she drove out, so I went up to the house and found the front door standing wide open. When I called inside, Haven didn't answer, so I went in to look for her. She was already dead when I found her lying on the bathroom floor. I may have leaked a few drops of blood when I checked to make sure, but Susan Gillette is your killer, not me."

"And you didn't bother calling the police because...?" Tony asked.

"Because I'd prefer that not all of Santa Barbara know my husband cheats on me. You're a man, maybe you don't understand that sort of thing, but I'm sure Miss MacIntire gets it."

"I do," Nola said. "But you're still lying. We already know Susan was there, and we know she conked Haven on the head with some heavy-duty art, but you're the one who polished her off with the tanning spray. Susan was home at the time of death, and there was no spray-tan spatter on her clothing. But there was on yours. I called your maid after our search. She told me you gave her a bag of clothes to take to the Salvation Army. Unfortunately for you, they were still in the trunk of her car. It's so hard to get good aiding-and-abetting help these days, isn't it?"

Jillian's voice was dry and metallic. "Larry, call Howard Anderson. I'm not going to listen to one more word of this."

"When you call your lawyer, or fixer, or whoever Anderson is," Nola said, "you can tell him the pattern the spray tan left behind on your pants is called blowback. It couldn't have happened unless the machine was on and you were operating it. It'll probably be Exhibit D, maybe E, at your trial. Funny sidebar, it was your wardrobe that gave you away on Charley's murder, too."

Larry came out of his shock coma long enough to choke out a question. "Wait, you're saying Jillian killed the singer too?"

"Well she does get consistently high scores for marksmanship at your gun club," Nola said brightly. "And the maid says she takes the .38 in her purse when she's going to be out late. But, like I said, it was really those gorgeous Louboutins she wore to the premiere that gave her away."

"Did the Louboutins confess? Or did you have to beat it out of them?" Monica said derisively.

Keep it up, Nola thought. *I'm sure the nice judge will find you just as contemptible as I do.* The pins-and-needles feeling in her limbs was dying away, and evidence summations were so much cooler standing up, so she decided to end on a high note.

"Actually, Monica, we do have a witness," Nola said, rising to her feet. "He kept telling us he saw a dude shoot

Charley, click, click, click. Naturally we took 'dude' to mean guy. Then this afternoon a young coworker called me dude on my car phone. I'm so ancient, I'd forgotten it's not just for guys anymore." Nola turned back to Jillian. "You were the dude, Jilllian. And 'click, click, click.' There were only two bullets, so it didn't really make sense till I remembered those beautiful Louboutin stiletto heels. 'Click, click, click.' He wasn't describing gun shots, he was describing the sound you made running away on the stone path under the archway in those, literally, killer shoes."

If Jillian bit her lip any harder, she'd be aspirating blood. Nola kept the pressure up. "Of course, Howard will tell the jury that a million women wear spiked heels, but you were the only one who had access to the murder weapon, and a brilliant motive in the form of a pretty nasty prenup."

"What has our prenup got to do with it?" Larry asked, still gob-smacked by the news that his wife was a murderer.

"I read it when I went through your financials," Nola explained. "Jillian gets none of the money you made before she married you, which is basically all of it. That's why she desperately needed this new development to go through. Monica knew it too, and she knew if Charley repeated his song in front of a judge, the whole project would collapse. Then instead of half of two hundred million, they'd get next to nothing if you ever filed for divorce. And with a serial cheater like you, divorce is really just a matter of gravity plus time. Right, Jillian?" Nola threw a sympathetic look Jillian's way.

Monica looked like she was weighing the pluses and minuses of throwing her mother under the bus, but Larry was still awestruck. "So, this was all about money?" he said.

"Oh Larry, it's always about money," Nola sighed. "'Behind every great fortune lies a great crime,' as Balzac said. Brilliant man, wrote about a hundred novels. Look him up in the prison library. You'll thank me."

She was still being glib, but she was running out of steam. The adrenaline rush that had carried her through the fun bit was waning. Tony winked her a "good job." It almost made up for his blowing the big reveal.

Jillian, Monica, and Larry sat stone-faced and silent. The Crawford-Wilsons were finally starting to realize that a little discretion might be in order if they wanted to avoid further incriminating themselves.

"Okay then, good talk," Tony said, pulling out his handcuffs. "I'm sure my partner's exhausted from being gassed and all, and I've got a wannabe girlfriend to break up with in the morning, so how 'bout we just arrest all of you now and sort out the bribery, murder, and gas-attack charges down at the station? Everybody good with that? Actually, even if you aren't, you have the right to remain silent, anything you say can and will be used against you in..."

Nola was particularly rough handcuffing Monica. If she hadn't shot off her mouth to Jillian about Charley, he might be standing outside in the forecourt now, smiling at people and making up songs. *Rest in peace, Charley Beaufort*, Nola thought as she snapped the cuffs shut. *Wherever you are.*

Fifty-Six

The drab walls of Bryan's office were covered with brilliantly colored photos of comets and supernovas. Astronomy was definitely his thing. As a little boy, he probably wore *Star Wars* pajamas and dreamed of being an astronaut with a rockin' nickname like Buzzman or Jetpack.

Nola hadn't called ahead to let him know she was coming. She was peeking at him through his open door. The front page of the *L.A. Times* was spread out on his desk in front of him.

The photo of Nola and Chris Marcil unconsciously entwined on the theater floor was making quite a sensation that morning. She'd turned down half a dozen calls to appear on the morning talk shows. Tony thought she was crazy not to go for her fifteen. "Do it. Why not?"

"Because I'll be introduced as the hero cop who saved the day, then peppered with a bunch of giddy questions about what it felt like to be lying on top of *People* magazine's sexiest man, and wasn't I just a little bit tempted to kiss him before I passed out."

"Were you?"

"No!"

She had been tempted, actually flattered pantsless, when *The Daily Show* called and asked her to be a guest. But since even iPhone cameras made her look away self-consciously, and sitting across from every smart woman's "Marry" in the Marry, Kiss, Kill game would be so surreal that she'd most likely have a stroke, she politely declined. Stewart would have to remain her dream husband till the real thing came along.

She watched Bryan reading about her and wished she knew what he was thinking about her. Unfortunately, with the photo right in front of him, only one of his thoughts went without saying.

"The camera adds ten pounds to everyone's ass, I swear," she said as she stepped into the office.

Bryan casually looked up and smiled. "I was wondering how long you were going to stand there peeking through the door without saying something." He stood up and walked around his desk to meet her.

"You knew I was there all along?" She frowned. "Well, that puts a wet weekend on all my dreams of becoming an international spy."

"Where have you been?" he asked with boyfriendly concern. "I've been calling and texting ever since I saw the news last night. Oh man, what color is that eye?"

"Lancôme bisque and blue. I tried covering the black with makeup, but it just made it worse. Upside, it was a movie star who hit me, so I'm already getting offers for my eyeball on eBay."

"You might look cute in a patch at that," he said. When he went to kiss her, she shied away. "Still sore?" he asked.

"You have no idea," she said, knowing that he really didn't...yet.

"Why didn't you at least text or email me back? I was worried."

"Actually, Bryan, I thought what I needed to say should be said in person." She paused to take a last look at his recruitment-poster-perfect face.

"Well, okay. Say it." He was starting to catch the vibe.

"We can't go look at the stars together. In fact, I can't see you at all anymore."

"Oh?" Silence settled like dust over the moment. "Is that it, or do I get an explanation?"

"Kari Kachchi."

His chiseled-from-handsome face remained impassive. Only his eyes gave him away.

"I saw video of the two of you together at that film festival you just 'wouldn't be caught dead at,'" she said. "Not good, Major."

Bryan shook his head at his own stupidity. "Yeah, I was afraid that giving you the idea to look at that footage might come back to bite me in the ass. Did it at least help you find your killer?"

"It did," she replied, with a small nod of thanks. At least he didn't try to bullshit his way out of it. She had to give him that.

"Nola, I don't know how much detective work you had to do to find out about Kari, but, you know, if you had just asked me, I would have told you."

"Actually, I went all Sheryl Crow cool about it. It was Tony who got curious. The festival people said she's a producer from Sri Lanka. Almost won for best foreign film."

"Would you believe me if I told you she's actually a Sri Lankan government agent posing as a producer, and our getting together was strictly professional?"

"In fact, I would believe you." She nodded. "I really do."

"That seemed a little easy, he said suspiciously."

"I believe you because I already know it's true. It seemed strange, you knowing a Sri Lankan filmmaker, so our resident tech genius dug a little deeper."

"If you know it was just military business, why are you

canceling our trip?"

"I didn't say I was canceling, I said we couldn't go. See, I also know you were meeting Kari to exchange two full canisters of SE40 for two empty canisters that the Sri Lankan military made up, per your specifications. I'm guessing it was your backup plan in case the bogus log entry was found out, which, of course, it was."

One Mississippi, two Mississippi...she got all the way to ten, but he was still just standing there calmly as ever, waiting for her to go on. "Really? No shocked denials? Not even a shot at a lie?" she asked.

"I get the feeling there's more," he said.

"There is. We searched her private government plane this morning and found the canisters hidden behind her inflight movie console. Kari was one hot Tamili when we arrested her. That's Tamili with an i. It's a sound-alike joke because she's Tamil. Although maybe she's Sinhalese. That's the other largest ethnic group in Sri Lanka, according to Wikipedia. In which case, the joke makes no sense."

"The trap's snapped, Nola. You can stop being glib now."

"Sorry. You know if Kari *had* been just another woman you were seeing, I couldn't really complain. We only slept together once and it was our first date — makes me sound kinda slutty, doesn't it? Oh well, moving on. Another girl would have been par for the course, but trafficking earth-killing bio-weapons — I like bad boys as much as the next gal, but there *are* limits."

"Nola, Sri Lanka is an ally. Until Congress nixed the deal, that's where the SE40 was headed in the first place. The Tamil Tigers have a drug-crops-for-weapons cash operation that's financing terrorist attacks."

"Yeah, I might buy the 'saving the world for democracy' bit if you hadn't taken money for it. The Sri Lankan government is fully cooperating in exchange for keeping the whole international incident on the down low."

"Right, yeah, okay. I took money. One paycheck, two ex-wives, and then my buddy tells me about this investment guru…" He didn't bother to finish the sentence, the inference was clear.

"Wipeout?" Nola said, sympathetically.

"Nose-in-the-sand broke." He nodded.

"Sorry, if it makes you feel better, I know a guy, smart, rich, same thing happened to him."

"How's he dealing with it?"

"He got murdered."

"How did you think that would make me feel better?"

"At least you're still alive. If you want to feel sorry for someone, how about me? You just have to go to jail, I have to keep dating."

Bryan didn't laugh. "Too soon?" Nola asked.

"A little." He winked. "You realize that if I'd never asked you to dinner, your partner wouldn't have cared about Kari, and I'd be golden?"

"I know. I figure you only asked me out because on some subconscious level you wanted to get caught."

"Right. 'Cause I could never have found that ruby-in-the-dust quality of yours just too likable to pass up."

"Okay, you have *no idea* how much I like it that you just compared me to a line in an old Neil Young song. Honestly," she sighed, "if you were just a teensy bit less treasony…"

He took her hand in his, and instantly great-sex sense memories came flooding back. "I'm sorry I messed up," he said. "Mostly because of the court-martial, but who knows, maybe if we'd connected another time…?"

"Maybe," she said. "Call me when you get out. I'll most likely still have a night or two free."

"Yeah, I'm not going to worry about you dating. I'm sure you have men lined up out the door."

"Actually, I do. Sorry about this." Nola turned and raised her voice. "Guys, you can come in now."

Three MPs who'd been waiting for her signal entered, sidearms drawn. Bryan let go of Nola's hand, and the gooey, marshmallows-in-heaven feeling gradually faded away.

"Hands down, worst breakup I've ever had," he said.

"Sweetie, if that's true, consider yourself lucky."

Fifty-Seven

Tony was already soaking up the sun in Carlito's courtyard when Nola sank into the soft Mexican-leather chair across from him. It had been a bittersweet ride back from Vandenberg. The new boy bounce was gone, but most women could only complain about their exes to their girlfriends. She'd gotten to throw hers in jail. Man jail, so she didn't even have to waste time imagining him with his new girlfriend. All and all, she decided to call it a win.

"Margaritas on their way?" she asked.

"Yep, double frozen for me. Tequila over ice, no triple sec so your food-diary, calorie-count bullshit doesn't spike — for you, my black-eyed girl."

Nola laughed and watched jealously as he scarfed a handful of homemade chips with the best hot salsa in town.

"So, how'd your major take being busted?" he asked through a mouthful of salty heaven.

"Handsomely. How did your pancake-making Chelsea take having The Talk?"

"Actually, she was surprisingly cool," he said. "I told her we needed to slow things down and set some boundaries, and she agreed."

"So you're back on Suffragette City?"

"*Then* she suggested we go antiquing this weekend in Santa Ynez."

"Oh, the horror," Nola teased. "So I'm guessing we can make this a nice, long lunch."

"No naked-woman-under-coats in my life to run home to," he said, breathing in the sunny winter air. "Ah, freedom and Mexican food. Makes you feel good just to be alive, doesn't it?"

"Does this whimsical mood mean any of the Crawford-Wilsons confessed?" she asked hopefully.

"No, on advice of counsel they all finally shut up. But the press has been mostly glowing — Santa Barbara Police Foil Bad Guys — so Sam's in a happy place. Did you know he was dating 911 Julie?"

"In secret, sure, I thought everybody did."

"Well now they've gone public."

"Good for them. Excellent match."

"And there's more good news," he said. "Our junkie came down enough to identify Jillian in a lineup."

"It is the age of miracles, dude," Nola said picking up her menu. "To celebrate, and to sublimate for all the great sex I'll no longer be having, I'm going to go nuts and order something crazy fattening *with* guacamole."

A young waitress, who weighed less than the tray she was carrying, arrived with their margaritas. It was clearly divine intervention. "Hi," she said to Nola. "Wow, Tony said you had a black eye, but wow."

"Tony? Do you two know each other?" Nola asked the pretty little beanstalk.

"We do now," she said. "I can't believe he's the guy who saved the film festival."

The waitress flipped Tony a Colgate Ultra White smile that was off the charts. Tony smiled back like the Italian *gato* that ate the canary.

"So what can I get you? Tony's having the Anaheim-chile

chicken," she added reverently, like it was the order of a true genius.

Nola put her menu down. "Broiled halibut and salsa, no guacamole, no sour cream."

"Seriously?" Tony said, turning to the waitress. "Elise, put her guacamole on my plate, I'll make sure she eats it."

"You got it." Elise flashed another memorable smile and drifted away, leaving only a trace of J. Lo's latest perfume on the breeze.

"I will not eat guacamole off your plate," Nola protested.

"History has proven otherwise," he said. "Halibut and salsa, no guac. Hmm, I wonder what skinny waitress brought about that sudden change of heart?"

"Don't be intuitive. It's time to toast." Nola raised her margarita on the rocks. "To the best partner ever, who, because he had my romantic back, exposed my new boyfriend as a weapons trafficker, his girlfriend as a foreign agent, *and* solved our biggest case to date. *Salut.*"

"*Salut.*" Tony started to drink his frozen happiness rimmed with salt.

"Hey, wait," Nola stopped him. "You're supposed to say something nice about me now."

"Okay. Let's see. To the oldest woman I'm still willing to be seen with."

"Aww. Remember when we were young and you weren't my partner?" she sighed. "Those were happy days."

"Oh, right," he said. "Back when you were perfect. Which reminds me, you might want to turn your chair a little — I see a wrinkle starting where the sun's hitting your uvula."

"My uvula's inside my throat."

"Then you might want to get it tightened. Maybe do some uvula Pilates or try a silicone martinizing treatment."

"Funny guy."

"I'm not kidding. I hear in Switzerland eighty-year-old women have the slim, trim inner throats of twenty-year-olds."

"Good news for their eighty-year-old husbands." Nola laughed. "Hey, do you think people really still do that in their eighties?"

"God, I hope so," he answered, fingers crossed. "In fact, I hope it's the main cause of knee-replacement rug burns. In fact, I hope some kindly nurse at the home is doing it to me when I die."

"Okay, okay, I get it. Girl…guy…whole different way of looking at things. Forget my last toast," she said, raising her glass again. "To crazy women, and the men who make us that way."

"Right back at ya."

The mariachis started up, and everything felt right with the world.

Acknowledgments

My deepest thanks to all my friends who put up with me or, more aptly, found me missing from their lives while I endeavored to write my first book. Stephanie, Pam, Kris, et al...I shall make amends.

Kudos squared to John Roshell for his kick-ass cover design, which perfectly brought to life what I envisioned in my head, only way better.

Love, laughter, and eternal happiness to Chelsea Myers for all her help in getting this thing proofed and distributed, and keeping her head while I was losing mine.

A million angel kisses to my wonderfully supportive agent, Paul Fedorko at Bienstock.

The universe and all its wonders to my editor, Colleen Dunn Bates at Prospect Park Books, for her enthusiasm, indulgence, and brilliant assistance all along the way.

Bowers of flowers to David Hyde Pierce, Jane Leeves, Wendie Malick, Valerie Bertinelli, Howard Korder, Tom Fontana, Kelsey Grammar, and Joe Keenan, who gave up big chunks of their holiday vacations to read about murder and mayhem. The only thing I loved more than your blurbs was the joy of working with you. I feel genuinely blessed.

An eternity of gratitude to my perfect, long-suffering friend and partner, Chuck Ranberg. His early retirement forced me to do something on my own — too bad, because I can guarantee the book would have been better if we'd written it together.

And last but not least, huge thanks to my husband, Arnie Giordano, for going out to play disc golf at Lake Casitas so I could work at home on weekends with no distractions. Arnie's friend Chris Workman ran into a man playing golf one day because his wife, another writer, wanted him out of the house while she worked. When Chris asked the man who his wife was, he answered, "Sue Grafton." I'm repeating the story because this may be the only time I can tenuously link myself with one of my idols and thank Arnie at the same time. I raise a glass to thoughtful husbands everywhere.

About the Author

Anne Flett-Giordano is a five-time Emmy-winning television writer and producer whose credits include *Frasier*, *Hot in Cleveland*, *Becker*, and *Desperate Housewives*. In addition to the three Best Comedy and two Best Writing in a Comedy Series Emmys, Anne (with her screenwriting partner Chuck Ranberg) has won a Producer's Guild Award and a Golden Globe and was nominated for the Writer's Guild Best Writing in a Comedy Series award. Anne divides her time between Los Angeles and Santa Barbara, California, where she shares a home with her husband, Arnie, and two book-blocking cats, Raider and Gracie.

Marry, Kiss, Kill is her debut novel and the first in a series.

www.anneflettgiordano.com
Twitter: @AnneFlettGiorda
Facebook.com/AnneFlettGiordano